PRAISE FOR THE FAMILY SKELETON MYSTERIES

"Adjunct English professor Georgia Thackery makes a charming debut in *A Skeleton in the Family*. Georgia is fiercely loyal to her best friend, Sid, an actual skeleton who is somehow still 'alive.' When Sid sees someone he remembers from his past life—who later turns up dead—Georgia finds herself trying to put together the pieces of Sid's past as she works to hunt down a killer. Amateur sleuth Georgia, and her sidekick, Sid, are just plain fun!"

—Sofie Kelly, *New York Times* bestselling author of *Faux Paw*

"No bones about it, Leigh Perry hooked me right from the beginning. An unusual premise, quirky characters and smart, dry humor season this well-told mystery that kept me guessing until the very end. It's too bad Perry's sleuth is fictional—I'd invite Georgia over for dinner in a heartbeat."

—Bailey Cates, *New York Times* bestselling author of
Magic and Macaroons on *A Skeleton in the Family*

"A delightful cozy with a skeleton who will tickle your funny bone."

—Paige Shelton, *New York Times* bestselling author of
If Onions Could Spring Leeks on *A Skeleton in the Family*

"An effortlessly narrated, meticulously crafted cozy mystery."

—*The Big Thrill* on *A Skeleton in the Family*

"I had a grand time reading this fresh, original novel peopled (and skeletoned) with enchanting characters and a warm, engaging story. The undercurrent of the gift of love and loyalty between friends and family members gives this book a burnished glow of strength and peace. I totally loved every page and want to visit with Georgia and Sid again and again."

—*Criminal Element* on *A Skeleton in the Family*

THE
SKELETON
PAINTS A
PICTURE

LEIGH PERRY

DIVERSIONBOOKS

FAMILY SKELETON MYSTERIES

A Skeleton in the Family
The Skeleton Takes a Bow
The Skeleton Haunts a House

Diversion Books
A Division of Diversion Publishing Corp.
443 Park Avenue South, Suite 1008
New York, New York 10016
www.DiversionBooks.com

For more information, email info@diversionbooks.com

First Diversion Books edition October 2017.
Print ISBN: 978-1-63576-046-0
eBook ISBN: 978-1-63576-045-3

Printed in the U.S.A.
SDB/1708
1 3 5 7 9 10 8 6 4 2

To the visual artists whose work brightens my home
and whose friendship brightens my life:

Kim Allman, Jerry Frazee, Brenda Holt,
Maggie Kelner, Valerie Kelner, Martha Lewis,
Mike Luce, and Stephanie Vinke.

CHAPTER ONE

Flakes had just started falling out of the slate gray sky as I walked to the faculty parking lot Friday afternoon, but since students were within earshot, I waited until I was inside my minivan to express my opinion of the swirling bits of frozen aggravation. The fact that only a couple of inches were expected that evening was no consolation.

It's not that I have anything against snow. I was born and raised in New England, and while my so-called career as an adjunct English professor has involved moving all too often, I've never lived anywhere that didn't require a winter emergency kit that included a fold-up snow shovel, a blanket, and a bag of cat litter for traction on icy roads. But not only was Falstone in the snowiest part of Massachusetts, with an annual average snowfall second only to nearby Ashburnham, this year was turning out to be one for the record books.

I felt as if I were driving through a tunnel as I pulled onto the street that ran past Falstone College of Art and Design—FAD to its friends. There had been five major storms in the past month, and the weather hadn't warmed up enough for appreciable melting, so the exhausted snowplow drivers were running out of places to push the snow. That meant the piles on the side of the road and in every available median strip were getting higher and wider, and the roads were getting narrower and narrower.

As I drove, I could see brush, rocks, even shopping carts partially buried in the icy piles. My students were starting to make jokes about missing classmates who wouldn't be found until the next thaw.

I just wish they'd been the only ones to get that idea.

Finally, I made it back to the bungalow I was borrowing from one of my parents' friends for the semester. Snow was still falling, and it was already half an inch deep on the long driveway I'd cleared the day before, meaning that another session with the snowblower would be in my near future. I trudged up the sidewalk—which would also need clearing—and was cheered to see two big packages waiting for me on the front porch. Both had my parents' house in Pennycross as the return address, but the labels were typed, so I didn't know if they were from Mom, Phil, or my daughter, Madison. Nobody had warned me they were sending anything, which was unusual, but maybe they'd wanted to surprise me.

I grabbed the box on top and left the other on the porch while I divested myself of the coat, hat, scarf, and gloves that winter in Falstone required. I was about to go back for the second box when there was a *ping* on my phone. I pulled it from my pocket and saw that my best friend, Sid, was texting me.

SID: *Hi, Georgia. Did the packages arrive?*

GEORGIA: *Good timing. They came today.*

SID: *Open 1 of 2 first!*

I checked the box I'd lugged in. It was labeled *2 of 2*. Of course. I dropped the phone on the table in the hall, opened the door just long enough to drag the package inside, and went to track down a pair of scissors. I was on my way back to the front hall when I heard my phone *ping* again.

SID: *Aren't you going to open the box?*

GEORGIA: *Give me a minute!*

There was another *ping*, indicating that yet another text had arrived. Only, it wasn't from my phone. It had come from inside Box Number One. I sent another text.

GEORGIA: *I'm trying to find the scissors.*

BOX: *Ping.*

I briefly considered shoving both packages back out onto the porch, but I knew that would only be delaying the inevitable. So I slit the tape on the top of the cardboard box and lifted up the flaps. Inside, nestled in a bundle of old T-shirts, was a pile of clean white bones and a cell phone. Plus a skull with a very big smile.

As I watched, the bones snapped together with an uncanny clatter, and within seconds, a human skeleton was standing in front of me with bony arms flung wide.

"Surprise!" Sid said.

CHAPTER TWO

It sounds scarier than it was. I admit that it would have been trauma-inducing for most people, but most people hadn't grown up with an ambulatory skeleton for a best friend. Sid had come to live with—or at least to stay with—my family when I was a child, so I was blasé about Sid walking, talking, and assembling himself at will. Mailing himself to me, however, was new.

"Sid, what are you doing here?"

"I came to keep you company!"

"Sid—"

"Don't I get a hug?" He gave me puppy dog eyes, an impossible feat for a bare skull that he was really good at. So, of course, I hugged him.

Hugging a skeleton is kind of like hugging a coat rack—only, a coat rack doesn't hug back.

I helped him step out of the box. "Do Mom and Phil know you're here?" I couldn't imagine my parents would authorize this shipment without checking with me.

"Not exactly, but... Hey, we can catch up later. I want a tour of your new digs!" He dashed away, rushing from room to room. I suppose it was pretty exciting for him. Sid only rarely left my family's home, for obvious reasons, and his opportunities to explore other houses had been limited. So he oohed and aahed over everything as we roamed through the eat-in kitchen and the living room. The bungalow had been intended as a summer cottage, and the decorations were determinedly rustic: exposed wooden beams, braided rag rugs, and vaguely Native American patterns on the upholstery.

"Is there an attic?" he asked.

"There is, but it's packed full of the owner's things."

"That's all right. I can bunk in the living room. Or the kitchen. I don't need a bed, right?"

"There's a spare bedroom, but—"

"Perfect!" He trooped down the hallway, opening doors as he went. "Only one bathroom? Well, it's not like I ever use it. I can tell this is your room. I recognize your mess. Maybe I can clean while you're at work. And this is my room! Kind of small—"

"Sid—"

He held up one hand. "No worries. I don't need much space. And bonus! The curtains are nice and thick, so nobody will see me in here. I'll go get my things."

"Sid, why don't we sit down and talk first?"

"Just give me a minute to unpack."

"Sid! Sit."

He plopped down onto the bed, and I sat next to him.

"Now talk."

"Okay," he said, with the tone of voice my daughter, Madison, uses when I catch her doing something she shouldn't have. "No, your parents don't know I'm here. I printed out postage and put the boxes in the front hall, then left a note asking Dr. T. to finish taping up the box and leave me on the porch for the mailman to pick up."

"And he didn't want to know what it was you were sending me?"

"He may have thought the note was from Mrs. Dr. T."

"Why would he have thought that?"

"Because I signed it 'Dab.'"

"But why—No, first things first. I need to let them know you're here. They must be worried sick."

"I doubt it," he said with a sniff. "They probably haven't even noticed I'm gone."

That didn't sound good. I got my phone from the front hall and texted home.

GEORGIA: *Sid is safe with me. I'll explain later.*

Then I went back to the bedroom that Sid had laid claim to. "So what's going on? Have you guys been fighting?"

"You have to talk to somebody to fight with them."

"Oh. Have they been working long hours?" My parents had only recently returned from an extra-long sabbatical and had restarted their jobs at McQuaid University after the first of the year.

"No, they're home plenty, but since they've already started collecting grad students, the house is always full of strangers. I think they're feeding a dozen students breakfast and dinner, and I'm pretty sure a couple of postdocs are spending half their nights on the living room couch."

My parents had always attracted and ministered to needy grad students, a hobby that had gotten more pronounced once I'd moved out. And of course that meant Sid was stuck up in his room in the attic, or if he got caught downstairs, he was trapped in the armoire in the living room where he could listen in but couldn't exactly socialize.

"What about Madison? Isn't she spending any time with you?"

"I'm sure she would, but you know how brutal sophomore year is. Between rehearsals for Drama Fest and choral ensemble, she's barely home, and when she is, she's got homework. And the mutt to take care of."

I suspected it was the time Madison spent with her Akita, Byron, that bothered Sid the most. He was never going to be a dog person.

"Deborah?" I asked.

"The only time I've seen her is when she came up to the attic to get one of her storage boxes."

My sister and Sid had never been as close as he and I were. "I thought you guys were getting along better."

"It's not that. It's because she's busy, too. Juggling two boy-friends is taking up a lot of her time."

"So what you're saying is that you've been lonely." After years of mostly being confined to the attic, circumstances had finally changed enough that Sid could hang around with the rest of the family. Having to go back to isolation must have been harder than ever.

He hung his skull. "I know I should have asked first, Georgia, but I was afraid you'd say not to come. And from your e-mails and all, I thought maybe you were lonely, too."

"Are you kidding? With texting and e-mail and Skype, it's practically like I haven't gone anywhere. And for the first time in years, I get to be on my own! I can set mealtimes by my schedule, go out whenever I want, stay up as late as I choose, pick what to watch on TV, and play my music extra loud. I can even use real cuss words, instead of skeleton-related euphemisms."

As I spoke, Sid's bones loosened, which was a sign that he was unhappy. Since he holds himself together by pure force of will, weakened will means weakened connections.

I went on. "And I have never been so miserable in my life."

It took a second for that to sink in. "Really?" he said tentatively.

"Really. Yeah, I'm glad to have a teaching job, and it's great that Madison didn't have to switch high schools, and I know my parents love having her to themselves. But I hate this. I know almost nobody in town and there's not much town anyway. I had no idea how much snow they get around here, and the weather has been so awful that I don't dare drive home on weekends for fear of not making it back in time for Monday classes and getting fired. Of course, we're going to have to establish some ground rules while you're here, but I cannot tell you how glad I am to see you!"

Sid's bones were tightly connected once again. "I'll go get my stuff."

It didn't take us long to unpack Sid's belongings because he hadn't brought much. He didn't wear clothes and didn't need toiletries, so all he'd brought was his laptop and accessories, a few books, and his favorite DVDs: *The Nightmare Before Christmas*, the *Toy Story* trilogy, and *The Lost Skeleton of Cadavra*. All of that was packed neatly in a small rolling suitcase that I used to tote Sid around when the need arose.

"Planning a field trip?" I asked, looking at the suitcase.

"I figured it wouldn't hurt to have it around. Just in case." He looked at me hopefully.

"We'll see," was all I'd commit to.

Just as we got everything put away, my parents called back for an explanation of why Sid had gone AWOL. That got tricky because Sid was at my elbow insisting that I not put the blame on them, but they finally accepted my excuse that he was feeling restless. The fact that there were three grad students at their house during the phone call provided a good explanation of why he'd felt hemmed in.

Once that was addressed, the evening was one of the best I'd had since arriving in Falstone. We made dinner—which only I ate, of course. Then we settled in to watch TV and I caught Sid up on my not-overly-thrilling adventures teaching Expository Writing at a school dedicated to visual arts.

When the snow wound down, we went outside to shovel. This was a new experience for Sid. My parents' house was in the middle of town, and though it had a good-sized yard, the fence wasn't high enough to allow him to move around safely out of doors. The bungalow was much more isolated, on a large lot with no neighbors within easy view. The grounds behind the house were filled with trees and stretched out for yards. Not that I had any interest in going back there, since the snow had already been too deep for easy access when I moved in at the beginning of the semester.

Just to be extra careful in case somebody randomly decided to venture down the driveway, I had Sid swaddled in a spare parka, jeans, boots, gloves, and ski mask so he looked semi-normal.

I expected him to fuss about having to wear all that, but he's always loved costumes. Even if he hadn't, he was having too much fun playing in the snow to mind. Sid actually enjoyed shoveling snow and liked running the snowblower even more. His snow angel didn't work out very well, but he loved throwing snowballs and was just as happy when I returned fire.

It was with the greatest of reluctance that I finally dragged him inside so we could thaw out. Or rather, so I could. Bare bones don't feel the cold.

After a cup of hot chocolate to warm me up, I headed for bed, and since Sid doesn't sleep, he settled in for an all-night session with the stack of books I'd bought since I'd been in Falstone. I didn't know about him, but I felt happier than I had in weeks. What with being kept inside so much by the weather, the house had been starting to feel claustrophobic. Now, with Sid in residence, it felt like home.

With one thing and another, we didn't get around to establishing any ground rules for his stay, which I had cause to regret at three thirty in the morning. That's when I woke up with Sid's skull hovering over me.

"Georgia, wake up! You've got to come right away!"

CHAPTER THREE

"What's wrong?" I sat up and flipped the switch on the bedside lamp. "Why do you have clothes on?"

Sid had on the same snowy disguise-slash-ensemble he'd worn earlier.

"Okay, I know I shouldn't have, but I went back outside after you went to bed."

"Sid!"

"I know, I know, but I figured nobody would see me. Anyway, that's not important right now. The thing is I saw something and I want you to come look. You better get dressed."

I was too befuddled to argue with him. "Fine. As soon as you turn around."

"Like you've got anything I haven't seen before," he huffed. "I've got access to the Internet, you know."

"Just turn around and explain."

"Fine!" He faced the wall and put his hands over his eye sockets.

I climbed out of the bed and yelped when my bare feet hit something cold and wet.

"What?" He started to uncover his eye sockets.

"There's snow on the floor!" I said.

"Sorry, I forgot to take my boots off."

"This better be a really good explanation," I said darkly, pulling on the first set of jeans and college sweatshirt I could find. "I'm listening."

"Okay, so I went outside after you went to bed."

"Obviously."

"And I know I shouldn't have, but I knew nobody would be out at that time of the night and even if somebody did drive by, I'd duck. Plus I wore my disguise just to be extra careful." He looked at me for approval, which I wasn't about to give, so he continued. "I didn't go far, just down the road a bit so I could enjoy the fresh air."

"Fresh air? It's in the teens out there."

"I'm not exactly going to get frostbite! Anyway, I came back toward the house, then went in the other direction, through the woods behind the house. With the snow, it's easier to see than you might expect."

Sid had excellent night vision, even without the benefit of eyes, which made about as much sense as anything else about him.

He said, "I walked as far back as that fence behind the house, where the ground drops off a little, and was just looking down at the landscape. The moon was up and it was so beautiful and peaceful. I was about to come back to the house because I was being careful—"

"If you were being careful, you wouldn't have been out in the woods in the middle of the night." By then I had everything but my outerwear on. "Why am I getting dressed?"

"Because I need you to come see what I saw."

He grabbed my hand and pulled me to the front door where my winterizing accessories were hanging. "Get your coat."

"Fine." I put on all the gear, then put my keys and cell phone into my pocket. "What did you see?"

"I'm not sure. That's why I want you to come!"

"Okay, okay." I followed him outside, wincing as the frigid air hit my face, and let him lead me around the rear of the house. The snow was close to two feet deep back there, and Sid had to help me make my way through it, all the while insisting that we needed to hurry.

Finally, we got to the fence, and he said, "See? There!" He pointed to the right.

"I see something," I said doubtfully and squinted. "It's a car, isn't it?" It was bright red or I might not have even realized what it was.

"I think so. Should there be a car back there?"

"I don't think so." There was definitely no road or house in that direction. It looked as if the headlights were on, but dimly, as if the battery had nearly run down.

"Could somebody be stuck out there? I've read about people getting stuck in the snow and not being able to get out. People have died that way!"

I took a long look, but if anybody was moving in the car, I couldn't tell. In retrospect, I realized I should have called the police right away, but at the time all I could think of was getting to whoever it was in the car. "Sid, I need you to boost me over the fence."

"Okay, but I'm coming with you."

Under the circumstances I should have told him to wait in case there was somebody in the car to see him, but I didn't want to go down there alone. "Just keep out of sight as best you can."

"You got it."

Since Sid's strength isn't defined by muscles, he's as strong as he believes himself to be, and that night he was feeling particularly brawny. He easily lifted me over the fence, then climbed over himself.

It turned out to be a good thing he'd insisted on coming. The snow beyond the fence was even deeper than it was in the bungalow's yard, making for slow slogging in snowdrifts that were up to my waist. Even with Sid's help, I just barely made it.

When we got close enough, I started calling out, "Hello? Is there anybody in there?"

There was no response, and a few seconds later, I saw the car—its hood was crumpled against a tree, and the windshield was shattered. There was a deep trough in the snow, showing where the red hatchback had plunged off the road several hundred yards away and down a steep drop-off.

When I finally reached the car, I saw it was halfway buried in the snow, making it nearly impossible to open the driver's door.

I peered in through the window and saw a deflated airbag on the dashboard and a jumble of things that had been flung around in the crash, including a pocketbook and a thoroughly battered laptop, but that was all.

"There's nobody here," I said in relief.

Sid walked around the car and said, "Over here."

The passenger door was open, with signs that somebody had scrambled out that way and then tried to get up the incline to the road. To my dismay, those signs included splashes of blood.

"It looks like she tried to get up to the road but didn't make it," Sid said, then pointed to another track, leading away from a rut in the snow, as if somebody had tumbled down.

"Hello?" I called out, but there was no answer.

Sid and I started following that second track of snow and more smears of blood.

She hadn't gotten much farther. There was a gully a few yards away, and a figure in a dark parka was lying, face down, at the bottom. It looked as if she'd lost her footing, fallen that way, and hadn't moved again. When I saw a coating of snow covering her arm, I knew she had to be dead, but I said, "We've got to make sure," and started to look for a way to descend safely.

"I've got it," Sid said and scrambled down so he could kneel beside her. He put one bony hand on her back and used the other to touch the little bit of bare neck that her short-cropped hair had left exposed.

Then he looked up at me and shook his head. "She's gone."

Chapter Four

An hour or so later, I was sitting in the back of a police cruiser. Though the heater was running and I had a cup of hot, overly sugared coffee in my hands, I was still shivering. I wanted to blame it on the fact that my clothes were wet from melting snow, but I was pretty sure it was more reaction than anything else.

Once we were sure the woman was dead, I'd sent Sid back to the house while I called the cops, making my best guess at where the car had gone off the road and then using the flashlight app on my phone to signal them. It hadn't taken them long to find me, and then to help me climb up to the road to get to one of the cruisers to wait while they dealt with the dead woman. Thinking about what that meant made me shiver worse.

Eventually a police woman with short blonde curls and a sturdy build knocked on the window, then opened the door. "Ms. Thackery? The chief says there's no need to keep you here any longer and that I should drive you home."

"That would be great, if I'm not taking you away from any-thing." I'd been hoping somebody would offer. I really hadn't wanted to go back the way I'd come, and the road twisted around enough that the walk home would have been a long one.

"Not much to be done, really. You want to stay back here or ride up front with me?" I hesitated, torn between curiosity at seeing the front of a police cruiser and wondering if that would be tacky. She added, "It's right much warmer in the front seat."

"Up front it is."

Once we'd both climbed in and fastened our seat belts, I said, "I'm sorry, I don't remember your name."

"Officer Ginny Buchanan," she said.

"Do you mind if I ask some questions, Officer Buchanan?"

"I'd be mighty surprised if you didn't."

"The woman I found. She was dead, right?"

"Yes, ma'am," she said politely but couldn't help her tone of voice, which implied that that was one the stupidest questions she'd heard in recent memory.

"I mean, of course she was dead, but she'd been dead for a while, hadn't she? Was it okay that I left her there, where she was? It didn't seem right to drag her out."

"Well, the medical examiner will tell us more, but it looked to me like she passed away several hours ago. So you did exactly right. You called us and didn't disturb the scene any more than you had to."

"The scene? It was an accident, wasn't it?"

"Even accidents have to be investigated."

"I suppose so."

"Anyway, we should be able to better work out what happened once it gets light. We're just glad you spotted her when you did. There's more snow in the forecast tomorrow, and if she'd been out there too much longer, she and the car would have been buried for sure. We wouldn't have found her until spring."

"Then I'm glad I could do that much. Do you know who it is?"

"You didn't recognize her?"

"I didn't look at her face. I would have had to turn her over and…" Sid and I had both agreed that it wasn't necessary. "Should I know her? Who was it?"

"We need to notify the next of kin before we release that information."

"Of course," I said, momentarily thinking of some poor parent or spouse getting that horrible phone call or police visit.

By then we were nearly to the bungalow, and as we turned down the driveway, Officer Buchanan said, "Mind if I ask you something? What were you doing out in the snow at this time of night anyway?" She sounded casual, or maybe she was working at sounding casual, but I knew it looked odd.

Fortunately, I'd had time to come up with an answer. "I couldn't sleep. I'm only living in Falstone temporarily, you see, and normally, I share a house with my teenage daughter, my parents, and a big dog. I'm just not used to all the quiet, and I thought some exercise would do me good."

"So you went out into the woods? I mean, I walked back up that direction, and I saw that fence—I wouldn't have been able to get over it without help."

I hadn't realized anybody had retraced my steps, and I could only hope Sid had covered his trail well enough that it hadn't been obvious that two people had climbed over instead of just one. "I only meant to walk to the property line, but then I saw the car, and I guess I got that adrenaline rush you read about. Of course, I should have just called you guys right away when I spotted it, but I couldn't tell for sure it was a crash until I got over the fence, and by that point, I had it in my head that I could help. Not too bright, really."

"Well, your heart was in the right place," Officer Buchanan said as she pulled up to the end of the driveway.

"That's a nice way to put it. Thanks for the ride."

"No problem." I must have been wobbling when I got out of the squad car because she said, "Are you going to be all right by yourself?"

"I'll be fine. I've got a friend with insomnia and I'll give him a call and get him to keep me company by phone if I need it."

"Okay, then." She waited until I was inside with the door shut before backing out again.

As soon as the cruiser's headlights disappeared, Sid came clattering toward me with his arms outstretched. "Are you okay? What happened?" Before I could answer, he said, "Wait, don't say anything until we get these wet things off of you." In no time he had me out of my coat and boots. Then he pushed me toward the living room, wrapped me in an afghan, and zipped off to bring me an enormous mug of hot chocolate, a ham sandwich, and a mountain of potato chips. "Eat first."

"Sid, you're the best," I said, taking a bite.

"You mean I'm the worst! Coccyx, Georgia, if I hadn't gone out tonight, you wouldn't have gotten mixed up in this."

"I'm not mixed up in it," I said, "and I'm glad you saw that car. Otherwise that poor woman could have been out there for months!" I repeated what Officer Buchanan had told me. "Can you imagine how awful that would have been for her family, not knowing where she is?"

"No, and I don't want to. I don't want you thinking about it, either. Now eat your sandwich, and I'll find something cheerful for you to watch on TV." He surfed through channels until he came across a station showing *Singin' in the Rain*, one of our favorites. It was definitely cheerful, but once I was fed and warm, I started drifting off to sleep. The last thing I remembered was the beginning of the "Gotta Dance" sequence.

CHAPTER FIVE

Sid's and my moods were subdued the next morning, but by lunchtime, we'd decided not to talk anymore about the poor woman we'd found. Maybe it was callous, but as Sid pointed out, there was nothing we could do for her.

Instead we focused on my normal weekend activities: laundry, house cleaning, and grading essays. Usually it took me most of the weekend to get all that taken care of, but with Sid's enthusiastic assistance, we were done by Saturday afternoon. I should have felt bad about him doing so much work, but he seemed to enjoy it. He could actually fold a fitted sheet, something I've never mastered. As for the essays, I used to feel guilty about letting him grade student work because he didn't have an English degree, but he'd taken some online courses and had spent decades with my parents and me—all three of us English professors. So he was really good at it. He sometimes caught things I'd missed.

The last item on the list was grocery shopping, and Sid tried to talk me into letting him come along, claiming that nobody would notice him with his winter paraphernalia on, but I put my foot down. I did let him ride with me, but he had to stay in the car and hide. That satisfied him, and he was fascinated with the scenery. Falstone is a pretty town, and with a new batch of snow falling, it looked like a freshly shaken snow globe. On the way home, we stopped at DiPietro's, the local pizza place, for my weekly pepperoni-covered treat, and then we went back to the bungalow for a video orgy.

Sunday was filled with more shoveling and snowblowing—

thanks to another snowfall overnight—a snowball fight, reading, and a nice long Skype conversation with the family. Having Sid around meant I wasn't nearly so lonely after talking to Madison, and I didn't sniff as long as I usually did.

Monday morning, I left Sid alone with his laptop and headed to campus with a much cheerier outlook than when I'd left it three days before.

Though I'd worked at a variety of colleges and universities during my nomadic adjunct existence, FAD was my first art school, so I was still getting used to the schedule. Every place I'd taught before had classes that either met on Monday-Wednesday-Friday or Tuesday-Thursday, but apparently the norm for art schools was Monday-Wednesday and Tuesday-Thursday classes. Friday was reserved for students to work on projects.

That didn't mean I got the day off, of course. Instead I kept office hours, graded papers, planned class discussions in my three sections of Expository Writing, and did all the other work that went into an adjunct's workload.

Or rather three-fifths of my workload. In addition to the three classes at FAD, I was also teaching two classes via the web.

After teaching and grading five sections' worth of essays each week, occasionally there was enough time left over that I could read a professional journal, or at least a paper. Maybe half a paper. Sometimes it was just a footnote.

Not that the conditions at FAD were any worse than at any other college. In some ways it was one of my better jobs. The department was almost all adjuncts—only Professor Waldron, the head of the department, was tenured. That meant I didn't have to deal with the caste system prevalent in some universities, in which adjuncts always ended up at the bottom. And for the first time in my career, I had my own office.

It wasn't large—the artist adjuncts' studios were twice as big—but I didn't need as much space as they did. Just having a desk, a file cabinet, two chairs, and a bookcase was a rare pleasure, not to mention the luxury of being able to meet students in private. I'd squatted in my parents' office at my last job, but that wasn't nearly so satisfying as having my own place. I'd even put up decorations: family photos, a map from *The Lord of the Rings*, and the movie poster from the Keira Knightley version of *Pride & Prejudice*. My favorite part was the door, complete with lock, which enabled me to shut myself off from students and other adjuncts when the desire arose.

My first class wasn't until eleven, but I liked getting in early to grade papers and deal with e-mails, many of which were from students asking for information that was spelled out in the syllabus I'd both handed out and e-mailed to my class members the first week of classes. I was just getting settled when there was a perfunctory knock on my door, followed by Mr. Perkins stepping in.

"Dr. Thackery? I'm sorry to interrupt, but Professor Waldron has called an emergency departmental meeting. It's right away in the conference room."

I knew he was lying. Sure, there was a meeting about to take place and I had no doubt some emergency had arisen, but the gray-haired, slender black man wasn't sorry about interrupting. If Professor Waldron asked him to, the English department's secretary would interrupt anybody, anywhere. His devotion was not, as far as I could tell, a romantic attachment, but it was intense. He considered her to be the most brilliant scholar ever to grace the halls of academe and seemed indignant that the rest of the world didn't share his opinion. He was amazingly efficient in providing support for faculty members who showed the right amount of reverence for her, so I made sure to do so.

"I'll be right there," I said.

"I've got coffee and Danish waiting."

Since Professor Waldron liked coffee and Danish, he assumed everyone else in the department would, too. Fortunately, I was fine with both.

I shut down my laptop and headed to the conference room, wondering what the problem was. Professor Waldron was a creature of routine, and she wouldn't have deviated from her usual schedule of Wednesday morning meetings unless it was important.

The English department wing, like all the departmental wings, was made up of a long corridor leading from the main building, which opened up into a round room that was sunny, spacious, well-equipped with chairs and couches, and nearly impossible to heat. Somebody in the early days of FAD had dubbed this hub the Roundling. Along the walls were doors to the faculty offices, conference rooms, and the Writing Lab, and there was a small snack bar and tables next to a door to the outside. A wide circular stairway in the middle of the Roundling led upstairs to the department's classrooms.

Naturally, given that FAD was an art school, the walls were hung with a frequently changing array of artwork, and there were even a couple of niches for sculpture. The selection that day seemed to be variations on a life model who was either slender, voluptuous, multicolored, or black-and-white, depending on the artist's vision. One creator had turned her into a "rubber hose" style cartoon character, like the early Disney films. I wasn't sure if the sculptors had used the same model as the other artists because they were going for the abstract. One was softly curved burnished metal and the other was angular scraps of wood tied together with blue and blood-red rope.

The English wing had both more and less space than strictly necessary. We needed all of the classrooms because every student was required to take Expository Writing as part of their core requirements, but we didn't really need the room for students to work or socialize. There was no degree program in literature or writing other than sequential art, so we didn't have many kids hanging around unless their own departmental hubs were too crowded for them.

That early in the morning, the Roundling was mostly deserted, except for a couple of students who were taking early morning naps on one of the couches, but the adjuncts were gathering in the conference room.

There were only five of us, plus Professor Waldron. FAD only offered a handful of English classes, primarily designed to help budding artists produce art history papers, grant proposals, and descriptions of their work. Waldron taught two sections of literature, but they were electives and not particularly popular. The rest of us mostly taught Expository Writing classes that weren't that much different from classes I'd taught at colleges all through New England.

My pal Caroline, who'd helped me get the job at FAD, was staring moodily at her Wonder Woman coffee cup while Owen was examining the selection of Danish. I noticed that he was filling two plates and sighed, knowing what was coming next.

Owen was a fan of Western literature. Not the James Joyce kind, but cowboy stories by people like Zane Grey and Owen Wister, with a good dose of Willa Cather. This had led him to grow a luxurious walrus mustache that he fancied made him look like a rough-and-tough cowboy instead of a WASP-y academic with a penchant for lip foliage. Owen and I had dated for a few months a couple of years earlier and at first I'd found that mustache attractive. Then my sister, Deborah, saw his picture, made a sound I can only describe as a guffaw, and said he looked like an adult film star from the seventies. I never could shake that image afterward.

"Good morning, Georgia," he said when he saw me. "I grabbed you a cream cheese Danish!"

"Thanks, Owen," I said and took the plate he offered.

"Can I get you some coffee?"

"No, thanks. I can get my own."

"I don't mind. Black, right?" He went for the coffee urn.

I stifled a second sigh and sat next to Caroline.

Owen was a nice enough guy, but there was no spark. I honestly hadn't given him much thought after we got new jobs and drifted apart. I'd assumed Owen felt the same, since he hadn't bothered to get in touch with me, but when I'd arrived at FAD, he said he'd been pining for me all that time. I rather thought my appeal had more to do with the fact that I was available. Caroline said he'd already cut a swath through several other departments at FAD, so now he was concentrating on ours.

Owen was straight, and since Caroline was happily married, Renee was engaged to an adjunct in the Painting department, and Dahna was seeing somebody off campus, that only left me and Professor Waldron. I couldn't imagine anybody flirting with Professor Waldron—Mr. Perkins would probably poison the coffee and Danish of anybody who dared to be so impertinent.

Fortunately, Dahna arrived before Owen could get back to the table, and sat next to me. Then Renee came in and sat next to Dahna. That gave me a two-adjunct buffer zone. Owen had to ask them to pass my coffee down to me, which I don't think he'd intended.

Mr. Perkins arrived, made sure we were all present and accounted for, carefully filled a coffee cup and prepared a plate with a pair of Danish, and left the offering at the head of the table. Then he sat down and stared expectantly at the door. A moment later, Professor Waldron made her entrance.

Professor Waldron—never Martha to anyone on campus, as far as I knew—was a well-built woman in her sixties, with tightly curled iron-gray hair and glasses that did nothing to lessen the power of her gaze. And she was always the last to arrive. I don't think she was trying to be a snob—she honestly believed that there was no reason for her to waste her time on small talk while waiting on other people. Caroline and I had repeatedly tried to figure out how she managed it. Was she hiding in some hidden corner where she could see us come in? Did Mr. Perkins have a signal ring to let her know the time was ripe?

She took her seat and nodded regally. "Good morning. If you don't mind, we'll move past the social courtesies and go straight into business."

Since her usual social courtesy consisted of saying, "I hope everyone is having a productive week," I didn't much feel the loss.

"I'm afraid I have some sad news for the department. I received word from the dean that Kelly Griffith has passed away."

"Oh no!" Caroline said, suddenly awake. "What happened?"

"I understand that it was a car crash."

"Did it happen Friday night?" I said with a squeak.

"Yes, it was." Professor Waldron raised an eyebrow. "Why do you ask?"

"I think I was the one who found her." I gave an abridged version of the story I'd told Officer Buchanan.

"I hesitate to criticize," Professor Waldron said, "but it would have been helpful if I'd been told slightly sooner. The school only notified me this morning."

"I didn't know it was her. I, um, didn't look at her face. I just… Anyway, the police didn't tell me who it was because they hadn't gotten in touch with the family yet."

I felt terrible for not realizing who the dead woman had been, though really there was no reason I should have. As far as I knew, I'd never seen Kelly's car before, and of course Kelly herself had been bundled in outdoor clothes.

Though Kelly was technically part of the department, she wasn't an instructor or a member of the administrative staff. Instead she ran the Writing Lab, a resource for students to get help with their papers. Given that FAD students were visual artists, not writers, she stayed busy and never seemed to have a free moment to spend with the rest of us.

"In that case, of course you have no reason to reproach yourself," Professor Waldron said. "The department will be sending flowers, once the arrangements have been made, and Mr. Perkins will pass around a condolence card for each of you to sign for the family."

"Please sign it promptly," he put in.

"I believe there will also be a memorial service here on campus. I will share those details once they are known."

We all nodded.

"Now in addition to the personal loss I'm sure we're all feeling, the department finds itself in an awkward position. I'm sure you're all aware of our Writing Across the Curriculum program."

We nodded again. The idea of the program was to ensure that all FAD graduates were thoroughly educated, not just trained in their particular art form, so every class included some sort of writing assignment.

"At this point in the semester, many of our students rely on the Writing Lab for help with their essays and papers, and it's difficult to know how long it will take to replace Ms. Griffith. The dean asked what can be done, and of course I assured him that we would staff the Lab ourselves as long as necessary." She looked at each of us briefly. "I can count on you, can't I?"

Of course she could. Since we were all adjuncts, any of us could be fired at any time, so we certainly weren't going to refuse. I was ashamed that under the circumstances, I was thinking about money, and I was relieved that plainspoken Renee asked, "Not to be crass, but we will get paid extra for that, won't we?"

Mr. Perkins pursed his lips, as if judging us for our unwillingness to serve the department in its time of need, but he could make that face all he wanted. While he got benefits like insurance and paid holidays with his job, we adjuncts did not.

Professor Waldron, at least, wasn't so judgmental. "Of course. Mr. Perkins will provide time sheets, and he also has a sign-up sheet so you can put your names down for the hours you are available. This will be considered hourly labor and will be paid from a separate fund than your teaching salary." In other words, even if we critiqued our hearts out, we still wouldn't get benefits.

Mr. Perkins placed some forms squarely in the middle of the table, though I noticed none of us reached for them. While I liked the idea of making extra bucks, I wasn't sure I wanted to add to my workload. Had Sid not arrived, I might have been more eager, but now that I had company, I was hoping for some fun time.

Professor Waldron said, "I do have another matter to bring up. I'd intended to wait for our regular meeting on Wednesday, but since I have you all together now, I may as well inform you right away. As you know, FAD is in the process of beefing up its core curriculum, and as part of that, there will be more rigorous requirements for graduation. Starting in the fall semester, students have to take another English course in addition to Expository Writing—either a writing course or a literature course. I explained to the dean that we were inadequately staffed to meet that need and he agreed that we need to bring more instructors on board."

That was good news. If they were going to hire additional adjuncts, then my job was safer. Like most businesses, when there's a need to reduce headcount, the newest hire is usually the first to go. Caroline had been hired a couple of weeks before I was, which left me at the head of the firing line.

Professor Waldron went on. "In fact, I was able to convince the dean that our reliance on adjunct faculty for essential goals could leave us in a precarious position. He agreed, and I have been given authorization to add one tenure track position. I would prefer to promote from within, so to speak, so I invite you all to throw your hats into the ring, should you be interested in the opportunity."

Tenure! With tenure came support for writing academic papers, applying for grants, and attending conferences; a budget for professional organizations and journals; travel stipends for conferences; the ability to sign time cards for student assistants; and a myriad of other perks. Tenure meant a guaranteed job until retirement—unless I really screwed up. Maybe a career at FAD wouldn't have been my first choice, but with tenure, even the insane amount of snow in Falstone wouldn't seem so bad.

Of course, from looking around the table, I could tell that the other four adjuncts wanted tenure just as badly as I did, and there was only one position available. We'd just gone from friendly colleagues to competitors. On the plus side, I was pretty sure that Owen wouldn't be saving the cheese Danish for me anymore.

Professor Waldron gathered her notes. "I believe that is all for today. Don't forget to sign up for any shifts you can manage at the Writing Lab. Unless something urgent occurs, we can forgo our Wednesday meeting."

She swept out, with Mr. Perkins bringing up the rear. We five newly made rivals looked at each other for a moment and Renee said, "You know, that announcement wasn't an accident. She wants to see how much extra work we're willing to take on to prove our worthiness for tenure."

"Oh yeah," I said.

"Completely transparent," Caroline chimed in.

We all nodded at the unfairness of it. Then Renee said, "And it's totally going to work."

"Oh yeah," I said.

"Completely transparent," Caroline chimed in.

To our credit, we did not go all Thunderdome with the sign-up sheets. We took turns like grown-ups and even signed up for the same number of hours each so nobody would get an unfair advantage. Of course, I thought it likely that somebody would approach Mr. Perkins separately to glom on to more hours. To get a better shot at tenure, I might even be that somebody.

CHAPTER SIX

After the meeting, I taught my eleven o'clock class, grabbed a bowl of corn chowder and a roll for lunch, taught my one-thirty class, and went back to my office to deal with assorted routine e-mails and memos. At least, I'm pretty sure I did. The vision of tenure kept dancing in my head like sugarplums running late for Christmas, so I mostly operated on autopilot until it was time to head home for the day.

I'd texted Sid that I was on my way back, so I wasn't entirely surprised to find him waiting for me. The fact that he had a tray with a glass of Dr Pepper and two Ritz crackers spread with peanut butter waiting for me was less expected, and the fact that he was wearing a ruffled floral apron was downright astonishing.

"Hello, dear. How was your day?" he said with a grin.

Of course I had to play along. "Traffic was terrible, and work was worse. This country is going to the dogs! And didn't I tell you I wanted my Dr Pepper straight up and not on the rocks?"

Laughter ensued.

"Seriously, though," I said when I was able, "what's with the faux fifties greeting? And where did you find that apron?"

"In a box in the closet. There's a surprising amount of storage space in this place."

"Space where we shouldn't be sticking our noses and/or nasal cavities."

"I put everything back exactly where I found it, and I won't do it anymore if you don't want me to."

"Is that because you realize you shouldn't have, or because you've already turned the place inside out?"

His grin was all the answer I needed.

"Just be sure the apron goes back where it belongs. The Benstommes are doing me a big favor by letting me stay here rent free." Then I casually took a sip of my soda and even more casually said, "I wonder if they'd know of a place I can rent long-term. You know, if I get tenure."

"Tenure? TENURE! You're getting tenure?" Sid hadn't spent his entire semi-life living with academics without learning what that meant.

"Maybe. It's not a done deal, not by a long shot, but at least I'm in the running."

"Woo hoo! So if you get this job, will we officially move to Falstone?"

"Sure, if we can find a place. Maybe in a few years, we could even buy a house."

"I'll check real estate listings tonight and see what's available. It would be great to have a place as isolated as this one so I could take care of the snow shoveling and stuff, but if not, that's okay. Is the high school in town good? Or would Madison stay with your parents during the school year?"

"I haven't gotten that far yet." On the one hand, I missed Madison dreadfully. On the other hand, I didn't want to tear her away from a school she adored for her last two years before graduation.

"What are salaries like at FAD?"

"I have no idea."

"You didn't check before you came here?"

I shook my head. "I used to check on average salaries every time I started at a new school. I even chose between two positions by taking the one that had the higher starting salary for permanent jobs, just in case. But after a few years, I stopped—it just depressed me to compare what they get to what I get."

"Not anymore!" Sid said gleefully. "You've got this in the bag."

"There are five other adjuncts who want it just as much as I do, and they've all been here longer than I have, so don't get your hopes up."

"Please! Professor Waldron wouldn't have thrown it open that way if she was just going with seniority. She wants the best candidate, and that's you. I think we need a dance party!"

"Sid, we don't need a dance party for a twenty percent chance of a—"

But it was too late. He'd already run off to get his laptop and came back with dance music playing loudly while he gesticulated wildly. What Sid lacks in grace and skill, he more than makes up for in enthusiasm and staying power, and his fresh moves led me to conclude that he'd been watching music videos on YouTube in my absence. After a moment I joined in, though I was hopelessly hampered by the need to follow the laws of biology, unlike my bony friend.

Eventually we got on to making dinner.

"So tell me about the competition."

"First up is Caroline Craig."

"Caroline? She's the one who scores us all the hot new graphic novels, right?"

"That's her. She helped me get this job, too." Caroline, a redhead who tied her hair back in a ponytail and hated to dress up even more than I did, was my best friend at FAD. Whenever her husband was away on business, she and I shared geeky movie nights. She'd been delighted to move to FAD because it gave her a chance to teach a course in graphic novels, something she'd been dreaming of for years. "She's a real sweetie."

"Are her credentials as good as yours?"

"It's tough to say. I think I've got my name on more papers than she does. She's been an adjunct longer and is a few years older than I am, but I'm not sure if that's a plus or a minus. Being married might make her seem more stable."

"But you've got Madison. Motherhood makes you stable."

"Unfortunately, single motherhood still raises the occasional judgmental eyebrow. Besides, I don't think having kids adds to psychological stability anyway. I mean, we're always saying, 'That kid drives me crazy!'"

"You never say that about Madison."

"Well, she's awesome. Anyway, I think somebody who specializes in graphic novels would be a great fit for FAD, but Professor Waldron does tend to prefer instructors who specialize in the works of dead white guys."

"What's the matter with dead white guys?" Sid said indignantly. "You live with one!"

"Point taken. Many dead white guys are charming, and if you write a book, I'll be happy to read it, but one does like to reflect diversity in the literature one presents to one's students."

"Ooo, you're going into professor speech. Practicing for tenure already! I think you've got the edge on Caroline."

"I think so, too, but it's close."

By then we were ready to settle at the table: me to eat a Caesar salad and spaghetti, Sid to keep me company.

"Who else?" he asked.

"Owen Deen."

"That name sounds familiar."

"I taught with him at Lesley, and we went out for a semester."

"Wait, not Porn Star Owen!"

"He's not a porn star—he just looks like one. At least his upper lip does."

"If you're going to start commenting on his other attributes, I'm going to leave the room."

"No comment on those," I said. "It's just that I still feel guilty for rejecting him over something as superficial as a mustache."

"Your instincts are good. If he'd been worth keeping around, you would have overlooked the lip caterpillar."

"I guess. He's been trying to get me to go out with him again ever since I started working at FAD."

"Tell him to buzz off!" Sid said heartlessly. Which only made sense, I suppose. "Is he a better academic than he was a boyfriend?"

"It's hard to be fair to him given our history, but I don't think he's that great. He's decent as an instructor but doesn't seem to keep up with current stuff in the field, and though he has some publications, they're not in the best journals. Plus I don't think Mr. Perkins likes him."

"Does Mr. Perkins's opinion carry that much weight?"

"It does with Professor Waldron. They have a strongly symbiotic relationship."

"Does Mr. Perkins like you?"

"I believe so. He doesn't dislike me, anyway. I think that's as far as he goes for anybody other than Professor Waldron."

"Then hooray for Mr. Perkins. Next?"

"Dahna Kaleka. She's a fabulous instructor. I sat in on her talk about 'The Lottery' once and was just enthralled. On a personal level, she's got no sense of humor and is perpetually earnest." Her big brown eyes shone with it, and her voice was solemn whether she was talking about literature or her large Lebanese family. "Professionally, her only weakness is that she hates to write. I don't think she's written a thing since her dissertation, and word is that it was the shortest one ever accepted at her school."

"How many publications do you have again?"

"Six," I said. "Of course, I'm only third author on two of them, and two of the others were poster sessions, so that's not a big deal."

"Six beats none. Who does that leave?"

"Renee Turner, who is a pretty good instructor, especially when she's teaching poetry, but she's not much of an academic. She went out for drinks a couple of weeks ago with me and Caroline, and she got buzzed enough to confess that she only works to support her real passion: raising Shiba Inus."

"Shiba Inus?"

"You know, the dogs? Madison almost picked a Shiba the day she went to adopt Byron."

"I know what Shiba Inus are. I'm familiar with most dog breeds."

"Really?" Sid was famous for not liking dogs and given his

bone structure—heavy on the bone—I didn't really blame him. The dogs he'd encountered had either barked in a frenzy, run away in fear, or tried to eat him. Byron was from the third category, and Sid had never forgiven him for their first encounter and the resulting tooth marks on his femur. The attack hadn't hurt him—Sid didn't feel pain, exactly—but it had offended his dignity. "Why would you read up on dogs?"

"Sun Tzu says, know your enemy," he said darkly. "If you ask me, the best part about coming here is getting away from the dog."

"I miss Byron," I said.

"Seriously?"

"There's something soothing about having a dog around. You know, they bring in a therapy dog at FAD every week or so, more often near the end of the semester when projects are due. Cuddling with a dog, even for a little while, reduces stress like you wouldn't believe."

"It wouldn't relieve my stress." He shuddered noisily at the thought. "But back to the Get Georgia Tenure Project…"

"Right. Anyway, perhaps Renee isn't a strong academic, but she's been at FAD a long time—she and Dahna started at around the same time. Her fiancé is another FAD adjunct, which could be a plus." She had blonde hair, a turned-up nose, and a sense of humor that rode a thin line between hilarious and malicious.

"You can take her," Sid said confidently. "You can take 'em all!"

"Maybe. I'm just worried about—" But before I could tell Sid what I was worried about, the doorbell rang.

Sid and I looked at one another in mutual panic. "Coccyx! Where can I hide?" he asked.

At my parents' house, there was an armoire in the living room reserved for Sid to duck into when somebody showed up unexpectedly. Since the mailman was the only person who'd come to the bungalow since I'd been in residence, it hadn't occurred to us to establish a hidey-hole.

"I can't go through the living room to get to my room. Whoever it is could see me through the window on the front door."

"In the cabinet?"

"Not enough space, and it would be noisy."

The doorbell rang again. Since my minivan was in the driveway, I didn't think I could fake being somewhere else.

"Dishwasher."

"Full of dishes. Same problem."

"Washing machine!"

He zipped over and looked inside. "Tight, but I can manage it. But make some covering noise."

"I'm coming!" I yelled loudly. "Just washing my hands." I turned the water on full blast.

In the meantime, Sid went into the washing machine skull first, letting himself fall apart as he went. There was a slight clatter, but I didn't think it was too noticeable.

Once I was sure he was out of sight, I went to the front door and looked out the window that Sid was afraid of being seen through. My guest was a surprise, to say the least. Officer Buchanan was standing on the porch, looking at me with a cheerful grin.

CHAPTER SEVEN

I tried to manufacture a welcoming smile as I opened the door, though I wasn't entirely sure it was the appropriate expression for when a police officer showed up unexpectedly. "Officer Buchanan. This is a surprise."

"Nobody ever expects me. I'm like the Spanish Inquisition," she said with a chuckle.

I laughed dutifully.

"I knew you'd get that reference. Too many people in this town don't appreciate Monty Python, which is a real shame if you ask me. Can I come in?"

"Please do."

"I'll just leave my coat and boots here—I don't want to track any snow in."

I knew that I should have asked for a warrant or some reason for her to be there, but she was so jovial I couldn't bring myself to do it.

So as soon as she had hung up her coat on the hall tree and carefully put her boots on the rubber mat next to where I'd left mine, I led the way into the living room.

"What can I do for you?"

"I was in the neighborhood and wanted to see how you were holding up. Finding an accident victim like you did would throw just about anybody for a loop."

"That's very kind of you, but I'm doing okay."

"Glad to hear it." She sniffed noticeably. "Something smells mighty good in here. I sure hope I didn't interrupt your supper."

"No worries. It'll keep."

"No, ma'am, there's no need to let your food get cold. We can talk in the kitchen just as easy."

The kitchen was the last place I wanted her to go, but she was out of the living room before I could think of an excuse to stop her.

She hesitated before she took Sid's chair, and she definitely put her hand on the seat, as if checking for body warmth. That wasn't going to be a problem, since he was noticeably free of both body and warmth, but I didn't like that she'd thought it was worth checking. It implied that she suspected I'd lied about being alone. At least there was only one place set at the table.

"Would you like some spaghetti? I made way more than I can eat—I'm not used to cooking for one."

"Oh, you don't have to do that. I can grab a burger from McDonald's after my shift ends. It'll probably still be warm by the time I get home."

"I insist," I said, knowing a hint when I heard it, and got a plate to load up for her.

"A hot, home-cooked meal is just what I need to warm up my insides on a night like this. The winters around here take some getting used to—you know, I'm not from around here."

"The accent was kind of a giveaway." My friend Caroline had a slight Southern accent, but her years away from Virginia had softened it. Officer Buchanan's, on the other hand, was so thick I could have spread it on toast, or more appropriately, a buttermilk biscuit.

I put the spaghetti, a glass of water, silverware, and a napkin in front of her.

"This is awfully kind of you."

"My pleasure. Having company for dinner is a nice change."

"That's right, you're here all alone. I thought I heard voices when I got up to the house."

Fortunately, I'd just taken a bite, which gave me time to come up with a good response. "They say talking to yourself is a sign of cabin fever, but I have an excuse. I was practicing for my lecture tomorrow. The textbook I'm using is new to me, so I have to do a fair amount of preparation."

"A teacher doing homework? Now that's something I would never have thought about. Why don't you use a textbook you already know?"

"It's all part of the glamorous adjunct lifestyle. I almost never get to pick my own textbooks. The departments that hire me make those decisions and it's up to me to catch up."

"Can you explain to me just exactly what an adjunct is? I'm not quite understanding the idea. How is what you do different from any other college professor?"

"It's the difference between a full-time receptionist and a temp. Both answer the phone and take messages, but a receptionist has job security and maybe even a contract, so she can't be fired at the drop of a hat. A temp gets hired as needed and is let go when the workload decreases. A tenured professor is like the regular receptionist—an adjunct is a temp."

"Why don't colleges hire all permanent professors?"

"Using adjuncts is cheaper. Colleges pay us per course taught and don't have to pony up for insurance and vacation and all that."

"And they can get away with working you full time without giving you benefits?"

"The thing is, I only teach three classes at FAD, which puts me under the legal limit for full-time work. To make up the difference in income, I teach two more classes at Montserrat College of Art in Beverly, Mass."

"That's a heck of a long way to commute."

"It would be if I taught in person—I teach those classes online."

"Is that easier than doing it face-to-face?"

"Kind of, once it's set up, but I don't enjoy it as well and I don't think the students get as much out of the classes. If there were another college nearby, I'd try to teach some classes there, instead, but Falstone is kind of isolated."

She nodded, as if trying to put all the pieces together. "Okay, maybe I'm missing something, but why don't you get one of those permanent jobs? Tenure, you called it. Or do you like roaming around?"

"Not so much. Moving as often as I do makes it a lot harder to do my job, and it's rough on my daughter, too."

"Where is she? Is she staying with her father?"

"With my parents, actually." Madison's father and I had parted ways soon after I found out I was pregnant, and he had never been a part of her life. "I didn't want to uproot her in the middle of the school year if I could help it. And the reason I don't have a tenured job is because they're hard to get. There aren't that many positions open, and there are a whole lot of candidates out there who are just as qualified as I am." Sid might not agree, but I knew I had stiff competition for the position at FAD.

"Sounds rough," Officer Buchanan said. "On the good side, you must get to meet an awful lot of people."

"I suppose."

"Is that why you didn't recognize Kelly Griffith's body when you found her the other night?"

"Excuse me?" All of a sudden the jovial woman didn't sound so friendly.

"It's just that when I went to the college this afternoon to see if I could track her movements on Friday night, I found out you work right there where she did. Your offices are practically next to each other."

"I didn't recognize her because I never looked at her face. She was lying face down, and I didn't move her. I thought I told you that."

"You did say something along those lines, but here's the thing: there are loads of people I recognize without seeing their faces."

"I could say the same, but I barely knew Kelly."

"Even though she was part of your department? A department that has, what, eight people?"

"First off, I've only been here a few weeks, so I only know a handful of people by their back view. Second, Kelly didn't spend much time with the rest of us."

"Why is that?"

"I don't know. Maybe because her job wasn't all that much like what we do. She didn't teach classes—she did one-on-one critique sessions and tutoring."

"So you never spoke to her?"

"Of course I spoke to her!" I took a deep breath. "I met her briefly when I started at FAD at the first of the semester, when Mr. Perkins was taking me and another new hire around to meet the rest of the department."

"The other new hire would have been Caroline Craig?"

She'd really done her background work. "That's right. Kelly also came to the first departmental meeting of the semester, but she didn't show up after that because we meet when the rest of us don't teach classes, which made it a prime time for her to schedule sessions with students. I saw her in the Roundling—"

"The what now?"

"That big round room that's the hub of the department. I saw her there and at the snack bar a few times, and we chatted a little."

"About?"

"The weather. The T-shirt she was wearing. Nothing important."

"Nothing more serious?"

"Not that I remember, but it sounds like you've got something in mind."

"I understand you and Ms. Griffith had a disagreement a couple of weeks ago, and it got pretty heated."

I thought back. "You're not talking about the problem with that kid's grade, are you?"

"You tell me."

"It was no big deal," I said in exasperation. "Kelly reviewed a student's paper and told him she was sure he'd get an A. Which she should never have said in the first place. Then I gave the kid a C, which was all the paper deserved. He ran and complained to her, and she came to my office to ask what the story was. I guess we got kind of loud because I didn't like her questioning my grading and she didn't like my not appreciating her critiquing. But we calmed down, and I showed her why I scored the way I did. It turns out the student had turned in the wrong draft, meaning that what I saw was the version before he implemented Kelly's suggestions. So we got the student to come down and explained it to him. He was able to pull up the corrected paper on his laptop, and I gave him a break by grading that paper instead. Since it was clearly just a mistake, I didn't even take off points. He got an A and a reminder that he should come to me first when he didn't think a grade was fair. He thanked me for being so understanding and apologized profusely, and so did Kelly. As I said, no big deal." I narrowed my eyes. "I'm surprised you even heard about it."

Officer Buchanan didn't respond to my unspoken question. "And you had no other interactions with her?"

But I was getting tired of the third degree. "Why do you need to know so much about somebody who died in a car accident?"

"There are accidents, and then there are accidents."

"What does that even mean?"

"It means that when it got light enough for us to get a good look at where Ms. Griffith's car went off the road, we couldn't see any reason for her to lose control of her car. No ice on the road, no skid marks from braking, no signs that somebody had hit her. She just drove into the woods."

"Could she have been texting?" It was against the law in Massachusetts, but that didn't mean people didn't do it.

"Nope, she left her phone at work. It was under her desk, so she most likely didn't even realize it was missing."

I had wondered why she didn't use it to call for help. "I don't want to speak ill of the dead, but it was Friday night. Had she been drinking?"

"Might could have been, and we're running tests, but the results won't be back for a couple of weeks. We'll be checking for things other than alcohol, too."

"Meaning what?"

"There are all kinds of things that will make a person wonky enough to run off the road."

"Oh. I never heard any rumors of Kelly taking drugs, but I suppose there's no particular reason I would have."

"Because you didn't know her that well?"

"Exactly," I said firmly. "I didn't."

Officer Buchanan shrugged. "As it turns out, nobody else— nobody who admits to knowing her, that is—had heard anything about her self-medicating either and there's nothing to indicate it in her apartment. But then again, maybe she didn't know she was taking them."

It took a minute to figure out what she was implying. "You think somebody drugged her?"

"I don't think anything for sure, not until we get that blood work back. The trouble is, even if we do find something, by then the trail will be stone cold. And not just because of the weather. So I'm just clearing the brush away now."

"So I'm part of the brush?"

"You're somebody who knew and worked with the victim but didn't recognize her when you found her body. And you were running around in hip-deep snow in the wee hours of the morning and getting over a fence without anybody to help you. You did say there was nobody else with you that night, didn't you?"

"That's what I said. From the time I got home that night, I didn't see another living soul until you police showed up." I said it forcefully, hoping the truth would shine through. That is what I'd said before, and though Sid having a soul or not was debatable, he most definitely wasn't living.

"Is that right?" she said skeptically.

"Do you think I'm lying?"

"Everybody lies to the police."

"Maybe that's because you ask questions that are none of your business."

She chuckled and said, "If I knew a way to get the job done without asking the wrong questions, I'd do it that way. Now I suppose I've worn out my welcome. Thank you kindly for the spaghetti. You sure I can't help you wash the dishes?"

"Positive." I didn't want her in my house a minute longer than necessary.

She chuckled again, but I didn't join in. After she retrieved her jacket and boots, I watched to make sure she actually got into the squad car and drove off before shutting and locking the front door behind her.

CHAPTER EIGHT

I went back to the kitchen and tapped on the top of the washer. "You can come out."

"Is she gone?" Sid said, his voice echoing in the drum of the machine.

"No, and now she knows there's somebody in there."

"Ha ha, you have struck my funny bone," Sid said. "Open the lid, would you?"

I did so, and in seconds he'd reassembled and climbed out.

"Seriously, Sid, did you think I'd tell you to come out if she was still here?"

"How do I know what you'd forget? Like, you know, the fact that you knew the woman whose body we found."

"I know, and I'm sorry. With the announcement about tenure, Kelly's death kind of got pushed to the back of my mind. Which is a terrible thing to say, even if I barely knew her. Not to mention my not recognizing her."

"How could you have? From the back of her neck and the color of her coat?"

"Still."

"Don't worry about that, Georgia."

I was comforted for two seconds, which is how long it was before he went on.

"What you should be worrying about is telling that cop your whole life story. Not to mention inviting her to dinner. Coccyx, Georgia, what were you thinking?"

"What was I supposed to do?"

"Ask her what she wanted and tell her that if she didn't have a warrant, she couldn't come in. You've got rights, you know. Does 'you have the right to remain silent' ring any bells? I mean, it's only in every cop show ever."

"One, I do know my rights, even though unlike some people, I don't have time to binge on *CSI* and *Rizzoli & Isles*. Two, I didn't know I was a suspect. Three, if I had made a fuss, that would definitely have raised suspicions."

"She's already got plenty of ossifying suspicions! She thinks you killed that woman."

"She doesn't even know for sure that Kelly was murdered," I protested. "She's just fishing."

"No kidding, but what she's fishing for is a killer. Why would she tell you all that stuff if she wasn't waiting to see how you reacted? But keep telling yourself that she just wanted to come for a friendly visit right up until you're arrested. Or until she does get a search warrant and finds me."

"Geez, Sid, I didn't think of that." Hadn't I read that once you allowed police officers inside your home, they were entitled to snoop around? What if Buchanan had suddenly become curious about my laundry? "Maybe we should ship you back to Pennycross, where it's safe."

"Not on your life! I'm not leaving you here alone. You're like a babe in the woods when it comes to protecting yourself."

"I've got nothing to hide, Sid, other than you." And technically, I didn't even have to hide him—it was completely legal to have a human skeleton.

"Cops are only human—sometimes they decide the wrong person is guilty. I should know—they thought I was a killer at Halloween."

"That was a special case. Of course they thought it was odd when you disappeared."

"And they think it's odd that you went out in the snow at O-dark-thirty. Though I suppose that's my fault."

"Of course it's your fault."

He looked taken aback. "It is?"

"Absolutely. It's your fault that you thought somebody might be in trouble, and that you didn't think about anything other than helping her, even if it was dangerous for you."

"But I got you into danger."

"I'm not in danger. I'm only under suspicion, and only until Officer Buchanan finds the real killer, if there even is one. For all we know, the blood test results she was talking about will come back negative, and they'll decide it really was just an accident. I can suffer a few slings and arrows of outrageous fortune in the meantime."

"While you're trying to get tenure?"

"Yeah, that. Tenure already sounds iffy if my colleagues are spreading dirt about me. Caroline is the only person I told about that argument with Kelly—I hate to think that she'd throw me under a bus."

"She could have told somebody else in the department."

"True. We adjuncts do love our gossip. She could have told plenty of people and not meant any harm by it." I was relieved by the idea. I liked Caroline. Of course, I liked the other people in the department, too, for the most part. The idea of any of them running around telling tales behind my back made me uncomfortable.

"Professor Waldron setting you guys against one another could lead to a whole lot of stories coming out."

"I'm afraid you're right." I had some odd ones in my background, too, mostly involving Sid and murder, but I didn't want him to think he was putting my career at risk. He was already feeling guilty enough.

"So what we're going to have to do is get proactive," he said.

"Sid, I don't want tenure enough to dig up dirt on my colleagues."

"We're not going to. Unless one of them is the killer, of course."

"The killer—?"

"Obviously the only way to get that cop off your back and clear your path to tenure is to find the killer ourselves."

"I don't know, Sid. My running around asking questions could make me look more suspicious, not less."

"Not when we figure out who the real killer is."

"Then what about Professor Waldron? Do you think she's going to want to give tenure to somebody who plays detective instead of publishing papers?"

"She doesn't have to know. We can be discreet. We've always been discreet in the past."

"Not that much. Some of the adjuncts here have heard rumors. Caroline was one of the people we called about the girl who was murdered in October, so she knows I got tangled up in that case."

He waved a bony hand. "You worry too much."

"Maybe you don't worry enough. This isn't a game."

He paused for a long time, and at first I thought I'd convinced him. Then I thought he was peeved. It turned out to be a lot more complex.

"I know it's not a game, Georgia. Murder is never a game. I may know that better than anybody."

"Oh Sid." I knew he was talking about his own murder, and he was right—nobody could better know than he did. "Do you... Are you starting to remember more?"

"No, my memory still starts on that day I met you, but sometimes I think about that guy I used to be, and what his life would have been. I wonder if he'd have met somebody and settled down, had a family."

"You have a family. You have us."

"But it's not the same. I mean, I love you guys, I really do, and I'm happy. For all I know, maybe I'm happier than that other guy would have been."

"But you'll never really know."

"That's right. And we'll never know what kind of life Kelly Griffith would have had. So if we can help figure out what happened to her, don't you think we should?"

"But the cops—"

"We can do things the cops can't, and you know it. You understand academia, right?"

"Right."

"And I'm me."

"Right again."

He held up a fist. "Which makes us what?"

I couldn't just leave him hanging, so I bumped his fist. "The team supreme."

So we were back in the sleuthing business. I reflected when I got to bed that night that I really should have seen it coming.

CHAPTER NINE

Despite our resolution, we didn't do a whole lot of detecting or investigating that night. Once the dishes were done, I had papers to grade while Sid went online to see what he could find out about Kelly's death. A couple of hours later, he regretfully announced that he hadn't found much. The death hadn't caused much of a splash and had only gotten as much play as it had in the *Falstone Journal* because Kelly had worked there several years earlier. The coverage didn't hint at it being anything other than a tragic accident, and I wondered if that meant the police were keeping it under wraps or if Officer Buchanan was working on her own.

The only new information Sid found was that Kelly had grown up in Wyoming and had no family nearby. That seemed to rule out any of her relatives as her killer, which was a relief. Not only would it have been really upsetting to find out that she'd been killed by a family member, but I would have had zero access to those people. And despite Sid's enthusiasm, we knew that anything face-to-face would have to be handled by me. Sid came up short in the face department.

Still, neither of us were discouraged. Sid is the most optimistic person I know, and when I went to work the next day, I knew he'd be spending his hours burning up the Internet to see what else he could find.

I only had one class on Tuesdays and Thursdays, but unfortunately for me and my students, it was at eight in the morning. Once it was over, I headed for the Writing Lab. At the staff meeting, I'd signed up for a two-hour shift starting at ten thirty. Since I knew almost nothing about how things worked there, I was hoping that if I arrived early, one of the other adjuncts would be there to enlighten me. I was right, but unfortunately it was Owen who was finishing up with a student when I arrived.

"Good morning, Georgia! I knew you were taking the shift after me, so I reserved some time to show you the ropes." He ushered the student out unceremoniously and shut the door behind him. "So we won't be interrupted while I give you the grand tour," he explained.

I didn't think the office warranted a tour even if it was twice as large as mine, but I nodded.

"That was Kelly's desk," he said, pointing to one end of the long rectangle of a room. "The cubbies are available for students to write in, but I don't think they get used much." Two of them were piled high with books and magazines, and the third was dusty, so he was probably right. There were more books on the shelves above each workstation, and a quartet of file cabinets separated the two halves of the room. "The books are old textbooks, guides to writing research papers, style books, and resource materials for generating ideas. Not that anybody uses them. Kids mostly just come here to get their papers proofread, and half the time, it's an hour before deadline."

"That's when I used to finish my papers," I said. "I bet you were the same."

He looked momentarily indignant, then relented. "You're probably right. Anyway, I don't know what's in the files—papers from years gone past most likely. You're welcome to look inside if you've got a week to kill."

"Maybe later," I said, thinking that Sid would like nothing better than to go through every single drawer and folder. "How does scheduling work?"

"There's a portal on the department's website for students to sign up for time slots, and Mr. Perkins set it up so we could all access the list. He e-mailed a memo with the passwords and so forth this morning, but in the meantime, he printed out today's schedule."

"Anything else I should know?"

"Just that if you see anything around that belonged to Kelly, pass it on to Mr. Perkins. The cops sent an officer over to examine her personal effects yesterday, and then Mr. Perkins boxed it up to send it to her family, but they might have missed something."

"Would that officer have been Officer Buchanan?" I asked.

"That sounds right. She questioned a few of us about Kelly. Did you talk to her, too?"

"She was the one who brought me home after I found Kelly's body," I said, which was true, if not complete. I didn't want word to get around the department that she'd come to my house to question me further.

"You should have called me that night, Georgia. I could have provided moral support."

"I appreciate the thought, but you wouldn't have wanted me to wake you at that time of night."

"I'd rather lose sleep than have you be all alone at a time like that." He paused. "You were alone, right? That cop asked if you had company in town."

"She asked about me?"

"She was asking about all of us, what Kelly was like, and how we got along with her. Nothing to worry about."

"Okay, good," I said, though I was still worrying.

"And you didn't have company over that night, did you?"

"Nope, no company," I said. I was being truthful again. Even if he wasn't a blood relation, what with having no blood, Sid was family, not company. It was none of Owen's business, of course, but I wanted at least the appearance of having no secrets to hide.

"Okay then, if you ever need me, don't hesitate to call, no matter what time of day it is."

"Thank you," I said, knowing I would never take him up on it.

"What are friends for? We are still friends, aren't we?"

"I thought so."

"It was nice when we were more than that, wasn't it?"

"Owen," I said with a sigh. "I'm sorry. I respect you and like you, but not in a romantic way." I'd told him that the first time he'd suggesting renewing our relationship, but somehow he hadn't gotten the message. He didn't get it this time, either.

"You can't blame a guy for not wanting to give up on the best thing he ever had." It would have been more appealing to me if he hadn't followed that up with a loving stroke of his mustache.

"So what's today's schedule look like?" I asked, eager to change the subject.

"Nobody is signed up for the next hour," he said. "We could go get coffee or—"

There was a tap on the door. "Maybe we've got a walk-in."

He looked at the list again. "Tell whoever it is to make an appointment and come back later. We aren't responsible for walk-ins."

I ignored him and opened the door. A young woman was standing there, looking around uncertainly.

"Hi. I'm Dr. Thackery, and this is Dr. Deen. We're filling in here." She just looked at me. "I assume you heard the bad news about Ms. Griffith." Actually I wasn't so much assuming as hoping, because I didn't want to have to break it to her if she hadn't.

Fortunately for me, she nodded, but she didn't say anything else.

"Are you Michelle?" Owen said. "Because if you are, your appointment isn't for an hour."

"Um... No."

I waited for her to offer a name, but she just looked at me. She was tiny in all dimensions, and her turquoise-blue eyes were the most vivid thing about her. "Do you need some help with a paper or something?" I finally asked.

"Actually I need to get something I left with Ms. Griffith. It's a sketchbook."

"Owen, was there a sketchbook in here?"

"Not that I know of. What does it look like?"

The student said, "Um, black cover. Spiral bound. Just a regular sketchbook."

"We haven't seen it," Owen said.

"Are you sure?" she asked. "Because, you know… It's kind of important?"

Owen looked uninterested, so I said, "The department secretary boxed up a bunch of Kelly's belongings, and it might have ended up in there. You can go check with him."

Her eyes widened, as if she were alarmed by the idea of speaking to yet another stranger.

I shifted gears. "Or I could ask him and get back to you if you'll leave your contact info."

"That's okay. Um, I'll check back later." She turned and fled.

"What do you think?" Owen said. "Freshman? Freshmen are always flaky, and freshman art students are definitely the flakiest. So, about that coffee—"

Before I could answer, there was another tap at the door and Owen made an exasperated sound.

I recognized the next visitor, a stocky man with reddish-blond hair and a matching beard that didn't quite conceal his freckles.

"Hi, Jeremy. Looking for some tutoring?" Renee had introduced me to her fiancé at a campus reception at the beginning of the term, and we'd discovered that we shared an affinity for cocktail wieners. He wasn't entirely humorless, but it wasn't easy to get a smile out of him, let alone a laugh. I had no luck this time, either.

He said, "I'd heard that somebody was taking over the Writing Lab, but I didn't realize it was you two."

"Actually, all of us in the department are taking shifts until they hire somebody new. Didn't Renee tell you?"

"She might have—I was working last night, so I was kind of distracted. Anyway, I wanted to tell you that I'm about to assign term papers to my classes, and I'm requiring them to have their papers vetted here."

"We should be able to handle it," I said. "What's the topic?"

"Their biggest artist influences among the Italian masters—though they can pick a Dutch master if they want." From the expression on his face, Jeremy had serious doubts about anybody who'd pick a Dutch master over an Italian one.

"And the crowd goes wild with excitement," Owen said sarcastically.

"Ignore him, Jeremy. Anyway, just tell your students to sign up sooner rather than later, and we'll get them taken care of."

"Great. Good seeing you, Georgia. And, um, Owen." He wandered off.

"And people say English professors don't live in the real world. What does Renee see in him anyway?" He paused and stroked his mustache, as if waiting for me to join him in mocking Jeremy and perhaps Renee as well. When I didn't, he went on, "So we've still got time for coffee."

After all Owen's sneering, the last thing I wanted was to spend more time with him, and I was trying to decide between a tactful answer and a truthful one when there was a third tap on the door. I think I actually heard Owen growl deep in his throat.

"There you are, Georgia!" Caroline said. "Ready for our meeting?"

We did not, as far as I knew, have a meeting, but before I could apologize for forgetting it, Caroline raised her eyebrows, glanced at Owen, and winked. So I looked at my watch and said, "Wow, I totally lost track of time."

"Let's go into my office for this one."

"Great. See you later, Owen. Thanks for the tour."

"Anytime," he said tonelessly. Even his mustache looked disgruntled.

Once the door to Caroline's office was closed, I said, "And thank you for the save!"

"I figured I owed you. I switched shifts with Owen today, not realizing he was planning to lie in wait for you."

"Ambush flirting is not my favorite courtship method."

"Why don't you tell him you're dating that carny. You are still seeing him, right?"

"You mean Dr. Mannix?" True, Brownie Mannix was a carny

from a longtime carny family, but he was also an adjunct professor specializing in American studies. We'd started seeing one another in the fall, and I had hopes that we would continue doing so, but he still had a job in Pennycross, which made it tricky. On those rare occasions that I'd made it back home before the snow set in, I hadn't been able to spend any time with him because I'd wanted to see Madison and my family. Since then we'd exchanged e-mails, texts, and phone calls, but the relationship was still too new to go long-distance successfully. We'd finally admitted that we were both interested but needed closer proximity before we could be sure we wanted to move forward. Therefore, we were free to date others. Unfortunately, I hadn't found anybody I wanted to date, and if he had, he'd had the good taste not to let me know. Rather than explain all that to Caroline, I just said, "We're still in touch, but we're not exclusive."

"You don't have to tell Owen that."

"One, I don't want to lie. And two, I should be able to say 'not interested' to a man without needing an explanation or an excuse."

"Well, yeah, you should be able to, but you know how some guys are. They'll only back off if you're already taken."

"If Owen thinks that way, that's his problem."

"Just make sure he doesn't make it your problem. With the tenure race off and running, we all need to be careful. Fighting among ourselves is not a good way to impress Professor Waldron. Speaking of which, have you seen Renee and Dahna today?"

"No, why?"

"They were sniping at one another in the Roundling this morning, which Mr. Perkins saw. You know he reported back to the Boss Lady right away."

"What were they arguing about?"

"I didn't hear the whole thing," she said with some regret. "Might have been about Jeremy."

"What about Jeremy?"

"Didn't you know? He and Dahna used to go out."

"Was it serious or an adjunct romance?" Since we adjuncts

change jobs a lot, our relationships often end when one of us moves elsewhere. My experience with Owen was a perfect example of that.

"I think it was just an adjunct romance," Caroline said, "and Dahna says she's over him, but it's got to be hard listening to Renee go on and on about wedding plans, and this tenure thing isn't helping."

"Speaking of the tenure thing, I hope it's not going to affect our friendship."

"I hope not, too. I sure don't want it to."

"I've never been in direct competition with a friend for a job before. Well, I suppose I have been, but it's been via resume and private interview, not this kind of situation." I was tempted to ask her who she thought had the best shot at the position, but I didn't think it would be diplomatic, so I changed the subject. "Have you heard anything about services for Kelly?"

"She's not from here, and the funeral will be held out of state, so we're off the hook for that. The campus memorial service will be Wednesday evening."

"That'll be good. I don't know who her close friends on campus were, but I'm sure they'll want to be there."

"I don't think she had that many friends," Caroline said. "Not to speak unkindly of the dead, but she wasn't all that friendly, at least not to me, and I never saw her with anybody else in the faculty or staff."

"I just chalked it up to her being busy."

"That may be it." She hesitated. "Was is it really awful, finding her?"

"Yes and no. At first when I found the car, I was thinking she might still be alive. So I had an adrenaline rush like you wouldn't believe. Then when I did find her and she was clearly gone, it didn't seem real. Maybe if I'd seen her face…"

"That sounds like a yes to me. Though I know it's not the first time you've seen a dead body. I mean, you found that murdered girl in the haunted house last year."

"I didn't find her. One of the people who worked there did. I just happened to be with my sister, who was in charge of the place."

"Wasn't there a murder at your daughter's high school? And didn't something happen at Joshua Tay University?"

"What did you do, Google me?"

"Come on, Georgia. You know how we adjuncts gossip. It helps distract us from our lack of a career path. You gossip as much as the rest of us."

"I guess it's more fun to gossip than to be gossiped about. Speaking of which, did you tell anybody about that kerfuffle I had with Kelly? Remember, when she lit into me for giving a kid a bad grade after she critiqued his paper?"

"I might have. It wasn't a secret, was it?"

"No, of course not. It's just that the police seemed to think it was more of a deal than it was."

"Oh, I wouldn't worry about that. The cop who was here questioned a bunch of us. If you ask me, she was just trying to milk the investigation to get out of traffic duty or clock some overtime. We all know it was just an accident."

"Are you sure?"

"Georgia, can I give you some advice?" Before I could answer, she went on. "I don't exactly know what went on at those other schools, but you might want to tread carefully around here. Tenure and messing around with the police don't really go together."

I tended to agree, and I sure wasn't going to mention the fact that I was afraid Officer Buchanan considered me a suspect.

By then it was time to report back to the Writing Lab for my shift, but as I left, I couldn't help thinking that Caroline never had said who she'd told about the incident with Kelly.

Chapter Ten

My shift at the Writing Lab matched Owen's predictions. Of the first three appointments, two of the students had papers due the next day while the third student's paper was due in an hour. Needless to say, that precluded prolonged discussions about the intricacies of structure or idea generation. The best I could do was help them edit their work and make it stronger, and in the case of Mr. My-paper-is-due-in-an-hour, I stuck to basic proofreading and making sure his citations were in the proper format.

My fourth appointment was late, and I spent the spare time rummaging around Kelly's desk, but either she hadn't kept many personal items at work, or Mr. Perkins had done his usual efficient job. Not that I expected to find an envelope marked "Read in case of my unexpected death," but I did have time to kill.

I gave up when my last appointment showed up, out of breath and apologetic. Walking her through her paper took the better part of an hour, which put me past the end of my shift. Once she was gone, I realized I was starving and locked up the Lab before anybody else could drop in.

On my way to The Artist's Palette, the best of FAD's eateries, I stopped by Mr. Perkins's office to ask if he'd noticed a sketchbook mixed in with Kelly's belongings, just in case that student ever came back, but he assured me he had not.

"Why would Ms. Griffith have a student's sketchbook?" he asked.

"I have no idea," I admitted. "All I know is that a student came looking for it."

"There's nothing in our lost-and-found box that matches that description, but if anything is turned in… Her name, please?" He reached for a pen to note it down.

"She didn't tell me. If I see her again, I'll tell her." I looked around his pristine office. "Have you already sent off the box with Kelly's things?"

"Of course. Why do you ask?"

I couldn't very well cop to the fact that my favorite sleuthing skeleton would've given a spare rib for a chance to look inside, so I said, "I just wondered if I could drop it off at the mail room for you."

He raised an eyebrow and frostily said, "That's not necessary."

I realized he'd decided that I was sucking up to try to influence the tenure decision. In a clever attempt to convince him otherwise, I said, "Okay."

His phone rang, saving me from having to feign an urgent appointment I'd just remembered, and I made a hasty retreat.

After a bread bowl of vegetable soup for lunch, I went back to my own office to my own work. I knew Sid wouldn't be happy with me, but with Dahna taking her shift at the Writing Lab that afternoon, I couldn't very well walk in and look through file cabinets, and that was the only idea I had. Plus I did have work to do.

Sid, on the other hand, had had all night and day to look for information online. I was sure he'd have something waiting for me when I got back home.

Unfortunately, all Sid had waiting for me was an air of dissatisfaction. "That's all you found out?" he said after I'd described the day's events. "Georgia, it's important to move quickly on a murder. We don't want the case to get cold."

I winced, thinking of how Kelly had died.

"Sorry," he said. "I didn't mean it like that. And I guess you did give me some stuff to work with. I mean, it's pretty suspicious, don't you think?"

"What's suspicious?"

"Everything and everybody!" He started counting it off on his phalanges. "Owen, Caroline, Mr. Perkins, the mystery student…"

"How was Owen acting suspicious?"

"Hanging around and watching you. He admitted he'd seen Officer Buchanan—maybe he sent her after you to keep suspicion from himself."

"And his motive would be what?"

"Maybe he threw a pass at Kelly, and she turned him down."

"If turning him down led to murder, I'd be dead several times over."

"Suppose he'd taken it beyond making a pass. He was actively harassing her and she threatened to have him fired."

"That's kind of thin. So what did Caroline do that's so suspicious?"

"The way she interrogated you about Kelly's body is pretty telling."

"Yeah, it tells me that she was curious. Which I would be, too, in her place."

"You said yourself she didn't reveal who she'd told about your altercation with Kelly. An incident you never told me about, by the way."

"There are a lot of things I do in my day that I don't tell you."

"Like what?"

"If I told you, it wouldn't be something I don't tell you."

"Touché." He steepled his fingers. "Maybe Caroline didn't tell anybody about it, other than Officer Buchanan. Maybe it was an attempt at misdirection."

"And what would her motive be?"

"I don't know yet, but I'll think of something."

"Let's just make it something reasonable," I said. "Mr. Perkins? Other than possibly suffering from OCD, what's he done?"

"How do we know he actually sent off Kelly's personal effects? He could have hidden them."

"Not in his office. It would have brought chaos to his carefully preserved order. And not to sound like a broken record, but motive?"

"Why do they say *broken record*? A broken record doesn't repeat—scratched records repeat. Why isn't it *scratched record*?"

"So you don't have a motive for him, either."

"Not yet. And then there's the mystery student. As Mr. Perkins wondered, why would an art student leave a sketchbook with a writing tutor?"

"Now that is interesting, but if she'd killed Kelly, wouldn't she have taken the sketchbook already?"

"Perhaps she was prevented from doing so. After killing Kelly, she attempted to break into the office but was stopped by a security guard. So she intended to sneak in today, but hadn't realized that the department would reopen the Lab so soon."

"You're really reaching, Sid. You didn't find anything online that would have led to Kelly being murdered, did you?"

"Not a single ossifying thing," he said with a look of pure disgust. "I read everything she ever posted on social media, and I mean since she started her Facebook account. I even went back to the articles she wrote for the *Falstone Journal* before she came to work for FAD."

"Nothing juicy in local politics or crime?"

"Oh yeah, hot-button topics like whether the stop sign on Pleasant Street should be replaced with a stop light, and a rash of shoplifting at the dollar store. I'm sure somebody would kill to hide the truth behind big stories like that."

"Then maybe it really was just an accident, Officer Buchanan is a loose cannon, and we're wasting our time."

He shook his head. "I'm sure it was murder, Georgia. I've just got a hunch."

"Really? Your spine looks straight to me."

"Oh so very droll."

"Oh, come on, Sid. It was a joke."

"Really? I thought jokes were supposed to be funny."

"Sid—"

"If you'll excuse me, I'm going to go back to my room and see if I can waste some more of my time."

"Sid—" But he'd stomped away already. Despite the fact that he only weighs about twenty pounds, Sid can stomp a mighty stomp when he is so inclined. His bedroom door slammed a moment later.

I knew I was in the wrong, but his walking off that way—not to mention the slammed door when he knows I hate door slamming—made me mad. So I ignored him and made a dinner I could barely taste, watched an episode of *The Flash* I didn't enjoy, and played a computer game that bored me. I started out stewing over his behavior, but as time went on, I moved on to stewing over my own. Finally, I went and knocked on his door.

"Yes?"

"Can I come in?"

"Okay."

I went in and saw that he wasn't at the computer after all. Instead he was sprawled on the bed with a Ms. Marvel graphic novel. And by sprawled, I mean his bones were so disconnected he was barely still a full skeleton.

"I'm sorry, Sid. That hunch line was a cheap shot. I'm kind of stressed over this tenure thing, but that's no excuse and I apologize."

"Apology accepted." His bones tightened somewhat. "Does that mean you believe that Kelly was murdered?"

"Honestly? I'm still not entirely convinced." Sid's bones loosened again, so I quickly went on. "But here's the thing. There have been other times when I wasn't convinced even though you were, and you turned out to be right. So I'm going to go with your hunch, Sid."

"Really?"

"Really."

Sid snapped together and jumped up. "You're awesome!"

"If I were so awesome, I wouldn't have doubted you."

"Forget it—I already have. What were we talking about? I

have no idea. My mind is a blank. See?" He popped his skull off and held it out so I could see inside. "Nothing."

"Nobody accepts an apology like you do, Sid."

He grinned. "So about tomorrow…"

"Wait, were you making a plan while you were in here with your feelings hurt?"

"I knew you'd change your mind. You can't resist the thrill of the hunt any more than I can."

"I'd be willing to try resisting," I muttered.

He ignored me. "I think a two-pronged approach is best. I'm going to go back online to do some more digging and put together a dossier on Kelly. I'm also going to see what I can find out about the suspicious characters you encountered today and write that up, though it would help if you could identify the mystery student."

"I'll try, but other than wandering around looking for her, I don't know what else I can do."

"Maybe she'll come to Kelly's memorial service. I saw online that it's tomorrow evening on campus. You're going, right?"

"I probably should. She was a member of my department."

"And?"

"And it would be politically expedient to attend to show my loyalty to the department. All the other people who want tenure will be there."

"And?"

"And fine, I do enjoy the thrill of the hunt. A little. And stop looking smug. It's impossible for a skull to look smug."

That only made him look more smug.

It was late, so I headed to bed shortly after that. I still felt a little unsettled about the disagreement with Sid. We almost never argued, and I hoped it wasn't going to be more frequent with the two of us being alone together.

At least we'd gotten past this one relatively unscathed. Sid was happily clacking away on his laptop. Nothing cheers Sid up like creating nice fat dossiers.

CHAPTER ELEVEN

In the interest of fair play, I got to FAD long before my eleven o'clock class. If Sid was going to be working on our investigation all day, the least I could do was snoop around campus. Unfortunately, the only idea I had was to get back into the dusty files in the Writing Lab. According to the online schedule, nobody was being tutored that morning, so I went over, expecting to find the door locked. Instead Caroline was at the door talking to a student who was wearing a flannel shirt and a knit cap pulled over dark blue hair.

"Oh Georgia, good news," she said. "It turns out Kelly had a student assistant. Dr. Thackery, Indigo Williamson. Indigo, Dr. Thackery."

"Pleased to meet you," I said, and Indigo nodded in return.

"Indigo is in one of my graphic novel classes, but I hadn't realized *they* were working with Kelly." I was grateful for Caroline's emphasis, which clued me in to Indigo's preferred emphasis. I was guessing they were gender fluid, but if there was one thing I'd learned from teaching at an art school, it was that I shouldn't make assumptions.

Indigo said, "Yeah, I worked here a few hours a week. I didn't know if you guys still wanted me to help or not."

Caroline and I looked at each other, and we both shrugged.

"Sure, if you're willing," I said. I hadn't realized Kelly could sign time cards—we adjuncts couldn't—but Mr. Perkins would be able to handle the details.

"Do you have a shift now, Georgia?" Caroline asked.

"No, I was just going to work in here if it's empty. My office is kind of chilly." It did run cold in there, especially on a bitter day like that one, though I'd never bothered to go elsewhere before.

"You know, the winters up here are usually pretty rough. You better make sure you can handle it if you want to stay here long-term." Then she laughed.

I laughed back, but it was a strain. Between Kelly's death and the tenure issue, I was starting to hear nastiness in every conversation, and I didn't much like it.

Caroline left and Indigo followed me into the Lab.

"Is this the shift you usually work?" I asked.

"It's kind of flexible."

"So do you help tutor or…?"

"No, I just kind of run errands—get coffee and stuff. Or watch the office while Kelly goes to the bathroom. Do you need to take a bathroom break?"

"No, I'm good," I said, amused by what the situation had to be. Somebody, somewhere must have owed somebody a favor to get Indigo a plum job like this one. I didn't know if they were getting credit or a stipend for "helping" at the Lab, but I wasn't going to mess it up for them even if I had been hoping for time alone.

Since I didn't feel comfortable searching through files with somebody else around, I pulled out my laptop instead and made a halfhearted attempt at making notes on next week's lesson.

Indigo seemed to be at loose ends as much as I was. They looked at the books on the shelves, opened a couple of file drawers to peer inside, then checked out the stack of papers on one of the worktables.

"Are you looking for something?" I asked.

"Just wondering where Kelly's stuff is."

"They packed it up to ship it to her family."

"I guess that makes sense." They sat down at one of the cubbies and pulled out their phone, so presumably they were going to hang around a while.

Maybe I could take advantage of that. "Had you been working for Kelly long?"

"Just this semester."

"Did you enjoy working with her?"

They shrugged.

"I didn't really know her well myself. Did you? What was she like?"

"She was okay."

"Her death must have been a shock to you."

They shrugged.

So much for getting a more personal view of my former colleague.

Indigo put the phone away, only to pull a sketchbook out of their green canvas messenger bag and start drawing.

That reminded me of something. "You wouldn't know anything about a sketchbook being left in here, would you?"

They straightened up and looked at me sharply. "Kelly wasn't an artist."

"I know, but another student came by looking for hers. I haven't seen it, but if you were working here—"

"I don't know anything about it."

"I figured it couldn't hurt to ask. You know, I could use a cup of coffee if—"

"Sorry," they said as they shoved the sketch pad back into their bag. "I've got to get going."

"See you later. Will I see you again this week?"

But they were gone.

"I bet Indigo and Kelly got along just great," I said to myself. On the good side, I could finally look at the files. On the bad side, by the time I had to leave for my class, I'd only made it through half of one drawer and had found nothing but copies of old essays.

After the class, lunch, and my second class, I would have liked to go back to the Lab, but it wasn't going to happen. For one, Dahna was on duty tutoring somebody. For another, Wednesday afternoon is one of the times I keep office hours to meet with students. I had a steady stream of them with questions about grades, assignments, how many classes they could miss without affecting their grades, and whether I would be willing to grant an extension to the current deadline. For the first three, I pulled out a copy of the class syllabus and pointed out the answer, printed in nice, plain type. For the fourth, I answered on a case-by-case basis, depending on the sincerity and creativity of the excuse offered.

By the time all that was done, it was almost time for Kelly's memorial service. I locked myself in my office and changed from my thick jeans and warm pine green sweater into a dark brown pair of wool slacks and a considerably less warm, but more formal, burgundy sweater. For the first time in a month, I switched out of my toasty UGG boots and put on a pair of moderately dressy flats. I wondered if I would ever get a chance to wear shorts again if I got tenure at FAD.

To keep from having to walk outside, where it was once again snowing, I made my way through the maze of wings to get to the campus chapel. Only, it wasn't called a chapel—apparently "chapel" had been deemed too conventional for art students. Instead FAD had a Sanctuary.

The Sanctuary was a round room with lightly stained wooden beams against cream-colored plaster. The floor was an ornate mosaic of wood with all manner of religious symbols: crosses, different varieties of stars, crescent moons, yin and yang, and tucked in here and there, what I suspected were Klingon symbols from *Star Trek*. Niches along the wall were filled with statues showcasing just as much religious variety, interspersed with student paintings of religious subjects. Included was a portrait of Luke the Evangelist, the patron saint of painters, but it was a variant on the traditional pose. Normally, he's shown painting the Virgin Mary, but this version had him drawing with a stylus on an iPad.

Several rows of chairs were set up in a half-circle, with a podium and a poster-sized photo of Kelly up front. I spotted Professor Waldron, Mr. Perkins, Caroline, and the others from our department clustered together near the front and I joined them, greeting them with the nods and half-whispers reserved for funerals and memorial services.

The chairs were mostly empty, but since I'd come a little early, I'd expected them to fill up before the service got started. In fact, only a handful of other people showed. I recognized some as faculty members and a trio of people from campus administration, and there were about a dozen students, including Indigo. I nodded at Indigo, but perhaps they didn't see me because they didn't nod back.

Then there were one or two people who looked like they might be connected with Kelly from outside the school, but I didn't identify anybody as family. Of course, I told myself, Kelly could have had dozens of friends who couldn't make it to Falstone, given the wintry weather, but it was a sad showing, just the same.

I'd had occasion to attend a fair number of academic memorial services over the years, but just as the Sanctuary was different from most campus chapels, the service was a bit unusual too. Kelly hadn't been an academic in the normal sense, so that meant nobody could talk about her contributions to the field. She hadn't had an advanced degree, either, so there were no jokes about how absentminded or focused she'd been when working on her dissertation. Those differences alone cut the service in half.

It was obvious from his generic remarks that the dean hadn't known Kelly other than as a line in the department budget, and he quickly turned things over to Professor Waldron. She did her best to stretch out the story of how she'd come to hire Kelly and spoke with sincere admiration for the work she'd done with students, but the closest she came to the requisite funny anecdote was something about Kelly double-scheduling two students for critiques, and it was so uninteresting that only Mr. Perkins could manage a warm chuckle.

Afterward came the usual invitation for others to come speak about Kelly, but when the only response was awkward shuffling, the dean came back to the podium just long enough to invite everyone to join him for refreshments in the Sanctuary's reception room. Even the music played for the recession had an impersonal feel.

As I told Sid later, I'd known people so disliked that any

number of people would have been willing to kill them and others so beloved that it seemed impossible that anybody would ever harm them. But with Kelly I couldn't see that anybody even cared that she was dead.

Still, Sid was sure she'd been murdered, and when I got up and turned around, I was reminded that he wasn't the only one. Officer Buchanan was standing in the back of the room surveying the sparse crowd. As soon as I spotted her, she saw me and gave me a grin that made chills run down my spine.

CHAPTER TWELVE

If that feeling of dread I felt when I saw Officer Buchanan watching me was typical of what an innocent person felt when confronted by a cop, I couldn't even imagine how a guilty person would feel. Of course, I knew it was impossible for her to prove I'd killed Kelly. For one, I hadn't done it, and for another, I had no motive. That didn't stop me from wanting to run and hide. Since I wasn't going to do that, I went the other direction. Meaning that I went right to her.

"Officer Buchanan, you've surprised me again. Did you know Kelly?"

"She and I lived at the same apartment complex, so I guess you'd call us neighbors," she said, "but mostly I thought it would be nice to have the police department represented here. There was plenty of room, wasn't there? Did she not have many friends?"

"Apparently not," I said. "Have you found out anything else about her death?"

"Not yet," she said. "Would you mind telling me who's who? I'd like to see some of the other people she worked with."

Did that mean I wasn't a suspect after all, or was this a test to see how I'd react? I had no idea, so I figured I might as well do as she asked. "The tall lady in the dark blue pantsuit is Professor Waldron, the chair of the English department. The gentleman with her is the dean."

"The little fellow?"

"No, the smaller one is Mr. Perkins, our departmental secretary. The taller one is the dean."

"Who else?"

"The crew of people trying to pretend they're not watching us is the rest of the adjuncts in the English department." I had a hunch Caroline was telling them how the police had already spoken to me, and I wondered how the rumor mill would mangle the facts this time.

"I met the guy with the mustache already," Officer Buchanan said.

"That's Owen Deen. To his right is Dahna Kaleka, in the mustard-yellow blouse. Next to her is Caroline Craig, and next to her is Renee Turner."

"What about the guy with the beard?"

"That's Renee's fiancé, Jeremy Nolan. He's not in our department—he's a painter."

"And those people over there?"

"Other art faculty, I believe."

"Who else?"

"Students. Some administrative people. I'm not sure who that guy in the brown sports coat is."

"That's the one I do know. He's a reporter from the *Falstone Journal*."

"That's nice, that he and Kelly stayed in touch all these years."

"He didn't know her—the people she worked with are long gone. He's here covering the services for the paper."

"Oh." So much for my getting background information about Kelly. "Well, those are the people I know. If you'll excuse me, I haven't had dinner and I'm going to get myself something to eat."

"You bet. Thanks for the help. I'll be seeing you."

I wasn't sure if she meant to sound threatening or it was my own anxiety, but I made myself head to the refreshment table at a sedate pace.

Thanks to the low turnout, there was an overabundance of food, rare at a college event, so I filled a plate with deli meats, cheese, crackers, and cookies. Even though I'd only mentioned food as an excuse to get away from Officer Buchanan, I really was hungry. Some of the students were hovering nearby, as if unsure of the proper etiquette, so I stopped by them long enough to say, "You know, they're going to throw out what doesn't get eaten, so you might as well dig in." Then I stepped back to avoid the stampede. FAD's dining facilities aren't bad, but I've rarely met a college student who couldn't use some extra calories, especially if the price doesn't get added to their tuition bill.

I considered joining the other English department adjuncts, but I'd have plenty of excuses to talk to them later, while I hadn't had a chance to meet as many people in the school's other departments. Luckily, I did know one of the art instructors in attendance: Lucas Silva. We had both worked at a community college near Boston a few years back and there'd been a bit of a mutual attraction, though we'd never progressed to anything beyond lunch dates. Still, it was enough to give me an entree into the group.

I stepped into range of their conversation and waited through a discussion of natural light at different times of year until Lucas noticed me.

"Georgia, how you are you holding up? It's such a shame about Kelly."

"Heartbreaking," I agreed. "I didn't know her well, but it's always sad to lose somebody so young."

"Georgia, this is Ashwin Inamdar from Illustration, Jacqueline Lewis from Sequential Arts, and Greg Azzopardi from Animation." Ashwin was a well-built Indian man, shorter than me, with a buzz cut; Jacqueline, who was pleasantly curvy and dark-haired, looked younger than most adjuncts; and Greg was an affable bald man with a slightly nervous smile. Lucas himself was curly-haired with improbably black eyes and long, elegant fingers ideal for holding the paintbrush that was his favorite tool. "Folks, this is Georgia Thackery from the English department."

We traded collegial nods, since the plates of refreshments prevented handshakes.

"Thackery..." Greg said thoughtfully. "Aren't you the one who found—"

Lucas elbowed him. "Come on, man."

"It's okay," I said. "Yes, I found Kelly's body. It was…not fun."

"Sorry, I shouldn't have said anything," Greg said, his smile more nervous than ever.

"It probably would have been worse if I'd known who it was—I didn't find out until much later. Was she a good friend of yours?" It was a rough segue, but he was feeling too guilty for bringing up the finding-a-dead-body thing to notice.

"Yeah, no, not really. Not lately, anyway. We went out a few times when she first started working here." He shrugged. "It didn't work out, but we parted friends."

Ashwin snorted. "You say that now, but that's not what you said then."

The smile faded as Greg said, "That was years ago."

It seemed unlikely that a long-ago failed romance would cause a murder, but I'd heard of stranger motives, so I mentally filed it away. I was going to try to think of a way to ask the others about their relationship, but Jacqueline helped out before I had to.

She said, "How did you know Kelly, Ashwin?"

"We went to the same gym. When we were both in the spinning class, we took turns driving because the parking was so bad downtown, but I when I switched to cardio, our schedules didn't mesh and we fell out of touch."

Sid would do something with that. No obvious motive, but Ashwin would have known where Kelly lived and what her car looked like.

"Lucas?" Jacqueline said.

"We met at a faculty thing. She mentioned she was interested in going back into journalism, so I tried to hook her up with a couple of reporters I know. Nothing came of it, unfortunately. The only time I saw her was at campus events, except a few times when she came by to ask about art concepts so she could do a better job with critiquing papers."

"It doesn't sound like she had any real buds," Jacqueline said. "That's really sad."

"So you weren't very close, either?" I asked.

She shook her head. "I only spoke to her a handful of times, and that was mostly for work. She didn't know comics, and we got together so I could explain enough of the common tropes for her to work with my students. I recommended some stuff for her to read, but though she didn't come out and say so, I could tell she thought sequential art was a waste of time and talent." She gave Ashwin a pointed look. "She's not the only one around here who thinks that."

"Hey, I never said comics are a waste of anything. I'm all for artists being able to make a living so they can afford to work on their real art."

"So comics aren't real art?"

"Oh please, don't start on *real art*," Lucas said with a groan. "I don't want Jeremy to come lecture us about how only FAD's fine art students are serious artists."

Apparently this was an old argument. The conversation moved to ridiculous prejudices against various forms of art, and after that, it meandered into mild complaints about being an adjunct. But as we chatted, I couldn't help thinking that Jacqueline was right. It sure sounded as if Kelly had had a lonely life. For a moment I felt guilty that I hadn't reached out more. Then I remembered how she'd blown me off when I'd tried to pass the time of day. Maybe, for whatever reason, Kelly had liked living alone. I just wished she hadn't died alone, too.

CHAPTER THIRTEEN

At some point, I looked around and realized the reception was pretty much over. The students and administrators had left and as I watched, Professor Waldron exited with Mr. Perkins in her wake. Several of the other English adjuncts were making a last raid on the refreshment table while campus catering waited impatiently to clean up. Officer Buchanan had slipped away without my noticing it, or for all I knew, she'd been eavesdropping while I'd been playing sleuth. The woman was downright disconcerting.

I said my goodbyes to the artist crowd, got an invite from Lucas to go to lunch very soon, went to throw out my empty plate, and was about to leave when I spotted Dahna standing near one of the sculpture niches, her face in her hands, sobbing.

I couldn't leave her like that.

"Dahna?" I said, touching her lightly on the shoulder.

"I'm sorry," Dahna managed to say, "I did not realize how much the service was going to affect me."

"Don't apologize. I just didn't realize that you and Kelly were close." I reached into my purse and found a much-needed tissue to hand to her.

She wiped her eyes. "We weren't, not recently at least, but she was very welcoming when I first came to FAD. I didn't have any friends here and it made my first few months so much more pleasant."

"Really?" I didn't intend to sound so skeptical, but Kelly had barely noticed it when I started at FAD.

"I know, she became more reserved as time went on. Isolated, really. I believe she grew weary of making relationships here—you know, adjuncts come and go, but she remained. And she was so terribly unhappy."

"Why did she stay? My friend Lucas said she wanted to go back into journalism."

"She did, very much, but she couldn't find a job. When she was hired as a reporter at the *Falstone Journal* right out of school, she was hoping to use the work there as a stepping stone to bigger newspapers. But then the paper was sold to a conglomerate—most of the content is generated elsewhere, with only one page that's specific to Falstone. So they only needed one person, and of course, kept the most experienced reporter."

"Last one in, first one out," I said, having experienced that a few times myself.

"Exactly. So many newspapers have been shut down, and Kelly couldn't find another reporting job, which is why she took the job at the Writing Lab. She was an excellent proofreader and editor, and she needed a job to pay her bills, but she never meant to stay here.

"When I first met Kelly, she was still sending out résumés daily, but as time passed, she lost hope." She started to tear up again, and I handed her another tissue. She wiped before saying, "When I first learned of her death, I confess I was afraid that she might have done away with herself."

"Was she that depressed?"

"No, quite the contrary. These past few weeks, she seemed happier than I'd seen her in ages. It was as if things were turning around for her. I hoped she had either found a new job or perhaps a new lover. But when Professor Waldron said she was dead, I remembered an article I'd read about suicide, and how people are almost relieved once they decide to kill themselves. Their friends and families interpret this as improvement in their moods, but in fact, it's a very dangerous sign."

"The police don't seem to think it was suicide." I hesitated for a moment. "I don't know if this will comfort you or not, but you know, I found Kelly out in the woods. Her car was stuck in the snow, and if she'd really wanted to give up, she could have just sat in her front seat and waited for the end. But she was trying to get out of there. There were marks in the snow that showed she'd tried to get back up to the road, and when she couldn't, she took off through the woods. She kept going as long as she could—she never gave up. I don't know if that makes it worse or—"

"No, no, it makes it better. So much better." I thought she was reaching for another tissue, but instead she reached for me and hugged me firmly. We had not been on hugging terms before, but if she felt it that strongly, I was willing to oblige.

We walked back to the English wing together and retrieved our coats, and then I made sure she was okay before I let her drive home. She rolled down her window at the last minute and said, "Thank you for your kindness, Georgia."

"Anytime."

"But I must warn you, I still want that tenure position."

"Bring it!"

She was smiling as she drove off, which I thought was an excellent sign.

Chapter Fourteen

Though I thought my gossip crop was pretty slim pickings, Sid was delighted to get even those scraps. Since I'd eaten fairly well at the reception, I didn't care about fixing dinner, so instead I got myself an apple and sat right down to tell him everything.

"A thwarted lover, a scorned artist, and an abandoned friend. This is great!"

"I don't know about the thwarted lover piece. Greg said they quit dating a long time ago."

"Perhaps he'd tried to rekindle it and was slapped down. That's what we crime-solving types call a trigger."

"You've been watching *Criminal Minds* late at night again, haven't you? Sid, you know the serial killer stuff gives you the willies."

"I can handle it," he insisted.

"As for the scorned artist, if Jacqueline killed everybody who dissed comics, she'd be the most prolific serial killer in history. Professor Waldron sniffs every time she says 'sequential art,' even though Caroline's class is already twice as popular as any of hers."

"Maybe Kelly did more than sniff. Maybe there was this huge Twitter flame war between the two of them and it ended… in death."

"Well, let me know if you find any screenshots of Twitter battles. As for Dahna, don't be mean. She was really distraught."

"It could have been crocodile tears."

"Sid, if you'd seen as many students as I have trying to cry about their grades or dead grandmothers to get a deadline extension, you would know the difference between real crying and the phony stuff. She was crying."

"I bow to your expertise—crying isn't my thing."

True. He had no tear ducts, after all.

"Still," he said, "the very real tears could have been delayed remorse about her crime."

"Motive?"

"Nothing yet, but it's still early days."

"I take it you didn't find anything online or you wouldn't be so excited about what I got."

"No, not so much. I printed out Kelly's dossier for you, but it's pretty skimpy." He handed it to me with a discontented look.

"If it's any consolation, it looks as if Officer Buchanan thinks it's murder, too."

"I can't believe you helped her."

"Don't you think it would have been suspicious for me to say, 'Sorry, I don't believe in helping the competition'?"

"I suppose not."

"Hey, maybe she's the killer. She's got that creepy smile going on."

"Georgia, that is ridiculous. She's a police officer."

"Yeah, but she did know Kelly—they lived in the same apartment complex. Maybe they had some sort of inter-apartmental squabble."

"You are really grasping at straws."

"Dude, you're the champion of straw graspers. I mean you— Wait, you already checked Buchanan out, didn't you?"

"Of course I did. It turns out she has an alibi. She was at a darts tournament in Fitchburg. A police darts tournament, followed by dinner with a bunch of cops. There are a dozen pictures on Facebook. Not even I can break that alibi."

"Then why was she at the accident scene?"

"I don't think there are that many cops in Falstone. When something major happens, they all come running, even if they have the night off. Anyway, she's not the killer even if she does have some strange power to make you tell her stuff you ought to be keeping to yourself."

Sid hates it when I blow raspberries at him because he can't return the favor, so of course I gave him a really long one.

He thunked me on the skull in reply.

This set the tone for our conversation for the next half an hour or so.

Eventually I got around to looking at the dossier on Kelly, and Sid hadn't just been being modest when he said it was skimpy. She'd only had two jobs since college—the newspaper job and the one at FAD. Her parents and one brother were in Wyoming, and there was no indication that they were anything but fond of one another. Plus there was plenty of evidence that they hadn't been in Falstone on the night of Kelly's death—there'd been a blizzard in their part of the state that weekend, and a number of pictures on Facebook proved that they couldn't have left town if they'd wanted to. Kelly had no current boyfriends or girlfriends, and no hint that she'd ever had a serious one. No court cases, no arrests, and she didn't seem to be particularly active on Facebook, Twitter, Tumblr, or Instagram, though she did like scoping out men in kilts on Pinterest.

"Of course, she could have all kinds of secrets," I pointed out. "Not everybody likes sharing on social media."

"Even so, I would expect to get something from her friends' electronic footprints, but I got nothing." He drummed his finger bones against the table, which makes an awful lot of noise. "What about those files in Kelly's office?"

"I just barely got started on them. It's going to be hard to get to the rest."

"Why don't I go tackle them rather than you wasting your time with them?"

"Do you think I'm missing stuff?"

"No, of course not. It's just that you've got enough to do already, whereas my schedule is wide open."

"We could try, but I don't know that it would be any faster.

I don't see how I could manage bringing more than a few folders home at a time, and there are four stuffed file cabinets."

"You don't have to bring anything home. Smuggle me onto campus and I'll do the work there."

"I don't know how we could swing it, Sid. It wouldn't be safe."

"You could leave me in the Writing Lab overnight."

"Too many other people have keys to that place—Mr. Perkins gave them to all of us who are helping out, plus he's got a set. The custodial staff must have a set, too, not to mention campus security. What would you do if somebody showed up? There's no handy washing machine to duck into."

"I could stay hidden in my suitcase until the campus quiets down and only work until people start stirring. And I could barricade the door with a chair or something so nobody could come in on me."

"At which point they'd know something was going on and break the door down. Then what?"

"Then they'd find a suitcase—a locked suitcase. Or if I didn't have time to get into the bag, they'd just find a bunch of bones. Weird, but it's a college campus. They'd blame it on student pranks."

"And what would they do with that pile of bones?"

He shrugged. "Put me in storage somewhere, and I'd get out. Eventually."

"You've got to be kidding me."

"Okay, I need a better plan. But between us, we can work out the details."

"It's not happening, Sid."

"But Georgia—"

"No. Period. Full stop."

I expected his response to be a rerun of the other night: stomping, door slamming, and so on, but he seemed more disappointed than anything else. Or maybe resigned was a better word. I should have been glad he didn't argue with me, but it made me uneasy, and the rest of the night was painfully awkward. I was relieved when it was time to go to bed, but kept tossing and turning, feeling as if I was doing something wrong even though it all sounded logical.

The next morning, I thought Sid would make another attempt to talk me into taking him along, but instead he'd left a note on the kitchen table.

Don't worry about me. I'm going to play Final Fantasy as soon as my party comes online—they're in England, which means I'll be busy when you get up. Enjoy your day.

Even though the message was entirely cordial, I still felt snubbed, so I didn't go by Sid's room. As I went out the front door, I yelled, "I'm leaving now. See you later."

There was no response.

As I was about to drive off, I pulled my phone out of my purse, wondering if I should text an apology. *Forget it,* I told myself and dropped my phone onto the seat next to me. Sid was only sulking in his room to make me feel bad. Which wasn't going to work! Or at least, not much.

Needless to say, I wasn't in the best of moods when I got to campus. I grabbed my pocketbook and satchel, slammed the car door behind me, and stomped toward the school. I was in the English wing and nearly to my office when I went to check the time on my phone.

Which I'd left in the minivan.

"Coccyx," I muttered, more or less under my breath, and turned around to go back outside. Just as I rounded the corner to where I'd parked, I saw the back door of the minivan swing open and a figure swathed in winter wear started to get out.

It took only a second for me to realize who it had to be.

"Sid, what the patella are you doing here?"

CHAPTER FIFTEEN

Sid froze for an instant, then jumped back into the minivan and locked the door. That might have been more effective if I hadn't had the key fob in my hand. As it was, I unlocked the door, climbed into the driver's seat, and started the engine.

"I hope you're happy," I said. "Taking you back to the bungalow is going to make me late at the Writing Lab."

"I don't want to go back—I want to go check out those files."

"I told you 'no.' What were you thinking? Sneaking into the car like this? Really?"

"Coccyx, Georgia," he bellowed, "you're not my mother! You don't get to tell me what to do!"

"But—" I went no further because I couldn't think of what to say. I'd never heard Sid bellow like that before.

"Even if you only count the years I've been a skeleton, I'm over twenty-one, and if you add in my previous life, I'm older than you are. So don't you think it's time for you to stop telling me what to do?"

I hesitated a long time. "How long have you wanted to say that?"

"A while, actually."

"Oh."

"More since I've been in Falstone, I think. I was used to somebody else being in charge at your parents' house. Dr. T. and Mrs. Dr. T. always made the rules, and when you moved back with Madison, we fell into that same pattern. But coming here made me start seeing things differently. I mean, you keep saying we're a team, but when it comes to what you think we should do versus what I think we should do, it's always your view that holds."

"That's not true," I said.

"Maybe not a hundred percent of the time, but most of the time."

I thought over recent conversations. "Yeah, you're right. Most of the time I do make the final decision. But I am trying to protect you. And me, too."

"I know that, but you know I would never do anything to get you into trouble and I'm not going to jeopardize my life either. Or whatever you call what it is I've got. It may be weird, but I enjoy it."

"Other than when I order you around?"

"Yeah, other than that."

Neither of us spoke for a while. Then Sid sadly said, "You don't have to drive me back right now. I'll just stay out here. It's not like I get cold."

"No," I said, and turned the engine off. "You're right. I mean, my motives were pure. I really have been trying to juggle your safety and my safety."

"I never doubted that."

"Thank you. Anyway, that's what I meant to do, but obviously I haven't been going about it the right way. Sid, you're my best friend. My brother from another mother, my bestie, my wing man, my BFF. What you're not is my child, but I've been giving you orders as if you were Madison."

"Well, I realize one of us has to be in charge."

"No, not really. We're adults. Sure we need ground rules just like any other roommates—" I stopped. "Okay, not like just any roommates. You're a special guy, in a special situation, which makes it trickier. But I shouldn't be making those rules, and you shouldn't be having them imposed upon you."

"Let's not forget that you're the one with the job. Doesn't that put you in charge?"

"That's a complication, for sure, but it doesn't make me the head of the household or anything like that. You'd be well within your rights to go live somewhere else." I was trying not to lose it, but the thought of Sid leaving me nearly brought me to tears.

"No! No, don't cry. I don't want to go anywhere. You're my family, Georgia, you and Madison and Dr. T. and Mrs. Dr. T. and Deborah. Even the dog. But especially you. Please don't cry!"

"I'm not crying," I lied, but when Sid handed me an old McDonald's napkin from somewhere in the back seat, I gratefully wiped my eyes and blew my nose. "Anyway, no more bossing around. You and I are a team."

"Team supreme?"

"You bet."

"Fist bump?"

"Fist bump." Once that was accomplished, I said, "So what's your plan?"

He outlined what he had in mind, I instantly agreed, and we went into the building, arm in bony arm.

No, not really. In reality, we spent half an hour quibbling over what to do next, but this time we both tried to be fair about it. The decision about Sid taking a shot at the files was a given—the fussing was over the details.

Sid had thought he could walk around on campus wearing a parka, snow pants, boots, gloves, and ski mask and nobody would think it odd. To be fair, he hadn't been around people all that much, and the times he had been, he'd been in a costume of one kind or another. From that perspective, this wasn't that much more strange. So I had to convince him that people would think he was nuts or a criminal or both before we finally settled on my carrying him inside.

Unfortunately, I didn't have the rolling suitcase I normally used to tote Sid around—that was still at the bungalow. And unless I was willing to be extremely late to the Writing Lab, a trip back home was out of the question. What I did have was a collection of reusable shopping bags. So half of Sid's bones went into the blue Stop & Shop bag, while the other half went into a bright red

Hannaford bag. I put other bags on top to hide the contents so I could get the bags inside without anybody spotting the bones.

Between my purse, my satchel, and two bags of bones weighing over ten pounds each, it was a considerable load for me to carry, and I was glad campus maintenance had done a thorough job of clearing the latest accumulation of snow. Slipping and spilling Sid parts all over the sidewalk would not have been a good start for his undercover mission.

Sid's idea had been to go to the Lab and work openly, albeit covered up in winter clothing. That wasn't going to work, and he couldn't work openly without winter clothing, either. Instead I installed him in my office and then went to the Lab myself to grab an armload of file folders from Kelly's file cabinets. I really didn't think he'd find anything worthwhile, given the layer of dust on the cabinets, but I'd been wrong before.

It turned out I was wrong this time, too, though it was several hours before I found that out.

In the meantime, I met several students and helped them go through their papers, but every time I got a break, I lugged another batch of files to my office for Sid to look through while retrieving the ones he'd already fruitlessly examined. If anybody wondered why I was moving files back and forth, they weren't interested enough to ask. Most of my colleagues were teaching during those hours, and the handful of students in the Roundling were either texting, sketching, or sleeping. Some seemed to be doing more than one simultaneously.

Just before my shift ended, I brought in an extra-large load, and went to plop it on the desk before I got the door shut completely. Sid looked up as I came in, then I saw his eye sockets go wide and his whole body went stiff.

From behind me, I heard a polite throat clearing, and then Mr. Perkins said, "Dr. Thackery, can you explain why you have a skeleton in your office?"

CHAPTER SIXTEEN

Later on, Sid congratulated me for my fast thinking, but I'm not sure I actually was thinking. I just blurted out words and hoped they would come out in the proper order.

"Oh, hi, Mr. Perkins. My bony friend here is for an experiment in writing prompts. There's something about the human form that inspires a wide variety of written responses: horror, melancholy, nostalgia, um…reflections on mortality. All kinds of…stuff." He looked completely unconvinced until I said, "It's a technique my parents use, and they thought a visual prompt might be particularly effective with visual artists. So they shipped me the skeleton for me to give it a try."

That soothed him. Professor Waldron had encountered my parents at several conferences over the years and spoke highly of them. If she approved of them, then of course Mr. Perkins would consider any suggestions they made to be excellent.

"Intriguing. I'd be interested in reading the results."

"Of course. I'll be sure to send you the best essays next week." I kept a manic grin on my face until he left and I'd locked up behind him.

"Oh Georgia, I am so sorry!" Sid said.

"It's not your fault. I'm the one who forgot to shut the door."

"No, you said something like this would happen. You were right and I was wrong. I should never have come."

"It's okay, Sid. We were afraid you'd be seen, but now you have been and we made it through. The only thing is, you won't have much longer to look through files before it's time to go to class."

"You mean you're really going to use me as a writing prompt?"

"I have to. Mr. Perkins will want to read the papers. Sorry."

"No, I don't mind. How often do I get to see you in action in a classroom?"

"Just keep in mind that this might not be my most polished performance. I've only got a few minutes to come up with a reason why I'm waving bones around!"

I was actually fairly proud of what I had concocted. First, though, I had to get Sid to class. I couldn't carry him up in the shopping bags because then I'd have to explain how I was putting him back together. Most skeletons on display in academic settings are articulated with wires, nuts, and bolts. Sid was articulated only because he felt like it.

I had Sid sit in my desk chair, wheeled him through the Roundling to the wing's elevator, and got him up to my classroom. Then I put him at the front of the class and positioned myself to make sure nobody examined him too closely.

A few students were already waiting, and when I saw more than one taking cell phone pictures, I resigned myself to the fact that Sid might be going viral. Once the class gathered, I took a deep breath and began.

An hour and a half later, I wheeled Sid back to my office to a smattering of applause. Only when I was safe inside, with the door thoroughly locked, did I take another breath. Okay, since I was not Sid, I must have breathed in the interim, but I didn't remember it. All I could recall was the panic coursing through my system in a way it hadn't since I'd been a grad student giving my first lecture.

I flung myself into my guest chair. "I can't believe I got away with that."

"Got away with it? Georgia, that was a virtuoso performance! I've watched a lot of lectures online, and that one was the best ever. Using the skeleton as a metaphor for the structure of a piece of prose or poetry? Genius."

"Tell me I didn't make a pun about humerus writing?"

"Are you kidding? You brought the house down with that! I almost laughed myself."

"It was really okay?"

"You are a brilliant teacher, Georgia."

"I guess it wasn't too bad," I admitted. "Though I thought I was going to lose it when that one student said, 'But this topic isn't in the syllabus.' The first time all semester anybody has admitted to reading the syllabus, and it was the worst time imaginable."

"Yeah, who let him into class? What kind of artist is he anyway?"

"Art history, I think. He wants to work in a museum, so attention to detail is important."

"I guess," Sid said with a sniff.

"Kudos to you, too. The lecture never would have worked without you holding yourself still all that time. I don't know how you did it."

"It was harder than I expected. I'm used to being ambulatory or collapsing into a pile. Just being still was different."

"I don't think you even changed your expression." For a second I considered the notion that some would say that a skull didn't really have expressions, but only for a second.

As part of our newly formed pact for equality, I gritted my teeth and agreed to let Sid stay at FAD overnight. In fact, I suppose I shouldn't even have been thinking I was *letting* him do anything. Instead I was assisting in his preparations for getting through the rest of Kelly's files.

Fortunately for our plans, yet another bout of snow was predicted for that evening, so the building cleared out earlier than usual. Owen was the last of my colleagues still around, staying even longer than Mr. Perkins, but once he finished his shift at the Writing Lab, he cleared out immediately. The custodian made a cursory sweep a few minutes later, and I guessed he was either eager to get home or had snow removal to attend to outside.

I waited another half an hour after that, as the building grew quieter and quieter, and only then did I wheel Sid over to the

Lab. Our plan was for me to retrieve him before anybody got to the Lab the next morning, but if I did blow it, Sid would do his mannequin routine again and I would say I'd left him there as a prank. If anything went wrong, he had his cell phone and would call for help.

I still thought it was risky, but the look of pride on Sid's skull when I left him convinced me that I'd done the right thing. As long as Sid had been part of my life, we were still working out the parameters of the relationship. Maybe that wasn't surprising. After all, couples, parent-child pairs, business associates, friends, siblings, roommates—they all had to work at getting along. It's just that, unfortunately for us, there were no advice columnists we could go to for expert guidance. That didn't stop me from imagining sending a letter along the lines of, *"Dear Prudence: My best friend is a skeleton. How do we organize our collaborations when we solve murders? Signed, Bone Buddy."*

The parking lot was empty except for my minivan and I quickly brushed off the half inch of snow that had already fallen and made my way carefully back to the bungalow. I felt a twinge when I looked at the driveway and realized that Sid wasn't going to be able to use his beloved snowblower that night. Or maybe it was a painful twang from my back when I realized I was going to be stuck with the job. Having Sid around had already spoiled me.

It was only worse when I got into the bungalow, which felt painfully empty. I'd spent over a month alone there before Sid arrived on my doorstep, and though it had been lonely, that was the worst night I'd had there. I texted him to let him know I was home and to make sure he was okay, but his brief replies made it plain that he was focusing on the files and that I should let him alone.

After dinner, I called my parents to warn them that they had loaned me a skeleton to use for their brilliant new technique, and in order to distract them from questions about why Sid was on campus in the first place, I told them about my shot at tenure. They were enthusiastic and encouraging, which was great. Less great was the avalanche of advice that followed. Since they'd been in academia for their entire working lives, they had strong ideas about how I should position myself to show my qualifications to their best advantage. They both knew Professor Waldron from shared associations, and my father offered to call her on my behalf, but my mother and I overruled that.

Afterward, I tried to be productive and catch up on some of my work that I'd let slide a bit because of the many recent distractions, but instead I kept picturing Sid in scenarios involving theft, vandalism, and/or fire.

I had another restless night, and when my alarm went off, the only thing that kept me from shutting it off and going back to sleep for an extra hour was knowing that I needed to sneak in and get Sid back before too many people were around.

Between the freshly fallen four inches of snow and it being Friday—meaning that there were no classes scheduled—the English wing was nearly deserted. I tapped at the Lab door with our oh-so-original secret shave-and-a-haircut knock before unlocking it. Sid was playing mannequin, a precaution I approved of, but as soon as I locked the door behind me and put a spare chair in front of it as an extra block, he let out a gasp of relief. It was purely for show, of course, but I felt the same way.

"Everything go okay?"

"More than okay. Nobody came by, and nobody saw me, and I think I found what we've been looking for."

"You've figured out who killed Kelly?"

"Okay, not everything we've been looking for, but I think I know why she was killed."

"You do?"

He nodded. "There's just one problem."

"What?"

"If I'm right, I'm not sure I blame the killer."

CHAPTER SEVENTEEN

"Sid!"

"Okay, okay, I'm overstating. What Kelly did was awful, but you're right, she didn't deserve to die."

"What in the patella did she do?"

"Let me start with what I found."

I sat down. When Sid took that tone, it meant that he was going to go through every step of his mental process and was not susceptible to being rushed. So I might as well get comfortable for his presentation.

"This," he said, waving a thick manila envelope, "was inserted in the middle of a big folder labeled *First Year Expository*. That folder mostly had the kinds of papers you'd expect: 'My Worst Memory,' 'My Happiest Memory,' and the ever popular 'Why I Became an Artist,' but the envelope held something very different."

I reached for the envelope, but he pulled it back and continued.

"Inside you will find a series of photocopies of artwork and a matching series of printouts from websites."

"What kind of websites?"

"T-shirt sellers."

"T-shirt sellers?"

"If you'll let me continue."

"Sorry."

He cleared his throat. Well, technically he made the sound of somebody clearing his throat, since he had no throat to clear. "As I was saying, there are photocopies and screen dumps—each photocopy is paired with a screen dump." He produced an illustration with three images: a sea lion frolicking on a beach, a tiger shark popping up from the surf, and a koala sitting in a tree. At the bottom of the page was a slogan: "Lions, and tigers and bears! Oh my!"

"That's clever! They're all Australian. The real land of Oz. Madison would love that."

"We're not shopping, Georgia," he said and held up a screen dump of a web page advertising a T-shirt for sale. "Note that the designs are nearly identical."

I compared the two images. "They look the same to me. Except for the comma." The one for sale said: "Lions, and tigers, and bears! Oh my!"

"We are also not proofreading." He took the pages away and gave me two more. "What about these?"

This time it was a cartoon cat curled up with a bunch of mice. "The one on the T-shirt is flipped in the other direction, but it looks the same otherwise."

He took them away and gave me another set. "And these?"

It was a wolf in a forest. "The colors are a little different."

"But it's clearly the same design, right?"

"It looks like it to me."

"Note that these three pictures are in markedly different styles. As if they were done by different artists."

"One artist can use more than one style," I objected, "but I admit that these do look a lot different." The Oz picture was fairly realistic, the cat was old-style cartoony, and the wolf resembled a Japanese woodblock print.

"I have reason to believe they were drawn by different people. Look at the signatures on the photocopies."

Sure enough, the signatures on the three designs were definitely not the same. One was a scrawled name, one was an interlocking set of initials, and the other was a stylized butterfly.

"Now look at the signatures on the screen dumps." He handed me those pages.

All three had the same signature, in a pretty script font. "Scarlet Letter. I'm guessing that's not somebody's real name."

"I doubt it, and yes, I did a search on my phone to check." He paused for me to admire his thoroughness, so I gave him an approving nod before he went on. "There were a dozen more examples like these in that envelope, everything from elaborate illustrations to simple graphics to comic book character action shots. Multiple styles and signatures, but the matching T-shirt designs were all signed 'Scarlet Letter.'"

"Okay." Sid was raising his nonexistent eyebrows, waiting for me to reach some conclusion that was painfully obvious to him. "Don't give me that look—how long did it take you to work it out?"

He ignored the question. "I've concluded that the photocopies are of the original artwork. Which means that the designs being sold were stolen."

"By Kelly?"

"What do you think?"

I could see it. Kelly working at a job that she hated, with nothing better on the horizon. She had no romantic relationships or even close friendships. It wasn't hard to imagine her doing something illegal. "So you think somebody found out?"

"I'd bet my femur—the one without chew marks—that somebody did and then made sure she never stole their artwork again."

Chapter Eighteen

No wonder Sid had said he wasn't sure he blamed the killer. I wasn't an artist, but I knew about intellectual property theft. I'd lost count of the student papers I'd received with huge swaths of text taken straight from reference books and *Wikipedia*. Some students managed to dig up obscure essays, thinking I'd be fooled into believing that from one assignment to the next, their writing ability had evolved from barely literate to academically excellent. And I still remembered the time a student turned in a paper that was not only plagiarized, but was plagiarized from one of my mother's articles. She'd written it under her maiden name, so he hadn't made the connection with me. I'd thoroughly enjoyed flunking him in my class, and I'd reported him to administration, which had put him on academic probation for the rest of his college career.

Still, as angry as Mom and I had been, neither of us had ever been tempted to do anything worse than flunking the guy. Okay, there was talk of kicking him in the shins super hard and/or violence against his laptop, but it had never gone beyond talk.

So I said, "I don't know, Sid. Would a stolen T-shirt design really be worth killing over?"

"Artists can be pretty intense."

"True, and I could understand an emotional outburst, but it would have taken serious planning to make it look like Kelly went off the road accidentally. Officer Buchanan seemed to think she might have been drugged, which caused the crash."

"Maybe the killer didn't expect her to die. It could have been just an attempt to scare her."

"That makes a little more sense." Then I had an awful thought. "Sid, you remember what I said about a student coming in to look for a sketch pad? Maybe she's the one."

"Did she look crazed and vengeful?"

"No, she looked as if she wouldn't say *boo!* to a mouse, but for all I know, she's an Oscar-worthy actress. Of course, I still don't know who she is."

"Or if her signature matches that on any of the stolen artwork."

I checked my watch. "I've got an appointment in a few minutes, so we're going to have to table this. Do you want to stay here or hang out in my office?"

"I think I'll stay here and observe your students. If any of them turn out to be a killer, you might need backup."

"Sure, that could happen. And Sid?"

"Yes?"

"You done good, partner."

He grinned and continued to grin as I critiqued my way through my shift at the Lab. The students might have found the view of a grinning skull disquieting, but I was glad to see Sid looking so happy.

By the time I'd pointed out three dozen comma splices and a misuse of idiom, and suggested that my final customer decide what the premise of his paper was before he worried too much about typos, my time was up and Renee was hovering outside the door to take her shift.

"I don't mean to rush you," she said, "but I've got a full slate today."

"You're welcome to it," I said.

"Georgia, why is the skeleton still here?"

"It was too much trouble to carry him home in the snow last night." That was technically true, because if I'd tried, Sid would have fought me the whole way. "You know, most people would have asked why he was here in the first place."

"News travels fast. I heard something about using it as a writing prompt. How did that go?"

"He was a big success."

"He?"

"He's male. I had him checked a while back."

"You have interesting hobbies."

"You are not the first to observe that." And presumably Renee didn't even know about the solving crime thing.

I wheeled Sid back to my office, but since it was time for office hours and I had a pair of students already waiting for me, we couldn't resume our earlier conversation for a while. Two repeat explanations of next week's assignment, two excuses for late papers, and four distributed copies of the syllabus later, I locked the door and Sid was able to relax.

"Man, would I have stiff muscles if I had any muscles. Do you know how hard that is?"

"Are you kidding? I couldn't even manage a good game of freeze tag back in the day. I wonder how FAD's life models manage it."

"At least I had plenty of time to think. If we assume Kelly was killed because of her art thieving ways, then we can safely assume that one of her victims killed her."

"Right."

"So we need to identify the victims."

"How? Some of those designs had an actual signed name, but most are illegible, and the rest were initials or symbols."

"I don't suppose there's a registry of artists' signatures."

"I have no idea."

A few minutes on Google informed us that there was not.

"So on to assumption number two," Sid said. "The killer must be an FAD student."

"Or an FAD professor. Most of the art profs here are working artists, too."

"Right, I didn't think of that." He tapped his chin. "I don't suppose you could ask people if they recognize the signatures."

"Not without some kind of an excuse," I said, "but an awful lot of students and teachers have work on display somewhere on campus. I could wander around, looking at pictures and comparing signatures. I might get lucky."

"I'm afraid I can't help with that, unless… What if you put my skull in your bag? Then I could go with you."

I wanted to refuse out of hand, but I couldn't without a good reason. Or better yet, a distraction. "Wouldn't it be more useful for you to go online and do the same thing? You could check the FAD website—they've got a gallery of student artwork."

"Good idea. And I bet lots of FAD kids are on Facebook, probably with links to blogs and Tumblr and Instagram accounts and such."

"Exactly. You can work in here on my laptop, and I'll go wander. Just be very quiet."

"Nobody will hear a thing," he promised.

And he was true to his word. I stood outside the door after he got started, pretending to check e-mail on my phone, and heard only the softest of typing. How he could be quieter with bare finger bones than I was with the padded variety was an eternal mystery.

While Sid worked, I put on my metaphorical detective hat to go looking for artists' signatures. I started in our wing, looking at the signatures on every piece I found, refreshing my memory as needed by comparing the signatures with those on the photos I'd taken with my phone. I was trying for a casual air, but nobody seemed to notice me. Apparently it took having a skeleton in tow to really get people's attention.

When I'd assured myself that none of the art on display in my wing was from any of Kelly's victims, I ambled down the corridor to the main building, then took an almost identical corridor to the Illustration wing. I had no luck there, either. After that, I went to Sculpture. I thought it was a long shot, since we didn't know about any sculptures being stolen, but it was next door and of more immediate interest. There was a sandwich bar in that wing that served terrific meatball subs.

Next up were Photography, Fashion Design, and Graphic Design. After that, I was heartily sick of looking at pictures, and

I decided to go through Sequential Art only because it offered the fastest route back to my office. I nearly changed my mind when I saw they'd put up a display of comic book pages. Lots and lots of comic book pages. I promised myself a chocolate chip cookie—one of the big ones—if I made it all around the room.

I was about a quarter of the way through when I spotted a superhero splash page with a signature that I thought was a butterfly like the one on the wolf illustration. I pulled out my phone to compare but decided they weren't the same after all. One was very stylized, while the other was cutesy. Either way, they didn't match. I was entering the name into my phone, just in case, when I heard somebody right behind me.

"Taking in the art?"

I jerked around, startled. Lucas Silva and Jeremy Nolan were standing behind me. Lucas looked amused—Jeremy looked concerned. "Oh, hi."

"You know," Jeremy said, "you shouldn't be taking photos of student artwork." He pointed to a prominent sign that said: No Photography or Video.

"I wasn't. I was writing down the name of the artist."

"Why?" he said.

"The story looks intriguing and I thought I'd see if the artist had posted any more online somewhere."

Jeremy frowned at the picture. "It looks like a standard comic book fight scene to me."

I started to tell him that I had a superhero fetish and that I was going to use this comic to fuel my sexual fantasies but remembered just in time that I was a professor and should aspire to decorum. Besides which, Jeremy probably wouldn't get the joke anyway and would spread the story via the adjunct gossip mill, which would not be a good thing for my tenure quest. Instead I remembered Sid's advice not to tell people anything I didn't have to. "What are you two doing in sequential art land? Are you planning to get your students to paint comic book covers? Alex Ross has made quite the career doing that."

Jeremy made a face. "I want my students to study real art, not so-called popular culture."

I was working on a scathing retort when he said, "Anyway, I need to head out."

"You and Renee go celebrate," Lucas said.

"We will," he said, looking inordinately pleased with himself, and left.

Since Lucas didn't offer to explain, I didn't ask what Renee and Jeremy had to celebrate. Besides which, I'd had a thought. Since he taught some introductory courses, it was possible that he might be able to identify one or more of the mystery signatures. "Can I pick your brain about something?" I asked.

"Sure. Why don't we go to my place?"

I followed him to the Painting wing, which was considerably busier than the English wing. In their central area every couch and work nook was filled with students who were working and/or socializing. I didn't bother to check for signatures because instead of being decorated with paintings and sculpture, the walls had been given over to mural painters who, as far as my uneducated eye could tell, had been inspired by urban graffiti artists.

We had to dodge two groups working on new murals and a bevy of photography majors taking pictures of them at work. To make the scene even more meta, another student was sketching the photographers taking pictures of the students painting the mural.

The door to Lucas's combined office and studio was closed, and he stopped to knock loudly.

"What's that about?"

"Just letting my model get dressed before I let you in."

I know I blushed because he started laughing.

"Just kidding," he said. "There's nobody in there." He opened the door and proved it.

"You are never going to let me live that down, are you?" I said as I followed him inside.

"Not yet, anyway," he said cheerfully.

Once when we'd worked together before, I'd come to Lucas's

office to meet him for a lunch date, and when I opened the door, found myself confronted by the northern end of a south-facing nude model standing on a stool. In other words, his well-muscled rear end was right at eye level. That was bad enough, but I'd distracted the model enough that he'd turned around, meaning that something else had been at eye level. And apparently the model enjoyed his work.

According to Lucas, I'd turned bright red before excusing myself and running from the room. I couldn't really blame him for bringing it up now and again.

"Come on in. Have a seat." He looked around for a stool that wasn't covered in paint or paint-related materials, then rolled his own chair out from behind his desk and waved me toward it while he took a stool, presumably unconcerned about any wet paint on it since his pants were already well-anointed. "So what brings you to my humble studio? Were you hoping to find more live models?"

"I try to keep my ogling separate from my job, thanks just the same."

"What a shame," he said, waggling his eyebrows, which reminded me that he had really nice eyes.

"Here's the thing. I've found some artwork that is signed, but I don't know who the signatures belong to."

"Meaning that they're 'signed' with a crest or symbol rather than something obvious."

"Right. Is there a registry or database to track signatures?"

"I don't know of one. I've heard that artists register trademarks, but I don't know of anybody who did. Is it somebody local?"

"I'm not sure. Can I show them to you?"

"Sure."

I pulled out my phone and flipped through the pictures of signatures for him. "Recognize any of these?"

He put his hand on his chin. "That stylized butterfly looks familiar, but I can't remember who uses it. Probably a student."

"A student here?"

He nodded. "I think it was somebody recent, but that's the

best I can say. I'll keep my eyes open and let you know if I see it again."

"Great."

"Do I get to know why?"

"Sorry. National security." I knew Lucas well enough to know he'd accept that.

"Fair enough. I actually have a work-related question for you."

"Work? You mean you've got a job? When did this happen?"

He put his hand over his heart. "My muse has failed me, and I have nothing left to live for but daily tedium. I'm even now deciding between retail and fast food."

"Then who is in the middle of painting that portrait behind you? The one with paint still wet?"

"Oh that? Paint-by-number. Anyway, what's the deal with the Writing Lab? With Kelly gone and all?"

"For now, we English adjuncts are taking shifts. Why do you ask?" I was hoping he wasn't leading up to a request for me to proofread a paper for him. I've been approached by more than one academic from another department asking me to "just take a quick look at" their papers, only to have those requests evolve into proofreading, editing, and even rewriting, all without pay or author credit. Even being treated to a cup of coffee and a muffin would have been nice.

"Next week I'm going to assign a paper for Advanced Life Painting, and I usually require my students to go by the Writing Lab for input, so I wanted to make sure you guys can accommodate them."

"It shouldn't be a problem. Is there anything special we should know about how you want the papers to be written or formatted or anything?"

"Not really. To be honest, I'm only assigning a paper because I have to for the 'Writing Across the Curriculum' program." He snorted.

"Ahem."

"No offense," he said. "I'm completely in favor of all of our students being able to write a decent paper. It's just by the time they make it to this class, they're pretty focused on painting. Having to write a paper scares them to death."

"I can see that. One time I asked a bunch of English majors to illustrate a paper about their favorite Shakespeare character. I was only asking for clip art or something online. Even a stick figure would have done. But they got so worked up you'd have thought I was asking them to re-create the *Mona Lisa*. I never did that again."

"I get that. Which is why I'm not going to be grading very harshly. The topic is 'My Favorite Pose,' so they don't even have to cite sources. As long as they can come up with two pages that explain why they prefer to paint models in a particular pose, they'll get an A."

"Good enough," I said. "I will spread the word. Do you have anything more difficult coming up for any of your other classes?"

"My Intermediate Painting class is going to write a finished artist statement, so that's a bit more serious, but it won't be assigned for another month."

"Then we'll talk about that later. Or maybe they'll have a replacement for Kelly by then."

"They would have had to replace her pretty soon anyway."

"How so?"

"I could be wrong, but she told me she was working on something that would be her ticket out of here."

"I didn't know that," I said, though I wondered if she'd been saving up her ill-gotten gains for a definite purpose.

"So she said. She wanted to move on to bigger and better things."

"Don't we all?"

"Not me," he said. "I mean, I don't want to count my chickens before they're hatched, but…"

"But what?"

"So the rumor has been going around for months that Professor Liederman is finally ready to retire, meaning that there would be an open tenured position in Painting, but nothing was definite until today. We just had a departmental meeting, and it turns out that Liederman is leaving at the end of the semester. So Jeremy is getting the nod, which we'd all expected because he's been here the longest. And he is really good."

"Okay, I see why you'd want him to celebrate, but I'm missing why you're so excited."

"That's because you weren't in the meeting. Administration has noticed that Painting is becoming a very popular major indeed, so they've decided to add another tenured position. Guess who's been here the second longest."

"Is it someone who is also really good?"

"Modesty forbids me from answering."

"Lucas, that's wonderful!" Almost shyly I added, "We're adding a position in English, too. Of course, we all want it, so my chances aren't good."

"None of that—positive thoughts only. Come on! Let's go grab a hot chocolate to celebrate. My treat!"

I couldn't very well turn that down. I didn't have any more sleuthing in mind anyway. Of course, I did have to endure more jokes when the snack bar special was a foot-long hot dog, but we still had a great time imagining a brighter, tenured future.

CHAPTER NINETEEN

When I got back to my office, I found that Sid had had even less luck than I had. He hadn't identified a single artist signature, whereas I at least got a "looks familiar" from Lucas. Plus hot chocolate and a cookie.

"It's even worse than I thought," Sid grumbled. "Did you know artists sometimes have more than one signature? Or they change just because they feel like it! Where's the continuity in that?"

"We'll go for a different angle," I said soothingly. "So are you coming home tonight?"

"Definitely. It's dead around here at night!"

Since I'd been hoping to bring Sid home, I'd brought his rolling bag, which was an old hard-sided one my mother had bought years before. The pattern on the side was called "Antelope," but it looked like bacon to me, which may be why it was such a good buy. Sid fit in neatly, and he was much easier to transport that way.

We packed up and I was locking up when Owen showed up. "Hey, Georgia! Where have you been all afternoon? A bunch of students were looking for you."

"Really? I was here for my office hours earlier and I didn't get any e-mail from anybody."

"Well, you know kids. They expect a lot out of us. I just hope Professor Waldron didn't hear them banging on your door, or worse still, Mr. Perkins. You don't want to make a bad impression at this stage of the game."

That was such an obvious dig that I didn't bother to respond to it. "See you Monday!"

"What's with the suitcase? Are you heading out to see the kid, or do you have a sleepover planned?" He waggled his eyebrows, which made me wonder how Lucas made that gesture look funny, while Owen made it sleazy.

"It's my skeleton."

"Oh, right. That was a smart move. You got some buzz going about what an innovative teacher you are. Kudos."

Since I couldn't very well explain that using Sid had more to do with improvisation than innovation, I accepted the compliment and repeated, "See you Monday!"

A student approached, luckily for me, and said, "Dr. Deen, can I ask you about this week's assignment?"

Owen looked momentarily annoyed but swiftly switched his expression to that of a devoted teacher and said, "Of course, *my* door is always open." That gave me and Sid enough time to escape.

I loaded Sid's suitcase into the front seat, and once the doors were unlocked and I'd checked to make sure nobody was nearby, I unzipped the bag and flipped one side up so Sid and I could talk on the way home.

"He's lying," Sid said immediately.

"Excuse me?"

"Georgia, I was in that room while you were gone. Nobody knocked on your door except Porn Star Owen—I could hear him calling your name from the hall. I think he thought you were ducking him. Which you should, permanently."

"He's not that bad."

"Yes, he is."

I thought about it. "You know, you're right. The adjunct biz is so dependent on networking that I hesitate to totally write somebody off, but it's time to quit making nice with Owen. The combination of constant come-ons and veiled insults is too annoying to put up with."

"Good. You're going to smoke him in the tenure race, anyway. His publications are crap."

"How do you know?"

"I may have gotten bored and prepared dossiers on all your colleagues. After all, they were suspects up until we discovered the art theft angle."

"Couldn't one of them still be the killer? Maybe one of them draws in his or her spare time."

"If one of them draws, there is no record of it or reference to it anywhere. Caroline loves her comics, but as far as I can tell, she's never tried to draw her own. Since I bet they'd draw attention to artistic ability while they're trying to get tenure at an art school, we can assume there are no hidden artists in the bunch."

"I guess that's a relief."

"It would have made a great way to get them off the tenure list, though."

We got home and I started rummaging around the kitchen to find something to eat. Friday dinners tend to be haphazard, since it's been so long since grocery shopping day, but I thawed a batch of chili I'd frozen a couple of weeks earlier and baked a can of rolls to go with it. Once I opened a can of fruit cocktail for dessert, most of the major food groups were at least nodded at.

Sid had been tapping away at his laptop while I thawed, baked, and opened, and by the time I was ready to eat, he had a report to share for our dinnertime conversation.

"I was thinking. A lot of those screen dumps advertising T-shirts are from a store called City Riggers. So I did a little research. You know, online art theft is a huge issue. All kinds of stores have been accused of swiping designs from artists to put on T-shirts, mugs, phone cases, just about anything you can print on. It's like people think that once it's on the web, it's fair game. And it turns out that City Riggers has been accused of foul play a lot. They claim that since they buy designs from third-party artists, it's impossible for them to know whether or not a design is stolen."

"If they hadn't seen the original, how would they know?"

"Fair enough. But when the original artists provide proof, they blow them off with a boilerplate we're-sharing-this-with-our-legal-team-for-review note. Or at the very most, they'll take the product off their site but won't provide information to the injured party or pay a fair share of the money they've made."

"Can't the artists sue?"

"Do you know of any FAD students who could afford to sue some place like City Riggers, which is probably owned by a big-money parent corporation?"

"Good point."

"Anyway, this is nothing new, meaning that Kelly even stole the idea of stealing. Which is pathetic, when you think of it."

I had to agree. "So any more ideas for more sleuthing?"

He considered it. "Not right now. You?"

I shook my head.

"Movie night?"

"Go see what you can find."

He went to the living room while I cleaned up from dinner, finishing just in time for my cell phone to ring.

"Hello, Thackery residence."

"Hi, gorgeous."

"Oh. Hi, Owen. What's up?"

"Just making sure you're okay. I know you've been a little nervous about being out there alone at night since you found poor Kelly's body."

"I'm not nervous, Owen. It happened nearly a week ago, and I wasn't nervous then, either."

"Good for you," he said as if he didn't believe me. "So I'm finally leaving FAD, and I thought I could grab some Chinese food at May Chung's and swing by your place so we could have dinner. Would you rather have sweet and sour pork or Kung Pao chicken?"

"I've already eaten."

"That's all right. I'm not that hungry anyway. I could just get some cannoli at Maria's Pastry and we could go straight to dessert."

I could just tell he was leering when he said it. "No, thanks. I've got plans tonight."

Before he could offer anything else, Sid clattered into the room, "Hey, Georgia, would you rather—?"

I held a hand up and pointed to the phone.

"Sorry," he whispered.

"Oh, you've got company," Owen said, sounding injured.

"Just the TV," I said. Sid made a face, but after Officer Buchanan's nosing around, I didn't want any rumors getting back to her about my having a houseguest.

"I thought I heard somebody say your name."

"It's a documentary about Georgia O'Keeffe. I was named after her, you know." Before he could ask what channel it was on, I added, "My parents recommended it, so I just finished downloading it."

"I love O'Keeffe's work," he said enthusiastically.

Of course he did. "I did not know that. I'll send you the link for the video and if you get a chance to watch it, you can let me know what you think. Goodbye."

He was starting to say something as I hung up the phone.

"Owen again?" Sid asked.

I nodded. "Why won't some people take a hint?"

"Maybe you're being too nice."

"Why should I have to be rude just because he is? He's the one whose behavior needs changing, not me."

"Okay, that's fair."

"So what do you want to watch?"

We decided to binge on *Community*, which rounded out the day with plenty of laughs. Honestly, I needed the distraction. Despite what'd I'd told Owen, I was feeling uneasy about Kelly. Not just because of finding her body, but because of knowing what I knew about her. I couldn't see how she could rest in peace when she'd been murdered by one of her victims, and though I don't believe in ghosts—Sid notwithstanding—I was restless.

Sid, bless his chest cavity, seemed to recognize what I was feeling and kept me supplied with hot chocolate and cookies until I was about to burst. I think he watched over me while I slept, too, which would have looked disturbing to anybody who wasn't us.

The rest of the weekend was a wash as far as investigating went.

Instead I was reduced to doing things like grading papers, laundry, grocery shopping, housecleaning, and catching up with the family. It snowed part of Saturday, which made Sid happy because he got to use the snowblower again. I even let him borrow the car keys to move the minivan in the driveway so he could clear around it. I told him I had complete trust in him, but I also knew that with the piles of snow lining the driveway, it wasn't like he could go far off track into the yard. As for the mailbox, it wasn't really damaged—I just had to set it back upright again.

CHAPTER TWENTY

Having finished going through Kelly's files, Sid was fine with staying home on Monday to catch up on his gaming, social media, and an online course in psychology he was taking. My own day was pretty normal, too. I did swing past the last couple of departments to check for artists' signatures and traded texts with Lucas to see if he'd remembered whose signature he thought he recognized, but nothing came of any of it.

My last task for the day was to take care of paperwork. I didn't have to fill out a time card for the classes I taught—I got a flat rate per classroom hour, no matter how much time I spent outside of class prepping and grading papers. But for the work in the Writing Lab, I had to turn in a time sheet to get paid. So I added up my hours, filled out the appropriate form, and went to Mr. Perkins's office to hand it in.

Mr. Perkins was typing as efficiently as he did everything else—only his fingers and eyes seemed to be moving. I know he saw me standing at the door, but he finished whatever passage he was working on before acknowledging me.

"Here's my time sheet," I said and handed it to him.

He inspected it as carefully as if I were getting paid enough per hour to bankrupt the college. "I'll turn this in right away."

"Thank you." Then I had a thought. Though Kelly's assistant didn't seem to be doing much to earn their pay, they had shown up during a couple of my shifts and actually brought me coffee once. "Is there anything special I need to do about Indigo?"

"I beg your pardon?"

"Indigo Williamson, the student assistant at the Writing Lab. I can't sign time cards, so I figured you'd have to handle it."

"There is no assistant assigned to the Writing Lab as far as I know. Certainly no funds were budgeted for that."

"But Caroline and Indigo told me—" What exactly had they said? "I must have misunderstood."

"Indeed?" he said with profound disinterest and resumed typing.

I peeked into the Lab on my way past, but Indigo wasn't around, which was probably just as well. I wouldn't have known what to say to them. Sid, on the other hand, had plenty to say when I got back to the bungalow and told him of my discovery.

"So you've let our star suspect hang around the Writing Lab? Because you realize that he is our star suspect now."

"They."

"They? You think he was working with somebody?"

"Indigo is gender fluid—they prefer *they* and *them*."

"Oh, right. So you let them loose in Kelly's office?"

"They said they were Kelly's assistant. How was I supposed to know any different? I mean, why would they spend hours in there for no pay or credit?"

"I think we know the answer to that. They must have been looking for the cache of artwork that I found. Somewhere in there is proof that Kelly stole from them."

"They did try to get me out of the Lab a couple of times," I said. "We're just lucky that they don't have a key."

I had work to do that evening, but it was hard because I was mightily distracted by Sid's scheming and plotting. He'd have cheerfully kept on discussing our plan all night long if I hadn't reminded him that one of us had to sleep. Fortunately, he decided to make a dossier for Indigo, which kept him from waking me up before I needed to be awake on Tuesday morning.

Though Indigo hadn't told anybody what their imaginary schedule was, they'd shown up for my shift on Tuesday the week before, and I was betting they would do so again. Sure enough, they showed up shortly after I did and looked around.

"No appointments?"

"Not for a while," I said. I'd canceled the one I'd had, rescheduling it for later in the day.

"I can hold the fort here if you want to go get coffee or something."

"No, thanks."

"Suit yourself."

I pretended to work until they were settled, sketchbook in hand. Then I said, "Can I ask you a question?"

"Yeah, I guess."

"Why have you been hanging around? I know you weren't working for Kelly."

They stiffened, and for a minute I thought they were going to bolt. But they must have realized it wouldn't do any good—one call to security would find them if I wanted them found. They relaxed again or tried to. "What I said was that I was Kelly's assistant, which I was. I never said it was a paid gig."

"So you volunteered to hang around here for hours every week out of the goodness of your heart? Because art students have so much free time? Try again."

"I was helping her," they insisted. "It just wasn't Writing Lab stuff. It was a private project of hers."

"Something to do with art theft?"

Sid kicked me under the desk. He'd insisted on coming to help in case Indigo went into a murderous rage, and was in his suitcase with the lid open so he could leap into action if it was called for. The kick was because he'd wanted me to finesse the information gathering, and I hadn't. I wasn't particularly good at finesse.

"What do you know about it?" Indigo asked.

"Enough. Did she steal one of your designs?"

"Excuse me?"

"Did Kelly steal your work? A T-shirt design? Is that why you were angry at her?"

They gave me that jeez-are-you-being-an-idiot look that teenagers do better than anyone. "You've got it backwards. Kelly wasn't stealing anything—she was trying to find the thief."

Chapter Twenty-One

"Say that again, slowly."

They sighed in exasperation. "Kelly found out that somebody was stealing designs from students and then selling them to stores. Which isn't really news because people in the art and maker community have known about this for years. But it was news to Kelly, and she started looking into it near the end of last semester."

"These designs?" I pulled out the stack of papers and spread them out on the desk, ignoring Sid's kick.

"I've been looking for those!" They narrowed their eyes. "Why do you have them? How do I know you aren't the thief?"

"Because I found them, and because I thought Kelly was the thief until two minutes ago?"

"That's what you *say* anyway."

"Okay, then how about because I wasn't at FAD last semester?"

"The stuff was on the web."

"Then how about because I wouldn't know how? The art wasn't simply stolen, right? The thief re-created the designs, and in some cases, made changes. Like here on this cat. I couldn't do that—I can't even draw stick figures."

"It's easy to pretend to be bad at something."

"Fine. Call my parents—they've still got some of the art I did in elementary school, mostly for the laugh value. Or you can track my professional career. I have a degree in English, and I've never taken an art class, nor have I ever taught at an art school before now. But sure, I could have been nursing a talent for copying art my whole life, just in case I ever got a chance to steal another artist's ideas."

"Okay fine, you're not the thief."

"Good. Now it's your turn. After all, you really can draw. How do I know Kelly was working with you and not investigating you?"

"Hey, I'm a victim. And I wouldn't steal somebody else's art!"

"Can you back that up?"

"How?"

"Tell me how you became a victim. When did you find out your art had been stolen? And what got stolen?"

"This is mine," they said, pulling out the lions, and tigers and bears picture. "Last year I put some designs up on my Tumblr, and this fall a troll posted that I was copying a shirt at City Riggers. I would have just deleted his comment, but he included a link, and it really was my design."

"How do you know it wasn't a case of two people coming up with the same design? That happens sometimes, right?"

"Seriously?" They held up the photocopy and the screen dump. "Same composition, same colors, same pose. Same typeface!"

"Except he used the Oxford comma and you didn't."

"Whatever. The point is that there is no way this could be anything but stealing. After it happened to me, I found out that there have been rumors for years that City Riggers and other companies have been stealing designs, but nobody has been able to take them to court. These guys have deep pockets, and most artists barely have pockets at all."

"What if you did have a lawyer willing to go after them? How could you prove you drew the design?"

"I've got the original sketches, and I date all the pages in my sketchbooks, and there's a creation date on the file. I don't know if that would be enough to convince a judge or not, but it's never going to come to that because I can't afford to sue. I sent a C&D letter—"

"A what?"

"A Cease and Desist letter. I told them that it was my design," and they said they'd investigate, but a week later they said they'd found no evidence of wrongdoing. I posted about it on my Tumblr, but half the comments I got said I was probably the thief. The only thing I could do was take my designs down."

"How did Kelly find out about this?"

"I had to write a paper for Expository Writing last semester, and it was supposed to be about an event that made me emotional. Being royally pissed off is an emotion, right? So I wrote about what had happened. Only, I'm not a great writer, so I brought it here to the Lab to get Kelly to take a look. She was really interested. I guess somebody had plagiarized an article she wrote back in college, but she couldn't prove it and was still mad about it."

"Then what?"

"She helped me improve the paper, I turned it in, and I got an A."

"That's it?"

"That's it for last semester. This semester Kelly e-mailed and asked me to come talk to her. This time she had all kinds of questions about my case—that's what she called it, my case. She wanted to know if I'd had any other designs stolen, if I was still posting my work online—all kinds of stuff like that."

"Did you ask her why?"

"She said she'd found another victim here at FAD."

"Who?"

"She wouldn't say. She said it was better if her sources were uncontaminated, which they wouldn't be if we compared notes."

"How did she find the other person?"

"No idea. All I know is that she was fired up about investigating and was planning to write this big exposé about it. Did you know she hated working here?"

"I'd heard that."

"She figured that if she could break this story, she would get some serious attention and then she could get a reporting job at a newspaper or magazine or maybe at a good blog. She thought this was her big chance."

"But why? I mean, I've done a little research into this kind of theft, and it looks like this topic has been written about quite a lot. Why did she think her story was going to make a splash?"

"No idea," they said again, "but she was spending serious time on it. She wanted to know if I knew any other people who'd had their work stolen, and if they'd be willing to talk to her."

"Did you?"

They shook their head. "I did try to help her, though. She had me going through websites looking to see if any of my other designs had shown up. I found one more for sure, and one maybe. The 'maybe' looked a lot like my idea, but it had been tweaked quite a bit, and I think the copy was better than my original, so I don't know if it counts. Anyway, she said it was corroboration.

"Then she gave me some scanned sketches like those and asked me to look at sites for those designs. She wouldn't tell me where they'd come from and had edited out the signature, but I guessed they were from the other victim she'd found. Whoever it is, they're good—really elegant work. And I found three of their designs for sale online. That was the week before last. Then last week I found out Kelly was dead and…I just wondered if it was connected somehow."

"Then you thought Kelly's death was suspicious?"

"I don't know. Maybe. Everybody said it was an accident, but I just wasn't sure."

"Why didn't you go to the police?"

"What would I have said? 'That woman who died in an accident? I think it could have been murder over some stolen T-shirt designs that were worth maybe a hundred dollars at best, and I have no idea how you can figure out who it was. So go investigate already.'"

"I see your point. Is that why you've been hanging around here?"

"Partly. Plus I wanted to see if Kelly left any notes. I thought maybe I could, I don't know, continue her work. Then I got suspicious about you."

"About me?"

"Just about the first thing you said to me was about a sketchbook, and I knew Kelly had been scanning somebody's sketchbook."

"All I knew is that a student came by looking for one."

"Yeah, but I didn't have any reason to trust you. Anyway, I figured it couldn't hurt to hang around and see if anything else turned up. I was going to give it up after this week, but now… Wait, you weren't looking for the thief, because you thought Kelly was the thief. What have you been looking for?"

"Would you believe a murderer? I think Kelly's death was suspicious, too."

I knew I was going to have a bruise on my leg—Sid whacked me a good one when I said that.

It took a while to convince Indigo that I really knew what I was doing, more or less, or at least had done it before. Of course I didn't mention my kicking partner, but given how hard it was for them to believe I'd solved murders, I didn't want to throw Sid into the mix. As it was, I had to go online to show them articles about previous murders I'd been involved in. I think they were actually a little bit impressed after that.

"So what are you doing next?" they asked.

I waited for Sid to kick me again, but there was no need. I didn't have any secrets left to spill. "Honestly, Indigo, you've thrown me for a loop. If Kelly wasn't the thief, then obviously she wasn't killed by one of her victims. That must mean that the thief killed her. She must have figured out who it was."

But Indigo was shaking their head. "No, she'd have told me if she had."

"Maybe she didn't have a chance to."

"Sure she did. I saw her that afternoon."

"You mean the day she died? What time was that?"

"Maybe two thirty?"

"What happened?"

"There's not a lot to tell. Kelly had asked me to put out some feelers with artists on Etsy and some other sites, but I hadn't gotten anything. I asked if she'd had any luck, and she said she'd been doing background research into copyright law and creator's rights and stuff like that, but even though she tried to make it sound important, I could tell she was stuck. I asked if she wanted me to hang around, but she said she had an appointment in a little while, and then she was taking the weekend off to clear her head."

"A tutoring appointment?"

"I guess. She didn't say. Anyway, if there's one thing an artist learns, it's body language—she was beyond tired and frustrated that day. She didn't have squat."

I was starting to feel the same way. "One more thing. Have you been talking about this with other students?"

"Yeah, some. Why?"

"I'm probably just being paranoid, but do me a favor and be really careful. Maybe Kelly didn't figure out who the thief was, but I've got to wonder if the thief found out what she was up to."

"Okay, now you're freaking me out, and saying it out loud makes it sound crazy, anyway. Why would anybody kill somebody else over T-shirt designs? We're not talking big bucks."

"People kill for stupid reasons all the time. Just be careful."

"Sure. Whatever."

"And let me give you my contact info in case you hear anything else."

We exchanged phone numbers and e-mail addresses, and they asked, "So you want me to keep working here?"

"You do realize that I can't pay you or get you credit."

"Yeah, but it's not a bad place to work—the light is good. And listening while you tutor people has been kind of okay. I've learned a lot more about writing papers than I did during the class I wrote the paper for."

"Thank you. That's good to hear. Who did you write that paper for, anyway?"

"Mr. Deen. Why? Do you think he's involved?"

"Not really—just nosy about my colleagues." After they left, I took a moment to gloat that they were learning more at the Lab than they had in Owen's class.

I only wished I were getting something worthwhile for my time. Sid's and my big theory had been blown to bits, and I had no idea what to do with the new one. We were back to square one.

CHAPTER TWENTY-TWO

Sid had come to the same conclusion, and even he was frustrated. Of course, he'd had nothing to do but stew over it while I finished my shift at the Lab before we finally got a chance to retreat to my office and have a real conversation, so he decided to take it out on me.

"Did you have to tell Indigo everything?" he demanded.

"I didn't tell them everything, but I had to tell them as much as I did or they never would have told me anything. And aren't you glad they did?"

"I can't believe we got it backwards! I am such a bonehead!"

"Hey, it did make sense given what we'd found out."

"Yeah, yeah. But so much wasted time. Where do we go from here?"

"We can hunt for the real thief, right?"

"How could we? You read those articles about art theft I e-mailed to you."

"Um… Not all of them."

He looked at me suspiciously. "How many did you read?"

"None. Look, you gave me such a good summary that I didn't feel the need."

"Georgia—"

"I know, I know, I should have done my homework. But can we drop the topic of Georgia-is-an-idiot for now? Tell me why we can't hunt for the art thief."

"Because if you'd read the research, you'd know that most art theft is done electronically. Artists post their work for critique, or for sale, or just to show friends what they've been up to. Then somebody downloads it and sells it as their own. They don't ever meet in person. It might be possible to lever that information out of City Riggers, but not without a search warrant or at least some serious clout."

"Which Kelly didn't have. Do you think she was just spinning her wheels?"

"No, you've said she was cranky and bitter, but you never said she was stupid. She wouldn't have been spending her time on this if she didn't have an idea that she could really figure it out. And it must be somebody local, or he wouldn't have been able to kill Kelly. If she could figure it out, so can we. Right?"

"Right." I thought there might have been some circular logic involved in that conclusion, but I was willing to go with it.

"I sure wish we had some kind of notes or something other than the art in Kelly's files. I've looked through every folder."

"Everything else was probably on her computer, which was smashed in the car wreck."

"That was awfully convenient."

"True," I said, thinking about how thoroughly the laptop had been destroyed. "She must have had backup somewhere, but if it was in the office, Mr. Perkins would have packed it up and sent it to her family. If it was in her apartment, the family got it, and if it was in her car, the cops got it."

"All we've got is the pictures."

"And Indigo."

"Right, Indigo… Didn't they say they told Kelly about the theft months ago, but that Kelly only got fired up to do something about it this semester?"

"Yeah, they did."

"So why the sudden interest? What changed?"

"The other victim she told Indigo about?"

"Possibly, but we still don't know who that is. I don't suppose you noticed anybody in particular hanging around the Writing Lab before the murder."

"Sid, there were students in and out all day. No, I didn't notice anybody." Then I remembered something. "Unless it was the sketchbook."

"What sketchbook? The one Indigo was talking about?"

"The day I started at the Lab, a student came by and asked if we'd found her sketchbook. Why would her sketchbook have been there unless she was the other victim Kelly told Indigo about?"

"That could be it. So who was she?"

"I have no idea. I don't remember ever seeing her before or since. I don't even know for sure that she was a student, though she did look like one."

"What does an art student look like?"

"The right age, a big bag because she's carrying around sketchbooks and pens and pencils, a knit cap, and ink on her fingers."

"Sounds like a third of the people I've seen around FAD."

"I know, so I don't think wandering around looking for her would be a good tactic. I could ask some of the other faculty members, but her looks just aren't that distinctive."

"And maybe there should be some things that you don't share with every Tom, Dick, and Harry."

"I thought we agreed to no more Georgia-is-an-idiot remarks."

"You agreed," he muttered. "Anyway, let's attack it from the other direction. If this girl had had designs stolen, how would Kelly have found out?"

"Saw her crying somewhere and stopped to comfort her? Not that I can picture Kelly doing that. Um… Gossip? No, she wasn't much of a gossip. All I ever saw her do was work with students."

"Students! That's it!" Sid snapped his fingers, which should be physically impossible for bare bones. "What if the girl did the same thing that Indigo did? Maybe she wrote about having been stolen from."

"That makes sense, but it doesn't help us much."

"Sure it does. My watching you at work has not gone to waste after all. Every time somebody presents a paper to be critiqued, it gets logged into the system, right? All we have to do is go through the log and figure out which paper was written about stolen T-shirt designs."

"Sid, how many papers did Kelly critique? There must be hundreds."

"At least, but we only have to go back as far as the beginning of the semester, when Kelly got back in touch with Indigo."

"How many papers is that?"

"A lot," he said, "but don't worry. I live for stuff like this."

He wasn't being sarcastic, either. Okay, maybe about the living part, but I could tell he was delighted to have something he could sink his gumless teeth into. I hated to dampen his enthusiasm, but I had to say, "You realize we may not be looking for a killer after all."

"What do you mean?"

"Well, if Kelly was the thief, then we would have had a murder motive. Revenge, stopping her, whatever. But if she was looking for a thief, what was the motive?"

"You don't think a thief would want to kill her?"

"For a T-shirt design? Unless it's sold by a big designer, T-shirt designs aren't worth that much."

"Maybe there's more to it than just T-shirt designs."

"Like what?"

"Like... Like we'll figure that out later. But for now, you just give me access to the Writing Lab database, and I'll find that second victim."

It was late, and we decided to head back home so we could work simultaneously rather than having to share my laptop. So I loaded Sid back into his suitcase and headed to the minivan. Though it wasn't snowing at the moment—something I appreciated—a dusting of snow had fallen at some point during the day, so I took a few minutes to brush it off. Then I got in and waited for the heater to start working.

Sid peeked out of the bag. "Georgia? We're not moving."

"I'm just letting the engine warm up."

"Really?"

"No, not really. I'm just tired. It feels as if we've worked so hard and gotten nowhere."

"We're getting somewhere! But if you're tired, I could drive."

"Being able to navigate up and down the driveway does not make you street-legal, Sid."

"I know, but I've been thinking. When I first woke up like this, I already knew how to walk, right?"

"Yeah."

"And talk."

"Most definitely."

"So obviously I retained some skills and knowledge from when I was alive. And we know I was in college before I, you know, died. So I probably knew how to drive. Maybe I still do."

"That's a big maybe."

"I moved the car in the driveway okay, didn't I?"

"More or less."

"And I've played a lot of driving games—I score really high."

"The roads around here are a little less forgiving that the ones in *Mario Kart*."

"Hey, I've played more realistic simulations. I think I can do it."

My first instinct was to say "No," or even to yell, "Are you nuts? NO!" but I thought that might be a bit undiplomatic. So I dodged it as if I were driving in *Mario Kart* myself. "The problem is, even if you can drive, you don't have a license, and needless to say, you can't get one."

"When was the last time you were stopped and asked for your license?"

"Almost never, but I do have one. Whereas if the cops stop you, not having a license is going to be the least of our problems."

"Yeah, I see what you mean. I just think it would be fun to try."

"Let me think about it and see if I can come up with a way," I said. A deserted parking lot might do the trick, if we were really careful. Or maybe I could borrow a golf cart or a riding mower—I didn't think either of those required a license, and I was pretty sure nobody had thought it necessary to pass a law requiring that golf cart drivers be living.

"Awesome!"

"But just so you know, I've never once had occasion to drive like they do in the movies."

"Got it. No wild chase scenes. Cross my chest cavity and hope to die. Again."

As soon as we pulled into the driveway, Sid popped out of the suitcase, fully formed.

"What are you doing?"

"You're tired and don't need to be lugging me. Nobody's going to see me."

The temperature was even colder than usual, so I was ready to make a mad dash from the minivan to the nice, warm bungalow, but Sid called out to me before I got halfway there.

"Georgia, whose footprints are those?"

"What footprints?" I looked where he was pointing. A clear track lead to and from the front door. "The mailman?"

"The mailman comes in the morning between nine and ten—he hasn't missed it any of the days I've been here. And the snow started after that."

"Maybe he was running late, or it was a substitute."

"Would a substitute mailman peek in our front window?" he said, pointing. Sure enough, somebody had walked right up to the window and back again. "I wish it weren't so cold—the snow is too fluffy to make a recognizable print."

I looked around, which was silly because whoever it was, he was long gone. Still I shivered from something other than the cold. "Let's get inside." Neither of us wasted any time doing so.

CHAPTER TWENTY-THREE

As soon as we were safely inside, Sid said, "Georgia, I told you that you shouldn't be telling everybody about our investigation! Now the killer knows you're looking for him."

"I am not having this conversation. If I hadn't told Indigo what I did, they wouldn't have answered our questions."

"And when Officer Buchanan was here?"

"I didn't tell her a thing she couldn't find out elsewhere."

"You told somebody *something*!"

"Sid, I realize you're nervous about somebody finding out about you, but—"

"Coccyx, Georgia, I'm not worried about me. I'm worried about you! You're all alone out here in the middle of nowhere."

"I'm not alone. I've got you. You are the best bodyguard anybody could ever have. You're strong, you're smart, and you never sleep. What more could I ask for?"

"Well, yeah, that's true."

"Look, I'm not happy about this, either. And I'm not saying we won't make sure everything is locked up tight and keep our eyes open, or eye sockets in your case. I just don't think we should panic."

"Fine, no panicking. But I'm going to stay on guard tonight."

I thought he meant he'd just be a little more vigilant than usual, but in fact, he patrolled the house all night long. He wouldn't even sit down and keep me company when I ate a stuffed baked potato for dinner—just kept roaming from room to room, peering out of the curtains. It was moderately annoying, and I thought about reminding him that he was supposed to be seeing if he could find the second victim of art theft but decided to let him work out his anxiety in his own way. I did a little work, watched a little TV, and listened to him clattering from room to room. The noise made me feel a lot more secure than silence.

I slept well, though not as long as I wanted to, because I had to be up early the next morning.

One item I'd originally thought of as a benefit to teaching at FAD was that I was invited to English departmental meetings. At many of my previous jobs, adjuncts weren't considered important enough, or perhaps permanent enough, to include. We were lucky if we got informed of departmental policy via memo.

Now, having sat through a number of department meetings at FAD, I was starting to miss the memos. Sure, we sometimes got into a spirited debate over the use of the Oxford comma, but most meetings were so dry that I needed two bottled waters to get through them. It didn't help that they were first thing Wednesday morning, one of the rare times when none of us taught a class. I'd asked Caroline why we didn't meet on Fridays—another time when nobody had classes and when we wouldn't have to get up so early—but her guess was that either Professor Waldron wanted us to be available to students all day, or she wanted to be able to sneak off for wild weekends in New York or Vegas, possibly taking along Mr. Perkins as arm candy. I thought the former was probably the real answer, but the latter was a whole lot funnier.

That day we actually had an interesting topic: the use of plural pronouns for gender fluid people, trans people, and anybody else who preferred to avoid binary gender usage. Professor Waldron came down hard on sticking with traditional usage, and I'd expected lively debate from the rest of the department. Instead they all nodded, not quite in unison. I couldn't help wondering if they really agreed, or if they were just sucking up for tenure. Since I had strong feelings because of some of my daughter's friends, I argued for the other side.

I said, "I went to a talk by Dr. John O'Neil, the linguist, a couple of years ago, and he had a very persuasive argument. If a gender neutral pronoun is needed—"

"Is it needed?" Professor Waldron asked.

"A lot of people think so—and not just people who feel excluded. At any rate, first person and second person are gender neutral. Why not third person?"

She nodded slowly.

"That means we can either make up a new pronoun and try to convince people to adopt it, or we can repurpose an existing one."

"If *they* were to become singular, what would we use for plural?" Dahna said with a tinge of horror in her voice. I hoped that meant she was really expressing an opinion as opposed to echoing Professor Waldron's thoughts to get ahead in the tenure race.

"*You* is both plural and singular," I pointed out.

"Except when y'all are in my part of the country," Caroline said with a grin.

Professor Waldron didn't seem convinced, but she said, "I will research the issue further. In the meantime, the language has not evolved yet, so remind your students that he—or she—may have to adopt traditional usage in most circumstances."

"Understood," I said.

She closed her notebook and said, "I believe that's all for today. Have a productive week, and we'll see everyone here again next week." She swept out with a rasp of tweed. Mr. Perkins, as usual, was right behind her.

Since the meeting had been a little shorter than normal, nobody else was in a rush to leave, and it gave me an opportunity to check on something. Maybe I could save Sid some drudgery in going through files in the Writing Lab database.

"Owen," I said, "do you remember a student named Indigo Williamson? You had them for Expository Writing last year, and they wrote a paper about having their designs pirated?"

"It sounds familiar. Why?"

"I was wondering if any of your students this semester wrote about it happening to them. Or if any of you guys have had papers turned in on similar subjects."

"You think somebody plagiarized a paper about intellectual property theft?" Caroline said.

"Funny, but no. I've been hearing some rumbling about other kids having their artwork copied."

Renee scoffed. "Kids believe every thought they ever think is original, so if somebody says anything like it, it must be theft. It never occurs to them that they had an obvious, wholly unoriginal idea."

"Granted, but I think this case goes a bit beyond that," I said. "I've seen some suspicious duplications of art and it does look like something might be going on."

"Here at FAD?" Owen said. "That's not good."

"I know, it's terrible. I've been trying to find—"

"If that rumor were to circulate, it could discourage people from coming here, and if enrollments go down, the dean might decide we don't need another tenured position in the department after all."

"I was thinking that it's terrible because students are having their work stolen," I said.

"That kind of thing cannot be stopped," Dahna said, waving it away as unimportant. "Once a piece of artwork is on the Internet, of course people are going to copy it. This is known."

"But it's not legal or right," I said.

"No, but it's hardly FAD's fault if people want to put their artwork online. They must learn to take responsibility for their choices."

"Sure, but—"

"Is this another one of these mystery things you do?" Caroline asked. "Like at Joshua Tay?"

I glared at her.

"What mystery things?" Dahna wanted to know.

"Georgia's got a strange hobby. She goes looking for criminals," Caroline said.

"I don't—" I started to say.

Renee added, "Yeah, I heard something about that. Didn't it have something to do with that skeleton she brought to campus?"

"Is that why she had to leave McQuaid?" Dahna wanted to know.

"Excuse me—I'm right here!"

But Renee talked over me. "There aren't any criminals here, and I don't like the implication that there could be."

"Look, I just want to know if anybody else has had a student whose art has been stolen."

"Georgia," Caroline said, "can't you find a better way to spend your time?"

Dahna added, "Perhaps you aren't likely to get tenure here, but please don't ruin it for those of us who do have a chance."

"Maybe she's trying to draw attention to herself again, like with the skeleton writing prompt." Renee smirked. "I didn't see anything about skeletons in the syllabus."

The other adjuncts actually laughed at that. Or rather, at me.

I was shocked into silence, but as it turned out, I didn't need to answer.

"What in all that is holy is going on in here?" Professor Waldron was standing in the doorway, her abundant eyebrows making her indignation all the more intense. "I heard your ruckus halfway down the hall, and students could, too!" She closed the door firmly behind her. "Now what is the cause of this unseemly behavior?"

The other members of the department exchanged glances, then all turned to me. Apparently they had appointed me spokesperson, or more likely, the scapegoat. I said, "This is kind of complicated—"

"I'm sure you can clarify it for me." She resumed her seat at the head of the table.

I took a deep breath and did my best to summarize my theories about the theft, ending with, "I've been asking around to see if I can find out more." I looked at my see-hear-speak-no-evil buddies. "My colleagues think I'm opening a can of worms that will just make FAD look bad."

"Of course it makes us look bad," Owen said. "What student is going to want to come here if he thinks his artwork is going to be stolen? These kids post their whole lives on social media, and then complain when they have no privacy."

"Work posted online is still protected by copyright," I reminded him.

"Then let the artists take it up with their lawyers," he shot back. "It's not our problem."

"Maybe it should be!" I said.

Professor Waldron held up one hand to silence us. "Let me recap. Dr. Thackery has found that the work of some of our students has been appropriated."

"That's what she thinks, anyway," Renee said, "but I don't find her 'proof' to be all that conclusive."

"I'm trying to find more proof, which is why I brought it up with all of you."

Professor Waldron held up her hand again. "And you others are concerned that her investigation could harm FAD's reputation?" She raised an eyebrow. "Perhaps your chances for gaining tenure here or at other institutions?"

There were nods all around the table.

"So in conclusion, you are more concerned with FAD's appearance of integrity than our actual integrity?"

Dahna and Owen started to nod again, but Renee nudged them and Caroline looked abashed.

Professor Waldron went on. "Moreover, you are willing to let your students suffer as victims of intellectual theft so that you can pursue your own ambitions. Is that correct?"

"It is not that simple," Dahna said.

"It seems that simple to me. Dr. Thackery, doesn't it seem that simple to you?"

It was my turn to nod.

"Look, these are our jobs I'm talking about," Owen said.

"Teaching in a university is not a job, Dr. Deen. It is a vocation, a sacred trust. As academics, your allegiance should be to the truth and to your students, not to your paychecks." She nearly spat out that last word.

"Maybe you don't need this job to eat, but—"

"If you want a job, go sell shoes or insurance! Go work at any of a thousand other careers where chasing the almighty buck is acceptable, even encouraged. This, sir, is a place of teaching truth as best we can determine it."

Normally, I would bristle at such an old-fashioned argument. It had been used too many times in the past to justify paying faculty members a pittance rather than a decent wage. This time, I kind of wanted to cheer.

"But Georgia doesn't know the truth," Owen whined.

"Then it is our obligation to help her find it, or at the very least, not to impede her in her search." She glared at the quartet of thoroughly cowed instructors. "Have I made myself clear?"

There was no response.

"Good. Dr. Thackery, I trust you will let me know if there is any aid I can give."

"Of course."

"Then our meeting is once again adjourned." She stood, and for once she wasn't the first to leave. Instead she waited for us to file out before following us, and turned out the lights behind her.

CHAPTER TWENTY-FOUR

Though I was gratified by Professor Waldron's support, I was still furious at my colleagues. I retreated to the restroom for a minute to pull myself together. Well, more like ten minutes, but I was fairly composed when I left and went toward my office. I might have maintained my calm had Owen not picked that moment to approach me.

"Georgia?"

"Yes?" I said as civilly as I could. For somebody who was supposedly infatuated with me, he sure hadn't bothered to defend me at the meeting.

"I hope you didn't take my comments personally. I really am just looking out for the best interests of FAD. Tainting the school's reputation wouldn't do any of us any good, not adjuncts or tenured faculty. In fact, it won't do anything for the students either if they graduate from a school that has endured a scandal."

"It doesn't do them any good to have their work stolen either."

"Actually, nothing was really stolen. I mean, if somebody copies artwork, the original artwork is still there, right? There's no real theft."

"I disagree," I said, not even bothering to argue further.

He blinked. "I mean, actually—"

"Owen, I heard what you said, but I don't accept your position."

"Maybe if we talked it out some more. Why don't we grab lunch later and discuss it further. Or even better, how about dinner tonight?"

He'd gone from mansplaining to flirting in less than a minute. Sid was right. Owen was not a nice guy. "No, thank you."

"Was that for dinner or lunch?"

"Both, and any other meal you might be considering."

"Look, I know you're angry that I don't agree with you—"

"No, I'm annoyed that you mocked me at the meeting, but I'm angry because you refuse to take 'no' for an answer. I've told you repeatedly, as nicely as I can, that I do not want to date you. Period. Full stop."

He squinted at me. "There was somebody at your house the night I called, wasn't there? Why didn't you tell me you're seeing somebody? I wouldn't have kept trying if I'd known you were unavailable."

"So it's okay to keep harassing me even when I made it perfectly plain I don't want to date you, but not okay when you're encroaching on another man's territory? Coccyx, Owen, were you always this sexist, or did—"

"It's not sexist to—"

"Don't interrupt. My relationship status is entirely irrelevant. I could be single, I could be dating, I could be married, I could be sleeping with half the men and women on campus. It would make no difference in my feelings toward you. I am not interested in dating you. After this, I don't even want to be your friend."

"But—"

I'll never know what Owen was going to say next because I went into my office and only resisted slamming the door because I didn't want to rouse Professor Waldron's ire again.

Chapter Twenty-Five

I hid out in my office until a few minutes before my eleven o'clock class, which gave me just enough time to grab a hot chocolate beforehand. I was relieved not to see Owen around. I did spot Caroline and Renee in line at the snack bar and got in line behind them without being noticed.

I heard Caroline say, "I can't believe she got her father involved."

"Problems with helicopter parents?" I asked.

Caroline jerked around. "Oh, Georgia. I didn't know you were there."

"Didn't mean to scare you. So is one of your students giving you a rough time?"

"Something like that," she said, looking as if she wished she were somewhere else.

Apparently I'd intruded on a conversation that wasn't intended for me, and though I was curious, I was going to let it pass until Renee said, "It's not a student's parents that are the problem."

Caroline gave Renee a look.

"What am I missing?" I said.

"Hey, you don't have to play innocent," Renee said. "If you think having your father call Professor Waldron will help get you the job, then more power to you. It's not something I'd do, but I guess all's fair in love and tenure."

"I have no idea what you're referring to," I said stiffly.

Renee rolled her eyes as if she didn't believe me. "Sure, whatever you say."

"Maybe it was supposed to be a secret," Caroline said, "but word has gotten out that your father called Professor Waldron."

"There's no secret that I'm aware of. My father does know Professor Waldron, and they're both peer reviewers for a couple of the same journals, so if he called her, it may have been something about that."

"Whatever you say," Renee repeated. She got to the head of the snack bar line then, but I decided to forgo the hot chocolate and head to my classroom. I thought that was a more diplomatic approach than getting hot chocolate just to pour over both their heads.

My students, at least, didn't seem to know anything was amiss, and I scraped up enough enthusiasm to do a passable job at the lecture. Then I wimped out and ate lunch in a different wing to minimize the chances of being ignored by anybody in the English department and made it back in time for my second class.

Then it was time for office hours, and fortunately I was busy enough that I was distracted. The brooding didn't start until after the last student left, and after a few minutes of that, I remembered the hot chocolate I hadn't gotten before. As it turned out, I got something even better and with fewer calories.

FAD arranges weekly visits from therapy dogs, with extra appearances during exam week. They're intended to be available for comfort and anxiety relief for students, but I often availed myself of petting time whenever possible. Given my mood after the trio of unpleasant confrontations, I was delighted to see our usual doggie therapist, Huckleberry the beagle, when I left my office. I was mature enough to give the two students nearby a chance to pet him first before swooping in for a belly rub and getting kisses in return.

By the time I let somebody else have a turn, I was feeling much more content. I hadn't realized how much I missed Madison's dog, Byron. I'd have to be sure not to tell Sid that, given his lack of affection for anything canine.

I headed to my office and worked for an hour or so, and by the time I remembered I still hadn't gotten my hot chocolate and headed for the snack bar, Huckleberry and his handler were long gone. I was on my way back to my desk, steaming cup in hand, when I saw a student in a paint-stained, oversized sweatshirt standing in the middle of the Roundling, looking around. "Is he gone already?"

Nobody else seemed to be paying attention to her, so I said, "You mean the therapy dog?"

She nodded.

"You just missed him."

She'd looked bedraggled before, but as I spoke, she seemed to deflate and sank down onto one of the chairs. "Oh no. I really needed a puppy break. I mean…I *really* needed…" Tears started to roll down her face.

"Oh, sweetie!" I said, and hurried over. "Are you okay? Is there something I can do?"

"No, there's nothing."

Other students were starting to stare, and I could tell the girl was becoming more and more distraught. "I'm sorry," she said, "I'm bothering you. I'm bothering everybody. I'll go… I'll go somewhere."

"Why don't you come with me to my office? I'm Dr. Thackery. Georgia."

She wiped her eyes on her sleeve and followed me. I closed the door behind her, then sat her down on the guest chair and handed her the box of tissues from my desk. After a moment I gave her my hot chocolate, too.

Once she'd used the former and had drunk down half the latter, she seemed calm enough for me to ask, "Do you want to talk about it?"

"You don't want to hear this."

Technically, she was right, because I didn't want to take on more emotional baggage, but part of being a teacher is being available to students in need. And she was definitely in need. Besides, though she looked nothing like Madison, my maternal instincts were aroused. "That's okay. If you need to talk, I'll be glad to listen."

"You're an artist, right?"

"No, I'm an English prof."

"Oh. Then you wouldn't understand. Nobody cares now that—" she said dismally. "Nobody cares."

"I do care, and I will listen."

She hesitated a long moment, but I waited her out until she spoke. "So I'm in Sequential Art. You know what that is, right?"

I pointed at the stack of graphic novels on top of my bookshelf.

"Oh, okay. So money has been really tight this quarter. My parents never have been sold on art school, and they help out with tuition, but they don't cover all my expenses. I worked all summer to make up the difference, and I meant to work during Christmas break, too, but I was waiting tables and tips were really bad. So I'd put some of my designs up on Green Globe. People can order T-shirts and other merch and I get a cut."

"Right," I said slowly, starting to realize just who I had in my office.

"It's not a lot of money, but it's enough to keep me in ramen noodles. I uploaded a batch of new designs last week, and I was hoping to get enough for a pizza once in a while. Only, I ended up getting an e-mail from Green Globe, and they said one of my designs was copied from a T-shirt being sold in a store!"

"The store wouldn't have been City Riggers, would it?"

"Yeah, how did you know?"

"Just a hunch."

"So Green Globe said I was an art thief! They're claiming some of my other work was copied, too, so they've blackballed me entirely and taken all of my designs off the site! And it's not true! I didn't copy anybody!"

She dissolved into more tears, making it hard for me to get a decent look at her face, but I was almost certain she was the girl who'd come looking for her sketchbook. Her hair was a different color from when I'd seen her—it had been dyed turquoise to match her eyes—but I was 90 percent sure. I was about to ask when a *ping* from my phone let me know a text had arrived.

SID: *Found the other victim! A sequential art major named Marissa Esqueleto.*

GEORGIA: *I found her, too. Will explain later.*

The crying was dwindling into sniffles, and I thought it would be safe to ask, "Is your name Marissa?"

She looked at me. "Yeah. Have we met?"

"Not exactly, but I was at the Writing Lab when you came looking for your sketchbook the other day."

"Oh, right, that was you. You didn't find it, did you?"

"No, sorry."

She sighed heavily. "That's another disaster. I had preliminary work for a project in there, and I had to do it all over again."

"Okay, this is going to sound out of the blue, but how do you sign your artwork?"

She looked surprised but said, "With a little butterfly."

I resisted the impulse to pump my fist in triumph. "Did you give the sketchbook to Kelly Griffith for her to use as part of her investigation into art theft?"

Her eyes went wide, and I think she was actually afraid of me.

"It's okay," I said. "I've taken over the project now that Kelly is gone."

"She never mentioned anybody helping her."

"How I got involved is a long story, but I've been trying to pick up where she left off. The problem is that we don't have her notes."

"We?"

Coccyx, I couldn't very well tell her about Sid. So I improvised. "Another student is helping me. They had stuff stolen, too."

"Who?"

"Indigo Williamson." Sid would probably have kicked me for giving up more information, but I thought maybe it would convince Marissa I was on the up and up. "Do you know them?"

"I've seen them around," she said with an oddly wistful tone, "but I've never spoken to them. Kelly said there was somebody else at FAD who'd had designs stolen, but she never said who."

"Kelly was big on protecting her sources." Which had been reasonable given what she was doing, but it sure was making things hard for me. "Do you think we can all three meet? Maybe together we can come up with some clues about who the thief is." Given Marissa's state of mind, I didn't think I should mention murder yet.

She looked at the clock on my desk. "I can't now. I've got class in a little while. Maybe later this week?"

"I'll text Indigo right now." It took a few exchanges back and forth, but we finally arranged to meet the next day at the Writing Lab.

Before Marissa left, I pointed out that FAD has a campus food bank for students in need and told her where it was. I really hoped she'd go—students can't live on ramen alone, even with an occasional pizza.

CHAPTER TWENTY-SIX

Between arguments and discoveries, plus moments of actually working, I was exhausted. So once Marissa had gone, I texted Sid that I was leaving campus and would be home after a stop to pick up a pizza. Marissa's comments had roused a craving for a DiPietro's double pepperoni that could not be denied.

I was intending to make a quiet exit, but as I left my office, Caroline walked by. I gave her a curt nod and would have kept going, but she said, "Oh, hi. I hear you finally had it out with Romeo Owen." She tried for a conspiratorial grin, or perhaps a congratulatory one, but the expression was sadly strained. "Good for you."

A dozen responses ran through my head, ranging from the snarky to bitingly contemptuous to outright insulting to cutting her dead. I just didn't have the energy for any of them. "If getting tenure here is that important to you, Caroline, I hope you get it." Then I walked away, both relieved and disappointed when she didn't try to stop me.

After that I definitely needed that pizza and I lucked out getting a parking place right outside DiPietro's. I considered just getting a couple of slices but convinced myself that buying a whole pizza would be more economical because I would get at least two meals out of it—the idea of eating the entire pie never crossed my mind. I even bought a Greek salad to go with it to prove that I was an adult.

I was paying when I saw that Sid had sent a text, but I waited until I got back to my minivan to take a look.

SID: *Did you forget your keys?*

Since my TARDIS key ring was currently in my hand, I replied:

GEORGIA: *No. Why?*

SID: *You're not outside the house?*

GEORGIA: *NO! HIDE!*

SID: *Already hiding.*

GEORGIA: *Sure you can't be seen?*

SID: *Under my bed. In the dark.*

GEORGIA: *What happened?*

SID: *Doorbell rang. Ran for my room, quietly.*

GEORGIA: *Sure it wasn't mailman? UPS? FedEx?*

SID: *Mail came hours ago. The other guys ring once and leave. This guy rang three times. Then I saw a shadow—he's walking around house trying to look in windows. Should I try to get a look at him?*

GEORGIA: *NO! Too risky. Stay put.*

SID: *Understood.*

GEORGIA: *ON THE WAY!*

I started driving. Minutes clicked by as I waited to hear more. Finally, Sid texted again.

SID: *He's gone. Heard car door slam and car drove away. But I'm staying under bed anyway.*

I wanted to answer, but it would have been both unsafe and illegal to do so while driving—just reading Sid's texts was technically breaking the law.

147

SID: *Probably nothing. Sorry to scare you.*

SID: *BTW need to dust under the bed. Found some-
            body's lost sock.*

I was driving safely despite everything, just a little faster than usual, and I may have been a little sloppier on the turn into the driveway than my norm. The driveway was too messy for me to be able to spot errant footprints, but it was obvious that once again, somebody had been walking around the house trying to look through windows.

Even though Sid had assured me the intruder was gone, I was extra careful on the short walk to the porch, trying to look in every direction at once.

"Sid, it's me!" I yelled as I came in the door and slammed it shut behind me. "Are you okay?"

"Dead as ever," he said as he came clattering toward me. "Were you speeding?"

"Of course I was speeding." I grabbed him in a big hug.

In a voice muffled by his skull being pressed against my coat, he said, "Georgia, I can't breathe."

"You don't breathe, and I need this hug."

"Okay."

We stood there a while longer. Then he said, "Your pizza is going to get cold."

That convinced me to disengage, and after I got rid of my winter gear, Sid helped me set the table for dinner.

"I'm fine, you know. He didn't see me, and he didn't even try to break in. He couldn't do anything to me anyway, right? I'm just glad you weren't here."

"If I'd been here, I could have called the cops, even Officer Buchanan. You don't have that option."

"And you can't give somebody a heart attack by your very appearance. Not even with your worst bed head."

I laughed a little.

Sid said, "So we know somebody thinks we're onto something.

Which is good. Not as good as if we actually knew anything, but maybe we know something we don't know that we know." He paused. "I think I lost control of that sentence."

"I'm afraid you're right. And we do know something. A couple of things, in fact. One, Professor Waldron is aware that we're investigating the thefts—though not the murder—and she approves. And two, I've finally spoken to the other theft victim."

"Start talking or I'm taking the pizza hostage!"

It took a while to get it all out, and Sid reacted in just the right ways, which cheered me even more than the pizza did.

When I had gone through it all, he said, "So to sum up, Owen is an ossifying piece of sacrum, Professor Waldron has a great skull on her shoulders, your other colleagues need to grow spines, and Marissa is in a bad place."

"That covers it nicely. I take it you found her paper in the Writing Lab database."

He nodded. "Only, you'd found her first."

"I'll toss you a bone and say it was a tie," I said magnanimously.

"As if I needed more bones," he said and thunked my head. "Since we both made progress, I think we deserve a dance party."

"I'm really not in the mood."

"Dance party!"

"Sid! Do not put on any music!"

"Classic rock? Techno pop? Power ballad?"

"No!"

"Owl City?"

"Coccyx," I muttered. He knows I can't resist Owl City.

Apparently he'd put together a new playlist, none of which I could resist, and several rounds of really bad but wholly enjoyable dancing and lip-syncing ensued. It was the most fun I'd had in ages.

We were interrupted in the middle of our Journey sing-along when my cell phone rang.

I checked the caller ID before answering. "Hey, Lucas."

"Did I interrupt something? You sound out of breath."

"Just working out a little," I said. "What's up?"

"I need a favor. My life model for tomorrow bagged on me and I thought of you."

"If this is a joke about me posing for you—"

"No, really, no joke. The guy is sick as a dog, and I can't find anybody else. And I don't want you to pose—I mean, I'm sure you'd be a fascinating study for my students, but that's not what I had in mind. Somebody told me that you have a skeleton."

"We're all skeletons under the skin, Lucas."

"True, but apparently you have a spare—I heard you brought one on campus the other day. Do you think I could borrow it for my class?"

"Oh. You know, it doesn't belong to me—it belongs to my parents—so I really need to ask them first. Can I get back to you?"

"Sure."

"Talk to you in a few."

"Since when do I belong to your parents?" Sid said when I'd hung up.

"I couldn't tell Lucas I have to consult with the skeleton itself, could I?"

"Granted. So what's the deal?"

I explained the situation. "You'd have to stay still most of the day in Lucas's studio."

"I think it's a great idea. I've had a chance to scope out some of your students, but this will give me a shot at some others. We're talking serious eavesdropping possibilities, plus I can take a closer look at Lucas himself."

"Do you think Lucas is our guy?"

"I don't know that he's not."

"That's fair. At this point, it's pretty much up for grabs. Just thinking about how many people it could be makes me dizzy."

"After his performance today, I'm hoping it's Porn Star Owen."

For once I didn't correct him for calling Owen that. "Anyway, if you think it's worth the risk, let's do it."

"It won't be that big a risk, and it might—Hey, wait. Why aren't you trying to talk me out of going on campus?"

"What you said. Checking out Lucas, giving you a chance to observe students." I tried to look innocent but didn't do a very good job.

"You're not fooling me, Georgia. You just want an excuse to take me to FAD in case the prowler comes back. Maybe it would be better if I stayed on guard."

"No, it wouldn't. I've got to be able to concentrate on my meeting with Indigo and Marissa, plus dealing with backstabbing colleagues. And I do have that job thing. I can't do any of that if I'm worrying about you. Now should I tell Lucas that you'll come?"

"Okay, but you're going to have to help me with a bath tonight. I want to look my best when I start my modeling career."

Calling Lucas back, helping Sid swab himself with diluted hydrogen peroxide to make sure he was good and white, and routine life duties took up the rest of the evening. Sid was still trying to pretend that he wasn't worried about the intruder returning, but I noticed that he was patrolling again, and I'm pretty sure he scoped out hiding places in every room.

CHAPTER TWENTY-SEVEN

As soon as my Thursday morning class was over, I wheeled Sid in his suitcase over to Lucas's studio.

"Interesting carrying case," Lucas said, one eyebrow lifted.

"A skeleton is surprisingly heavy. Where shall I set him up?"

"Oh, I can do that. Is he wired together or—?"

"My father made me promise to set him up for you. One of his students broke one of the ribs once, and we had to glue it back together, and ever since then, he's been really particular." Actually, it was a pillow fight in which that rib had gotten broken, but sometimes the truth doesn't sound nearly as believable as a lie, especially when Sid is involved. "Just tell me where and how you want him."

The Painting department's wing was arranged differently from the English wing, reasonably enough. Lucas's studio had an adjoining classroom, and then Jeremy's office opened off the other end of the classroom—Lucas explained that the two of them shared the classroom. There was a platform in the middle of the room, with easels in a circle around it.

Lucas lifted a table onto the platform, then covered it with a dark blue fake fur cloth. "Let's put him on here."

Once again, Sid was pretending to be wired together like a normal academic specimen, so I had to kind of unfold him from the suitcase, a process that took much longer than just letting him pop back together. "Lying down, sitting, what?"

"Reclining, on one side, with his head propped up on his elbow. Will he stay in that position okay?"

"Sure, no problem." I got Sid into place, and for once, he

was on his best behavior—no funny noises or whispered remarks. "How's that?"

"Now bend the right leg a bit so he looks more comfortable. Tilt the chin down so he's looking at the students. Good. Just push—" This went on for several minutes, enough so that Sid and I were getting annoyed. That is, I know I was getting annoyed, and when Sid's hand started easing into a rude gesture, I thought it was a safe bet to say that he was, too. I lightly thumped his skull and fixed his hand back the way it was supposed to be. Finally, Lucas was satisfied.

"That's great! I think the kids will get a kick out of this." And I promise, no touching will be allowed. If I leave the room, I will lock the door to the hall, the door to my office, and even the door to Jeremy's office. Okay?"

"That should do it. I hate to sound paranoid about it, but—"

"No, I get it. I had to borrow my father's car when mine was in the shop once, and I was petrified that something would happen to it and he'd never trust me again."

"I appreciate your understanding. Where should I leave the suitcase?"

"Here, I'll stow it under the table."

That suited me fine. Sid's phone was in there, on silent mode, of course, and I wanted it within easy reach if he needed to call me.

"Well, happy painting or sketching or whatever." I hesitated. "Can I ask you a question?"

"Sure."

"If all of your students are going to be drawing the same thing, won't the pictures all look alike?"

"You mean like plagiarism?"

I blinked. "Wow, rumors spread fast."

"Telephone, telegraph, tell-an-adjunct." He grinned. "But in answer to your question, not really. For one, each student is sitting in a different spot—they have slightly different views. For another, they'll paint as much of themselves as they paint what they actually see. Some will draw this guy as horrific, some as sad, some as happy, and so on."

"That's kind of what I told somebody when he asked why I wanted to use a skeleton as a writing prompt."

"Did any of your students come up with the same piece of writing?"

"Not even close. I got some funny pieces, some scary ones, one kind of clinical, and even a limerick."

"A limerick? Do tell?"

"Later. It's not really work-appropriate." Besides which, Sid had been offended by it. I was tempted to ask Lucas what else he'd heard about my snooping, and from whom, but decided not to bother. As fast at the adjunct grapevine transmits data, it was probably all over campus already. I wasn't entirely happy with people knowing, but at least I wouldn't have to try for subtlety anymore.

"So will I get a chance to see what your students come up with?"

"You bet."

I took a last look at Sid, who managed to wink despite his lack of eyes or eyelids.

Chapter Twenty-Eight

To make our meeting appear less suspicious, I'd signed Marissa up for a one-hour critique session, and Indigo was going to pretend to be an assistant again. They were both waiting for me outside the Writing Lab, trying to look as if they weren't totally checking one another out. If I interpreted their expressions correctly, both of them seemed satisfied with what they saw. Maybe Kelly had kept them separate partially to forestall romantic complications in her big story.

"Hi, guys. Come on in, and we'll get situated."

"You want some coffee or anything?" Indigo said, presumably getting into character as a student assistant.

I was about to refuse when I wondered how much Marissa had had to eat since I gave her my hot chocolate. "I don't know about you guys, but I'm starved. Could you get me a Dr Pepper and one of those bacon-and-egg English muffins? What will you have, Marissa?"

"I don't—" she started to say.

"My treat."

"Are you sure?"

"No big," I said blithely.

"Then a breakfast sandwich sounds great. And maybe some orange juice?"

"Plus whatever you want, Indigo." I dug into my purse for my lunch money and handed it to them, and they headed off.

"Have a seat and I'll take a quick look at your paper," I said to Marissa in case anybody was listening.

Neither of us said much until Indigo returned with a tray covered with food, drinks, and the appropriate utensils. I cut my sandwich in two and only ate the first half, just in case, and after I saw Marissa wolf her food down, I made an excuse about being full and pushed the second half toward her. She looked a little bashful, but she ate it, too, and afterward her face looked considerably less pinched.

I closed the door and said, "Okay, maybe the best start is for each of you to tell your stories. Indigo?"

They went through what they'd told me, and then explained how the two of us had each decided the other was trustworthy. I listened carefully, hoping they'd share a new detail they'd inadvertently omitted before, but if they did, I missed it.

"Now, you, Marissa. Did Kelly find out about your work being stolen via a paper, too?" Of course, I knew the answer via Sid, but I couldn't exactly cite him as a source.

She nodded. "It was a personal issue paper I had to write for Ms. Turner."

"Okay, tell us what happened with Kelly." I listened intently, but there was no eureka moment. Marissa's story wasn't that different from Indigo's.

"So that's where we are," I said once she was finished. "Kelly was trying to find the thief, but I don't think she had yet. Do you guys agree?"

They nodded.

"Yet she seemed pretty confident she would be able to do so eventually, and that the thief was at FAD. Or maybe somebody local." I didn't know how I'd ever get a line on a local unaffiliated with FAD, but I had to admit it might be a possibility. "I still don't know how she was able to conclude that when you two are the only victims here, as we know. Maybe it was something computer-related. Was she computer savvy?"

Indigo shook their head. "She could use a word processor and a spreadsheet and was decent with online research, but she couldn't even crop a scanned photo until I told her how."

"Then I'm lost," I said.

"Wait," Marissa said, "didn't I tell you that part? How Kelly knew it was somebody on campus?"

"I am all ears," I said.

"Okay, after I found out I was ripped off the first time, I took all my stuff off the web."

"Indigo did that, too, but it was shutting the barn door after the horse got out. The thief had already stolen their designs."

"But that design with the wolf? In woodblock style? I drew that *after* I quit posting online. It was never anywhere on the web."

"That means the thief had to be somebody who saw it personally," I said excitedly.

"Right."

"No wonder Kelly thought it was someone on campus. So who did you show it to?"

"Well, lots of people," she admitted. "It was for a school assignment, so my professor. And we critiqued it in class, so everybody in my class. Plus I made T-shirts with the design to sell at the Holiday Fair in December."

"Then it could have been anybody at the fair. I read online that some thieves intentionally target art and craft shows to steal designs. The FAD fair isn't just for students and faculty, is it? Don't parents and people from town come, too?"

"Usually yes," Indigo said, "but not this year. The blizzard, remember?"

"I wasn't here then," I said.

"Oh, right. So there was this blizzard that weekend, and the roads were a mess. But the fair was already set up, and most of us students were stuck on campus anyway, so we went ahead and held it, but nobody but students, staff, and faculty came."

"Which means that somebody here at FAD had to be the thief," I said. "Unless somebody gave one of the shirts to somebody for a Christmas gift and…"

"Nobody bought any of the shirts," Marissa said sadly.

"I'd have bought one if I'd seen it," Indigo said. "That design is sharp."

"You think? I kind of liked it." She looked down, smiling.

"Okay then. Now we know why Kelly was focusing on FAD people. Maybe we should start with Marissa's professor for that class."

"It was Mr. Silva."

Lucas? With whom I'd just left Sid? I was ready to go rescue him until sanity reminded me that Lucas wasn't likely to try to kill Sid, what with Sid being dead and all. "Okay, we should look at him. He would have had your drawing when you handed it in, so he could have taken a photo or scanned it then."

Both of the students were looking at me as if I'd said something really stupid.

"Um… Not exactly," Marissa said gently.

Indigo didn't waste time being gentle. "He wouldn't have to scan anything. Almost everybody does digital submissions, right to the teacher's Dropbox."

"Oh. Yeah. You have to remember that my art career mostly involved construction paper and crayons."

Now they were looking at me pityingly.

"Anyway," I said, "we need to look at the professor. Indigo, were any of your stolen designs drawn for one of Mr. Silva's classes?"

"No. One was for Mr. Inamdar and the other one was for Mr. Azzopardi."

"Okay then." I would like to have concluded that Lucas was innocent since other professors had had access, but I didn't think I could do so quite yet. "What about the other students in your classes? Could they have taken a picture or hacked into the Dropbox or… Okay, don't give me that look. I freely admit I don't know the nitty-gritty of how your courses work."

Indigo tried to stifle another snicker. "There are private discussion boards online, and a lot of us post our art there for feedback before we hand it in. So sure, another student could copy our art that way."

"And the professors can get to that area, too," Marissa put in. "Probably even you English profs, if somebody told you how."

I wondered if I should get instructions. Though I didn't want to pore through those boards, I knew a skeleton who would be willing. "So any student and any teacher can get to those boards. Were any of your stolen designs on the FAD board?"

They both nodded.

"Any student, any faculty member. Plus somebody could have taken a picture of the T-shirt at the holiday fair, even if they didn't buy one."

"A cheapskate thief," Indigo said. "It doesn't get much lower than that."

"No argument here. Students and faculty, plus probably administration, too." I was confident that Mr. Perkins could find his way into any FAD database he wanted to see. "I don't even want to try to add up all the possibilities."

"Kelly was getting pretty frustrated, too," Marissa said. "She said that it was so easy to steal art around here she wouldn't be surprised if every student had at least one piece of work stolen."

I ran my fingers through my hair. "I don't suppose either of you has noticed anybody showing more interest in your work than they should have."

"Kelly asked me that, too," Indigo said. "Not a clue."

But Marissa was looking at her hands and fidgeting.

I said, "Marissa, what are you thinking?"

"Okay, I never told Kelly because it happened after she died, and I hate to tell on people, but one day I came back to my room and my roommate was looking at my sketchbook."

"Seriously?" Indigo said. "Man, that is so uncool!"

This was a form of etiquette with which I was unfamiliar, but from Indigo's reaction, clearly Marissa's roomie had violated artist-to-artist protocol.

"I felt, you know, violated," she said. "A person's sketchbook should be private. And then she, like, made fun of some of my stuff. It's not like I don't already know I'm bad with hands."

Indigo said, "Hands are hard! Everybody knows hands are hard."

"Well, they're hard for me. She actually started lecturing me on how to do them better. I was so mad—I took my sketchbook back and left, but I never got around to asking why she thought she had the right to look at my stuff."

"Did you have T-shirt ideas in there?" I asked.

"Some. It's a new sketchbook though, so not a lot. None of the pictures in it have shown up online, at least not that I've seen."

"Still, we should talk to your roommate. What's her name?"

"Bobbie Fitzpatrick."

"Oh, her," Indigo said with obvious disdain.

"You know her?" I asked.

"Bad Bobbie was in my Intro to Sequential Art class."

"Bad Bobbie?" I said.

"There's another student named Bobbie majoring in sequential art, but she's cool. So now it's Bobbie and Bad Bobbie to keep them straight. Not to her face, of course. Anyway, Bad Bobbie made sure we all knew she was just taking the class as an elective because she is a 'serious' artist and obviously serious artists don't draw comic books."

"How many more graphic novels like *Maus* do we need to shake that rep?" I asked.

"I know, right?" Indigo said. "I liked the class, but the critique sessions were torture when she was participating."

"Was she too hard on the other students?" I said.

"I wish. That would have been something. Bad Bobbie gave us nothing."

"I'm not sure I understand."

"Okay, do you know how our critique sessions work?"

"Only in theory."

"Basically an artist goes to the front of the class and displays the assignment on the big screen, and the rest of us are supposed to give comments and suggestions. And we're not thin-skinned about it. We know the only way we're going to improve is through hearing different perspectives and getting constructive criticism. So we can handle harsh feedback."

Marissa was nodding emphatically as Indigo went on.

"Yeah, it sucks when you get called on something, but that's okay, if it improves the work. Positive comments are good, too— we need to know what we're doing right as much as we need to know what we're doing wrong. But what Bad Bobbie did was basically no feedback at all. All she ever said was, 'I like it,' or 'It's really creative.'"

"That sounds kind of useless." If I handed out that kind of "advice" in the Writing Lab, the students would revolt.

"Completely! I don't think Bobbie gave me a single useful comment all semester. Worst of all, she always had this smug little smile on her face, as if she was doing us a favor by even looking at our stuff."

"She had that same smile when she was looking at my sketch-book!" Marissa said indignantly.

"Meanwhile, the prof and the rest of us were trying to give her useful information about her stuff, which wasn't really that great, and all she ever said was, 'That's interesting, but I don't think it's the way I want to go with this piece.' She never changed any-thing! Why go to art school if you're not going to learn? After a while, I quit bothering. I'd say, 'It's unusual,' and she took that as a compliment."

"Okay, Marissa, you've been rooming with her. Do you think she'd steal from other artists?"

"In a heartbeat. She stole my pads!" Then she colored and looked away from Indigo. "You know, my sanitary pads. She never even told me, so when I needed some, there were none left. And she didn't pay for them, either. She just said I must have forgotten using them. Anybody who'd do that has no shame at all."

I had to agree. My sister, Deborah, and I had occasionally borrowed each other's supplies when we were both at home, but never without letting the other know. There were some things that should be sacred.

Indigo seemed to agree but said, "Okay, I can see her as a rip-off artist, but a murderer?"

I winced, since I'd been planning to avoid the M-word with Marissa because she seemed so fragile. But apparently Indigo had a more accurate read on her than I did.

"Wait, then you guys think Kelly was murdered?" she asked.

"I do," I said. "I've got no proof, but—"

"No, that makes sense," Marissa said. "Her dying when she did was too much of a coincidence, you know. And that explains why you haven't found my missing sketchbook. This wasn't the new one Bad Bobbie stuck her nose into, but one that was filled with designs, including some that had been swiped. Who else would have taken it than the art thief, and the only way that could have happened is if the thief killed Kelly."

"So do you guys think Bad Bobbie could kill somebody?" I asked.

The two of them looked at one another, then shrugged.

"I've heard anybody can kill, given the right circumstances," Indigo said, "and if Kelly had outed her as an art thief, she'd probably have been kicked out of school."

Marissa said, "Even worse, she'd never be able to go to another art school. She told me how her parents wanted her to study nursing. She had to beg and beg to come here, and her parents still talk about this just being a phase she's going through. The day she told me that was the only time I almost liked her. Then when I tried to tell her my story, she said I didn't really need art school anyway because what I was doing isn't 'real art.'"

"What a piece of sacrum," I said. They looked at me funny, but any mother of a teenager is used to that.

Obviously Bad Bobbie was now at the top of our list of suspects, and Indigo was all for confronting her right that minute. I pointed out that as a faculty member, I couldn't just barge in on a student, because it was a good way for me to get fired. If Indigo or Marissa went after her without me, she'd just deny everything. No, we needed to do something a little more subtle.

Normally, *subtle* was not a word I'd use to describe Sid, but in this case, I thought he'd be perfect for the job. Without telling them exactly who—or what—my accomplice would be, I made plans with Indigo and Marissa for Saturday morning. I figured that Sid and I could plot out the rest of the details that night.

Chapter Twenty-Nine

After Indigo and Marissa took off, I finished my shift at the Lab, then went back to my office to grade papers. I was managing to keep up with my work, even with the extracurricular activities, but it didn't hurt to have an uninterrupted afternoon to buckle down and get a lot off my plate. Needless to say, I was not interrupted by fellow English profs wanting to chat, nor did I feel a pressing need to seek anybody out.

Around four, I was starting to feel lonely but knew it wouldn't last because I was going to get Sid. I locked up and went back to Lucas's studio, and when I saw him in the adjoining classroom, I went on in. Sid was exactly where I'd left him, which was good news. Lucas was focused on sketching at his easel and didn't notice me at first.

"Hey!"

He jumped, saw me, then looked at the clock on the wall. "How did it get so late?"

"I didn't know you were drawing Sid, too."

"Sid?"

Coccyx! "The skeleton. I call him Sid."

He raised one eyebrow but didn't comment further. "Yeah, I got inspired. I've sketched bones and skulls before but never a whole skeleton, and this one just seems to have character, you know?"

"He is a friendly-looking guy, isn't he?" I said affectionately. "And excellent company."

Lucas laughed at what he thought was a joke. "Georgia, can I ask a favor?"

"Sure."

"Can I keep Sid overnight?"

I blinked.

"I know, it was supposed to be a one-day thing, but I'd really like to finish this piece. And if we move him so you can take him home, I'll never be able to get him in just the right position again, even with reference photos as a guide."

"I don't know, Lucas. You know, a human skeleton is an expensive item. As in three or four thousand dollars."

"I know, but the studio is completely secure. I'll tell the cleaning staff to stay out—they're used to that when we've got scenes set up for the students to draw—and it'll be locked all night. I'll even tell security to take an extra sweep or two past the room, but they won't come in. Your skeleton will be as safe as houses."

"Well..." What I really wanted was a chance to ask Sid, but that would have been awkward. I glanced over at him and realized one thumb bone was held up, and he was nodding his skull ever so slightly. "Okay, I guess it'll be all right."

"Thanks, Georgia. I owe you. Hey, are you up for dinner tonight? As payback for loaning me Sid?"

Now Sid was nodding, and I knew it wasn't because he was invested in my love life. He wanted me to pick Lucas's brain. That didn't thrill me because I liked Lucas, but eating alone didn't thrill me either, so I said, "That would be great."

It took a little while for Lucas to get ready to go, and unfortunately, he never left the room, so I didn't have a chance to talk to Sid privately. The best I could manage was a pat on his skull, which I could tell he appreciated.

Parking being scarce in what passes for downtown in Falstone, we left my minivan on campus and Lucas drove us to Antonio's, the town's best Italian restaurant. Antonio's is also Falstone's only Italian restaurant, but it is actually pretty good. The decor is bare brick with out-of-focus photos of Rome, Venice, and Tuscany hanging on the walls. It was early enough that we had our pick of tables, and we were soon enjoying steaming plates of lasagna. Since we were both driving, we regretfully passed on the wine.

After the requisite amount of small talk, I asked, "So how's tenure process going on your side of the campus? Are you still feeling confident? And Jeremy, too?"

"The chair assures us that the positions are ours to lose," Lucas.

"That is so exciting."

"I know! I never really intended to spend life teaching, but at FAD I don't feel like just an academic."

"Not that there's anything wrong with being an academic," I said dryly.

"Sorry, no offense meant," he said with a grin. "It's just that academics—real academics like you—are into research and writing papers. Right?"

"Yeah, that's fair."

"I never cared about any of that. I just wanted to paint. But somewhere along the way I realized I really like teaching, too. It makes me feel like the Italian and Dutch masters with their studios, sharing their expertise with young painters. I've had some incredibly talented students, and nurturing their talent is amazing. I'll always be an artist first, but teaching doesn't take away from that, and having a secure income is only going to make it easier for me to focus on the art. Being broke all the time is kind of a distraction."

I toasted him with my soda. "To the end of distractions!"

We clinked glasses.

"So how goes the tenure battle in your department?"

"It started out being kind of awkward," I said, "but now it's getting downright nasty."

"So I've heard."

"Oh? What have you heard?"

"Look, I don't even know if it was true."

"Lucas, you can't leave me hanging."

"Somebody—and I don't want to say who—somebody said

your father called and tried to influence Professor Waldron to give you tenure."

"Does anybody seriously believe that? How could my father influence anybody? He can't afford to bribe her. If he did call Professor Waldron, it had nothing to do with me. Feel free to spread that around!"

"Hey, I didn't believe the rumor. I'm just telling you one of the ones I heard."

"One?"

He hesitated.

I just waited.

"Okay, did somebody really accuse you of trying to spread rumors that FAD is a hotbed of art theft just to make points with the department?"

I sighed.

"I'm sorry," he said. "I shouldn't have brought it up. Let's talk about something else. I hear we might get more snow."

I was tempted to go along with him—okay, perhaps not to complain about snow, but tackling just about any other topic. Then I decided I might as well face it head-on. It wasn't like my interest was any secret. "Given that you've already heard a lot, I may as well give you my side of the story." I was fairly thorough, though I didn't bring in Indigo or Marissa by name.

By then we'd finished our meals, but since we hadn't been able to have wine, Lucas insisted we should order dessert and I respected him too much to argue. As we ate our tiramisu, I concluded, "So that's what's been happening. I'm not doing this to make myself look good or to make FAD look bad. I just don't think stealing art is right. I wouldn't have thought that was a controversial position."

"It is and it isn't."

"Seriously, Lucas?"

He held his hands up defensively. "Hear me out. First off, copyist artists have a long and honored tradition. Some instructors think it's the best way to learn how to paint. The idea is that after copying the work of the masters, an artist will be prepared to develop his or her own style. Some museums still have copyist programs, and Ashwin teaches a class on it. Of course, copyists usually sign their copies with their own names, and then on the back put something like 'Copy of Leonardo da Vinci's *Mona Lisa* by Georgia Thackery,' so it's not forgery."

"Okay, I can see that."

"Then there are professional copyists who make replicas of art to sell for decoration. Some of them even use the same kinds of canvas and pigments so the copies are as close to the original as possible, but they do that thing with signatures, too."

"So still not forgery."

"Right. Then you get your homages, your parodies, your pastiches, and your swipes."

"Swiping sounds like theft."

"It's a particular usage. You read comics, right?"

I nodded.

"You know that pose with two opposing superhero teams facing one another? That's shown up in plenty of comics, and I don't even know who the first artist to use it was, but it's not considered plagiarism."

"'It had to happen,'" I said. Fortunately, Lucas read enough comics himself to get the joke.

He went on. "There's also something called—and I'm probably pronouncing this wrong—*détournement*, which is when you take a well-known image like an ad or logo and warp it to make it mean something else."

"Like when somebody took the HOPE graphic with Obama and made it NOPE?"

"Exactly. And another mouthful for you: cryptomnesia. That's when you saw something but forgot it, then remembered it later and thought it was your own idea. That does count as plagiarism, but at least there's no malice in it. So all of those are kind of like art theft, but not really."

I thought about it as I ate my last bite of tiramisu, then shook my head. "I get what you're saying, Lucas, but none of those apply.

The designs I saw are direct copies—same subjects, same poses, same composition. I don't even know exactly what composition is in the art world, but I do know you're not supposed to duplicate somebody else's."

"Generally speaking, you're right."

"And you're definitely not supposed to commercialize somebody else's work. This is theft."

"Given all that, I wholeheartedly come down on the side of 'this is wrong.' Is there anything I can do to help you track the guy down?"

As much as I liked Lucas, I had to shake my head. I could only imagine Sid's conniption if I brought somebody else to the team, especially somebody who could be a suspect. "No, thanks. It's bad enough that people are talking about me—I don't want to risk your shot at tenure."

He agreed with obvious relief and went on to other topics, including his insisting that I quote the limerick my student had written with Sid as a writing prompt:

"'A lonely young skeleton named Cheech
Found romance was out of his reach
Though longing for dating
He kept hesitating
Boner's only a figure of speech.'"

Lucas burst out laughing, and I grinned, too, though Sid hadn't been nearly as amused when the student read it out loud. I suppose it had cut a little too close to the bone.

We finished the evening on a convivial note, and when Lucas drove me back to FAD to pick up my minivan, I was glad to accept the offer of a kiss on the cheek. Had I been able to discuss it with Caroline, I was fairly sure we'd have decided that it was a "maybe" kiss, meaning that it was the kind that could lead to more serious kissing at a later date. Unfortunately, after the way she'd been acting, that was out.

Thinking that Madison might like offering dating advice to

her aged mother, I did call Pennycross as soon as I got back to the bungalow, but she couldn't talk long because she had an essay due in world history the next day. I would have spoken to my parents instead, just to check on that phone call to Professor Waldron, even though I knew they hadn't been trying to talk her into giving me tenure, but they were at a concert on campus and wouldn't be back until late. I even tried to call Deborah, usually the last person I would go to for dating advice, but she was out bowling.

And of course, I couldn't talk to Sid.

Despite getting home later than usual and going to bed sooner, it was a long night.

CHAPTER THIRTY

Friday did not get off to a promising start. There was no Sid to help me clear the snow off the minivan, and when I got to campus and went to buy a cup of hot chocolate at the Roundling's snack bar, Dahna and Renee were conferring with one another, only to stop when they saw me. Though it was nice that they were friendly again, I had a hunch that I was the reason. There's nothing like a shared enemy to bring old adversaries back together, but I really didn't like being the shared enemy.

To cap it all off, after I got back to my office, Caroline marched in.

"We need to talk," she said.

Surprisingly, I was ready to talk, too. "Yes, we do."

She pulled the door closed and sat down on the guest chair without being invited.

"If this is about my father calling Professor Waldron, let me say again that I knew nothing about it until after the fact. Actually, I still don't know what it was he called about. All I know is that he would not call to try to pressure Professor Waldron into giving me the tenure job, even if he could. He doesn't play that kind of game, and neither do I." I was pretty sure my eyes were snapping with righteous indignation.

"I know that."

That pretty much killed the righteous indignation. "You do?"

"Okay, I admit I believed the rumor at first, but Harry Potter showed me the way."

"He did?"

"Last night I went home and I was still furious at you. But my husband was out of town, so while I was eating dinner, I turned on the TV. *Harry Potter and the Goblet of Fire* was on."

"Didn't we just watch that a couple of weeks ago?" *Back when we were friends?* I finished mentally.

"That's right. And remember how we both decided that Ron Weasley was being an idiot? Harry told him he didn't put his name into the Goblet, but Ron was sure he had, even though he had no reason to distrust his best friend. And we threw popcorn at the screen every time Ron showed up until he apologized, because he was being such a dink. Well, here." She pulled a snack-sized bag of popcorn out of her pocket. "I think you should throw this at me."

"Are you saying you were being a dink?"

"I was being a big old dink. I know you, Georgia, and you are not the kind to take advantage of having parents in the field to get a job. Yeah, sure, you'll get gossip and introductions from them. That's called networking. You wouldn't try to use them to crowd other people out."

"No, I really wouldn't. And they wouldn't do it, either. Unless maybe they're really sick of having me live with them, which I don't think they are. With me they get Madison."

"So whatever your father called Professor Waldron about, tenure wasn't it."

"Right."

"Besides, anybody who knows Professor Waldron knows that she would not respond well to either a carrot or a stick."

"You're right again. And now I've got a whole head of anger going wanting. There must be somebody I can yell at. Wait, who started that rumor?"

"I heard it from Owen, but I don't know where he got it."

"Can I throw popcorn at him? Or maybe something heavier?"

"No, let me handle Owen. Maybe I can get the source of the rumor out of him." She looked hesitant. "So anyway, I let the whole tenure thing go to my head and I'm really sorry. Can you forgive me?"

"Harry forgave Ron, so I think I would be a dink if I didn't do the same for you."

"Does that mean you forgive me?"

"Of course I forgive you."

Caroline smiled, I smiled, and we went for the awkward friend hug. She didn't stay much longer, but when she left, it felt as if we were back to normal.

After that I was feeling downright cheerful during office hours, despite having to hand out three copies of the syllabus to students, and my mood only improved when it was time to go retrieve Sid. I even waved at Renee when I saw her going into Jeremy's studio. There were two students still working feverishly on their portraits of Sid, and Lucas seemed to be putting last touches on his, so I found a stool I hoped was free of fresh paint spatters and watched them work. I was tempted to make faces at Sid, since he wouldn't be able to reciprocate, but decided I was too mature. Besides, Sid is skilled at revenge.

Lucas finally noticed me sitting there, finished up his piece, and came over. "I've got two artists working—are you in a hurry?"

"'You can't rush art,'" I said, then was disappointed when Lucas showed no signs of recognizing the source of the quote. "Can I see the ones that are finished?"

"Sure, but don't touch. Some of the paint is still wet."

"I'm not the one whose fingers are covered in paint."

Lucas looked down at his hands. "I see what you mean. You better not touch me, either."

I resisted a flirtatious response both because students were around and because Sid would give me a hard time about it later if I did. We took a spin around the room and I was pretty impressed by the work. A couple, including Lucas's, were so good that I could clearly recognize the form shown as Sid and not some random skeleton.

By the time we were through, the last artist had finished and I could finally pack Sid up in his suitcase and wheel him away. Lucas invited me to dinner again, but I told him I had a previous engagement. I wouldn't mind another date sometime but not that night. I had too much news for Sid, and I wanted to know what he'd been up to as well.

It was early, but I had no appointments and whatever work I needed to get done could be done just as easily at home as at FAD, so I stopped at my office just long enough to grab my things and headed for my car. It was not, for a change, snowing.

When I got into the minivan, I said, "Sorry, Sid, I can't open your bag. There are too many other cars around."

"That's okay," he said from inside the suitcase. "I can wait."

We got to the bungalow, and after a quick look around for more footprints, I wheeled him inside. Once the door was shut, I turned to let him out, but he was unzipping the bag himself.

"How are you doing?" I asked.

"Other than a desperate need to stretch, move, and talk, I'm fine. You?"

"Good." We moved into the living room and I told him about Caroline's visit, but he wasn't overly impressed.

"It's great that you worked out your interpersonal relationships," he said, "but can we get back to the case?"

I stuck my tongue out at him, which he hates even more than he hates raspberries. "Fine. What did you see and/or hear and/or find when you snooped around? I am assuming that you snooped around Lucas's studio last night."

"Of course I snooped around! I wasn't there for my beauty sleep."

"True. You're beautiful enough already."

His eye sockets narrowed. "You're sucking up. Why?"

"I'm just in a good mood."

"Whatever. So I searched the studio first, but there really wasn't much there. Just art supplies and half-finished portraits of me. Some of which are wonderful, by the way. Then there are others I barely recognized as me."

"Art can be very subjective."

"Easy to say when you aren't the subject. Anyway, after that I went into Lucas's office."

"I thought he locked the door."

"Georgia, what does your sister do for a living?"

"Yes, I know Deborah is a locksmith, but I didn't know she'd taught you."

"She didn't, but she's been teaching Madison, and as part of that process, she bought Madison an instruction book, which Madison left unattended where I could read it. The rest was just practice."

"Don't you need lock picks?"

"I had my set in the suitcase."

"You have lock picks?"

"They're easily obtained online. Which reminds me. You may notice some odd charges on your PayPal account."

"It's your stipend—you can do whatever you want with it." Sid couldn't make money, so I gave him access to my accounts for those things he wanted. He preferred that I not refer to it as an allowance.

"I started with Lucas's office. His computer has lousy security, which I really appreciated. I searched through as much of his hard drive as I could but found nothing relating to art theft. Nothing in his paper files, either, which are surprisingly well-organized for an artist, despite a lot of multicolored fingerprints on everything. Then I searched for secret hiding places under furniture and behind file cabinets and in heating vents. I was very thorough, but there was nothing."

"I'm glad. I like Lucas."

"One, just because I didn't find anything that doesn't mean he's not Scarlet Letter. And two, will you stop having the hots for our suspects?"

"Just as soon as you stop suspecting guys who are hot."

He sighed. "Next up was Jeremy's office. There was no computer, so he must have carried it home, and nothing suspicious in his paper files, which aren't nearly as nicely organized as

Lucas's. No hidden compartments that I could find." He looked at me significantly.

"What?"

"Isn't he hot?"

"He's okay, but he's engaged, so I'm not interested."

"Good. On to the other offices in the Painting wing."

"Wait, how far did you wander?"

"Georgia, when am I going to get a better chance to snoop? It was midnight by then. The building was empty, security hadn't come by in hours, and it was completely dark, so nobody could have seen me. It's also in the past, so do not get hysterical."

"I think I'm entitled to a little hysteria."

He gave me a look.

"Fine, I will be serene. Just tell me what you found."

"Nothing."

"Nothing at all?"

"Nothing related to the case. I did learn that one instructor has a fondness for fifties pinups, especially Bettie Page; another has a stash of dark chocolate hidden in her desk; and a third is way behind in his grading. Then I headed for the English wing."

"You went—?" I stopped when I saw his expression. "I mean, wow, you were moving swiftly to get as far as that."

"I only got to two offices: Renee's and Mr. Perkins's. Bad news for Renee—she's had to scale back on her original wedding plans. I never realized how expensive weddings are."

"It makes me glad I never had one."

"Ditto, though I do look good in white. She's also got scary taste in office decorations."

"Renee? I thought she had pictures of her dogs."

"That's what I said." He shuddered noisily.

"What about Mr. Perkins?"

"Had there been any dust, it would have been filed in alphabetical order. Even the lost-and-found box is neatly arranged—he folded lost mittens. But I did find something interesting. Have you ever heard of Pteriwinkle Gleam?"

"Periwinkle? Like the color?"

"Pteri as in pterodactyl. Winkle and gleam as in…winkle and gleam, I guess. Pteriwinkle Gleam is, or was, a glam rock band back in the eighties. The lead singer was a cross between David Bowie and Alice Cooper—big into spandex, platform boots, and sparkly makeup. Their biggest hit, which came the closest to actually charting, was 'Glitter Games.'"

"Why are you telling me this?"

"Because your prim and proper Mr. Perkins has their entire oeuvre on his hard drive, and it looks as if he's been splicing together performance clips to make YouTube videos. He even runs a fan site for the band."

"Really? How active a site is it?"

"It has a small, but enthusiastic fan base."

"Okay, hilarious, but not particularly suspicious."

"Not unless he's stealing T-shirt designs to finance his video-making activities, and I found no signs of that. Anyway, it was getting late, so I went back to Lucas's studio after that. I was back in position long before he arrived."

"Good work, Sid." Okay, the idea of him wandering around the campus where he could have been caught gave me the wiggins, but if there's one thing being a parent has taught me, it's that sometimes you have to sit on your hands and let things happen.

"I don't know about that," he said. "I didn't find anything, and we can't really rule anybody out yet."

"Okay, it would have been great if you'd found a smoking gun, but we come up empty most of the time."

"True. What about you? Did you use your feminine wiles to get anything out of Lucas?"

"Sure, let's call it that. Anyway, I learned a lot of stuff about copying art when it isn't exactly theft, but not a lot about copying when it is." I gave him a brief recitation. "It turns out that Ashwin teaches a class in copying."

"Does that make him more of a suspect or less?"

"I'm not sure. On the one hand, he'd be able to re-create the designs he sees, but on the other, he'd surely realize that he'd be a suspect. And here's a fun fact: when I was at Kelly's memorial service, it came out that Ashwin doesn't appreciate comics and at least one of the stolen designs is from an online comic book."

"Interesting."

"And according to some of the other art adjuncts, Jeremy doesn't really appreciate what most FAD students are doing. He's all about fine art painting, not the kinds of things that would go on a T-shirt."

"So would either of them bother to steal something he doesn't value?"

"He might, for the same reason I've been known to grab an extra couple of straws at McDonald's. A straw isn't worth anything, so I don't feel as if I'm really stealing. Since the T-shirt ideas aren't anything important, he wouldn't feel guilty about taking them."

"Also interesting. But if he doesn't think they're worth anything, why would he be so worried about being caught that he'd kill Kelly?"

"I don't know much about Ashwin, but Lucas said the tenure gig is Jeremy's to lose. I bet that if he were caught stealing from students, he'd lose it."

"That's a nifty motive, but I bet we could find evidence for half the people on campus if we looked hard enough." He drummed his fingers on the coffee table. "Coccyx. More possibilities, but nothing exciting."

"Not true. While you were posing for the benefit of Lucas's students, I located a red-hot suspect with the aid of Indigo and Marissa. And we have a plan—it's crazy, but it just might work."

"You hatched a crazy plan without me?" he said, and I noticed that his joints loosened.

"Only the bare bones," I said. "I've been dying to get together with you and really flesh it out."

"You are so humerus," he said, but his bones snapped back together and he rubbed his hands together in anticipation. "Let's hear what you've got."

CHAPTER THIRTY-ONE

After plotting Friday night away, with many texts to Marissa and Indigo, we thought we had all the wrinkles ironed out.

Sid and I got to my office at ten Saturday morning and texted our junior associates to get things moving. If all had gone according to plan, Bad Bobbie would just be waking up and realizing that her dorm room was ice cold. Marissa would then confess to "accidentally" turning the heater off the night before, and after Bad Bobbie complained loudly and profanely, would offer to take her to The Artist's Palette in apology. Since Bad Bobbie hated the food at the dorm cafeteria and could rarely afford to eat elsewhere, she would be sure to accept. Needless to say, I was financing the meal, which I would have done even if Marissa hadn't been short on funds. The typical college student was even more broke than the typical adjunct.

As soon as the two girls left their dorm room, Indigo—who was supposed to be lurking nearby—would use the key Marissa had provided to sneak into the room and grab Bad Bobbie's computer.

My part of the first phase was to wait. Impatiently. Thirty minutes later, Indigo showed up at my office and pulled a laptop out of their bag.

"Did everything go according to plan?" I asked.

They nodded. "Are you sure you can crack this? Bad Bobbie is bound to have password protection."

"I've got a friend on call who can handle it," I assured them.

"Okay, I'll hang in the Roundling until I hear from you or Marissa. You need anything?"

"Nope, I'm good to go."

I locked the door behind them and said, "The coast is clear."

"Excellent! Sid emerged from his suitcase. "Hand it over, stand back, and let me get to work."

Sid had explained to me that while he wasn't a true hacker, he did have a few tricks up his nonexistent sleeves. He'd spent most of the night before poring over Bad Bobbie's social media and Internet footprints, looking for clues to things she might have chosen for passwords and he had a list of pets' names, nicknames, important dates, favorite TV shows, beloved movies, and admired books—all gleaned from Bad Bobbie's background.

"What if none of those work?" I asked.

"I've got some online sources that might be able to help." He made an expression I think was an attempt to lift an eyebrow, which would have been more meaningful if he'd had eyebrows. "Nothing too shady, but it's better that you not know the details."

"Okay, fine. I'll just stay out of your way."

He cracked his knuckles, which was a lot louder for somebody with no flesh to dampen the sound, and opened the laptop. Seconds later, he said, "I'm in."

"What? You didn't even type anything."

"The system was never shut down—it just timed out and went into energy-saving mode. Doesn't this kid know anything about personal security?"

"Don't waste time complaining! Check for stolen art files!"

He'd only been at it a few minutes when a text arrived on my phone.

> MARISSA: *Coming back! Artist's Palette was full. BB wouldn't wait. Wanted takeout to carry to room. It'll be ready in ten minutes. Five more minutes to get to room.*
>
> INDIGO: *Abort?*

"Coccyx!" I said. "Sid, we've got to give the laptop back to Indigo."

"What?"

"No time to explain. We'll have to try again later."

"Forget that. She might put the password on next time. Hang on." He reached into his suitcase and produced a thumb drive. "I'll copy all her files."

"Is there time?"

He plugged it in and started the process. "It says it's going to take twenty-five minutes."

I texted back.

GEORGIA: *I've got the files copying to a thumb drive.*
Marissa, can you drag it out for twenty-five
minutes?

MARISSA: *Doubt it.*

INDIGO: *I can carry it open, so it'll keep copying. It'll just*
take longer to get back to the dorm that way.

GEORGIA: *Give me a minute. Marissa, STALL!*

"Okay, Sid, get back in the bacon bag and give me the laptop."

"Done." He fell apart into the suitcase, and I grabbed the laptop, draped my coat over it, and went to the door. Indigo was right outside.

"Bring back the thumb drive. And my coat!" I handed the awkward bundle to them and they took off at a good pace, but it was definitely slower than they'd been going with the laptop safely tucked into their bag.

I didn't want to distract either of my co-conspirators with more texts, so all I could do was pace back and forth in my office. When I heard a throat-clearing noise, I locked the door again and Sid got out to pace with me.

"Do you think Indigo got back in time?" he asked.

"I don't know." I looked at my phone again.

Forty-five excruciating minutes later, there was a tap on the door. Sid dove into the suitcase, breaking apart as he went, and managed not to make much noise. Then I opened up to find Indigo and Marissa. Marissa was wearing my coat, which was far too large for her, and Indigo was triumphantly holding up the thumb drive.

"Nailed it!" they said in unison.

I ushered them inside and asked, "What the patella took so long?"

Marissa looked confused by my phrasing, but Indigo was getting used to me. They said, "So I made it back to the dorm room maybe a minute ahead of Marissa and Bad Bobbie."

"You're just lucky the elevator was in use and we had to take the stairs," Marissa said.

"Lucky nothing! I took the elevator myself and pushed all the buttons before I got out to slow it down."

She punched their arm admiringly. "You are brilliant."

They grinned. "Only, when I got to the dorm room, the copying wasn't done yet. The status bar said it needed five more minutes."

"Meanwhile, Bad Bobbie and I got to our door, and there was Indigo, leaning on the wall and acting like they were waiting for me."

"I was waiting for you, wasn't I? Anyway, I said you'd left your coat in my room so I'd brought it by. Bad Bobbie didn't notice the coat was covering something."

"I think she was too surprised by my being in Indigo's room." She colored. "I mean, about my knowing them and all."

There was a tiny chuckle from Sid's suitcase, which I ignored and apparently the others didn't hear. "How did you get the laptop back where it was supposed to be without Bad Bobbie noticing?"

"Easy. I let Marissa and Bad Bobbie go into the room first, and on my way past the switch, I 'accidentally' turned off the light and pretended I couldn't find it again."

"Meanwhile, I figured out what they were doing and got in Bad Bobbie's way to distract her," Marissa said.

"You, too, are brilliant!" Another arm punch was exchanged. "By the time the light got turned back on, the laptop was on Bad Bobbie's desk and I had the thumb drive in my pocket. I'm ninety-five percent sure it was finished copying." They presented it to me proudly.

"But what took so long to get back here?" I asked.

Marissa colored again. "Well after that, we had to pretend like we're really, you know, seeing each other."

"We were making cute," Indigo explained.

"I was afraid Bad Bobbie didn't think we were really dating, so I wanted to be convincing."

"Why would she be so sure we're not dating?" Indigo asked.

"Because, you know, you're—" She swallowed visibly. "Because you're an upperclassman."

"As if that matters," they scoffed. "Anyway, I hung around while they ate breakfast and then asked Marissa to hang with me for the afternoon. And here we are."

"You two are awesome," I said. "If I could give a grade for this, you'd both get A's."

"So do you want us to help go through the stuff on the thumb drive?" Indigo asked.

There was a Sid-like rumbling from the suitcase.

"No, that's okay. You two probably have projects you need to work on."

"Yeah, kind of," Indigo admitted. "I've lost a lot of time working at the Lab with you."

I thought calling what they'd been doing *working* was a bit of an exaggeration, but given how well they'd done with their first attempt at espionage, I wasn't inclined to point it out.

"I've got assignments to finish, too, but I probably shouldn't go back to my room yet," Marissa said. "Bad Bobbie would wonder."

"You want to come chill in my room?" Indigo said. "My roomie is working in the animation lab all day."

"I don't want to be in the way," she said shyly.

"As if! Besides, I want you to show me how you drew that woodblock wolf. That's really good work."

They smiled at one another, and I just barely got my coat back before they wandered away together.

LEIGH PERRY

"Ah, young love," the suitcase said with a happy sigh.

After Sid climbed out, he got to work on the thumb drive in my office to see what he could find out from Bad Bobbie's files. Fortunately, he'd brought his own laptop to use, so I wouldn't have to twiddle my thumbs in the meantime.

Knowing that he hated to be distracted when he was in info gathering mode, I went to work in the Writing Lab and used every bit of self-control I possessed to keep from texting him every few minutes. I did check my phone repeatedly, but that wasn't interrupting. I was just about out of patience when I finally got a text from Sid.

SID: *Done.*

I didn't bother to reply, just locked up the Lab and headed to my office. After I tapped shave-and-a-haircut on the door, I let myself in, making sure nobody was close enough to see Sid at my desk.

When I saw him myself, I wasn't sure what to think. He was sitting with his skull in his hands. Not in the normal face-palm way—he was literally holding his skull in his lap.

"Sid, are you okay?"

"Georgia, there are things that once seen, can never be unseen."

"Okay."

"Do we have any more hydrogen peroxide at the bungalow? Tonight I'm going to need a good bath—I want to rinse out my skull."

"We can grab some more on the way home. Now are you going to tell me what's on that thumb drive, or should I look for myself?"

"Coccyx, Georgia, promise me never to look at those files. In fact, I don't think we should ever use that thumb drive again. Does the fireplace at the bungalow work? Or maybe we can bury it."

"Sid! What did you find?"

"You are familiar with fanfic, are you not?"

"Sure." Fan fiction is stories and even novels written by fans of a show or book to continue or expand upon the original work.

"And that sometimes fanfic combines fandoms, such as *Star Trek* meets Sherlock Holmes."

"Right."

"There is illustrated fanfic, as well, and of course you've heard of slash."

"Yes, Sid. I've been a nerd as long as you have." Slash is a subset of fanfic in which the fan imagines a romantic and/or sexual relationship between two characters who are not shown to be involved in the original work. The classic example was Kirk and Spock as lovers, but that was just the tip of the slash iceberg.

"Now extrapolate from that."

"So illustrated slash crossing over fandoms? I suppose that could be done tastefully, or at least artistically."

"It could be. Or it could be like Bad Bobbie's work. Trust me when I say that she has earned that nickname with her X-rated blend of *My Little Pony*, *Supernatural*, *Adventure Time*, *Homestuck*, and just a soupçon of Harry Potter."

"Oh."

"Well you might 'oh.' Bad Bobbie has a vivid imagination, and while a purist would have some quibbles with her anatomy and perhaps the scale of certain appendages, she knows how to get her point across. She is also apparently familiar with a wide variety of sexual practices."

"Kinky?"

"Kinky is such a mild word."

"Yow, Sid, is it that bad?"

He shuddered, which set all his bones to rattling. "Femur and phalanges, Georgia, I'll never get those images out of my skull. The only good side to this is that I can safely conclude that Bad Bobbie is not our art thief. Not a single one of the T-shirt designs shows up on her hard disk, and given the amount of time she spends posting her…work, she wouldn't have time to troll for designs to steal."

"Then I put you through this for nothing? I'm so sorry, Sid."

"No, she had to be eliminated as a suspect. But you know what the worst part is—the absolute worst part?"

"What?"

"She posts her work online regularly, and her followers number in the thousands."

CHAPTER THIRTY-TWO

While Sid made sure no vestiges of Bad Bobbie's files had tainted his laptop, I texted Indigo and Marissa.

GEORGIA: *Bad news. Bad Bobbie has no T-shirt designs on her hard drive. Unless she has another laptop, she's not our thief.*

INDIGO: *Now what?*

GEORGIA: *Marissa, you said your designs were critiqued in class. Do you have a list of the other students?*

MARISSA: *Can it wait? About to go to a movie.*

GEORGIA: *Sure. Enjoy.*

Sid put his skull on my shoulder to peer over it. "Their first date?"

"I'm not sure. It could just be chilling, or hanging. Do college kids date? As in, 'Would you like to go to a movie with me?'"

"You're asking the wrong guy. I'm more an Internet kind of dater."

"I suppose. Wait, have you been flirting online?"

"A gentleman never texts and tells."

Sid wanted to discuss next steps, but I was worried that somebody might hear the two of us talking. So he got back into his bag, and we headed back to the bungalow. Since it was daylight, I told him we should again hold off on conversation during the drive. But honestly, both of those decisions were just delaying tactics. The fact was, I was feeling discouraged.

Sid being Sid, he'd figured it out and as soon as we were home and he was out of the suitcase, he said, "Come on, Georgia, it's not that bad. I mean, Bad Bobbie's work is that bad, but finding out that she's not our murderous thief is a good thing. One less suspect."

"That's not a big help, Sid. Even with her eliminated, we've still got so many suspects. Do you know how many students, instructors, and admin staff members are at FAD?"

"Too many."

"Face it, Sid, we are a bust at catching art thieves."

"Hey, we've never tried to find a thief before. And we've only been at it a couple of weeks. Kelly was a trained reporter and she hadn't cracked it in a month."

"No, she just got herself killed, which is not something I aspire to."

"Yeah, she did get herself killed, didn't she?" Sid said speculatively. Then he actually smiled. I know, with the skin and such out of the way, human skulls have no choice but to smile all the time, but experience has taught me the difference between a default expression and a real grin. Sid was delighted with himself.

"Sid, stop that. You're creeping me out."

"Sorry. I was just thinking about what you said. You know, you're right. We suck at catching art thieves."

"This is a cheerful thought?"

"Shush. So we don't know how to catch a thief, but there is something we do know how to do. We know how to catch killers."

"Isn't that what we've been trying to do?"

"Yes and no. You don't even believe it was murder, do you?"

"I do now." I hadn't wanted to accept it at first, but something about the timing of Kelly's death combined with the overall nastiness at FAD had convinced me.

"Really?" He looked pleased. "That makes it easier."

"How?"

"Remember, we decided we couldn't do much without knowing a motive, but once we found it, we got sidetracked: first into thinking Kelly was a thief, and then into realizing that she was, in fact, going after the thief. So we've been doing that, too: looking for a thief."

"Don't you think the thief is the killer?"

"Absolutely, but we've been trying to work out the thefts, not the murder. The problem is that apparently our guy is a pretty good thief. I've found designs with the Scarlet Letter signature going back several years, so he's had time to perfect his technique. I'm guessing, however, that this is his first murder, which means mistakes were probably made. So let's look at the murder."

"That's what Officer Buchanan has been doing."

"I think she's given up. There's been nothing on the web about an official investigation. Have you heard anything more from her?"

"Now that you mention it, no." She'd paid me no more unexpected visits, and as far as I knew, she hadn't been on campus since the memorial service. Admittedly, I hadn't been entirely tuned into the rumor mill, but I think I'd have heard something.

"So forget her. She's a small-town cop, anyway—I bet we've got more experience with murder than she does."

"So what are do we going to do?"

"We'll do what we always do: nose around, ask stupid questions, speculate wildly, and argue about everything!"

CHAPTER THIRTY-THREE

Given that no opportunities available for nosing or asking presented themselves, we jumped right into speculating and arguing. Honestly, that was the part we were best at anyway.

"Okay," Sid said, "let's start with how Kelly was killed."

"She froze to death."

"Not according to the *Falstone Journal*. She died from a combination of injuries and exposure, which is a little different. But that's not what I meant anyway. I was talking about how the murderer killed her."

"Officer Buchanan said there was no sign of another car running into Kelly or anything like that. She just ran off the road."

"Normally, you'd expect to see skid marks if she'd hit a curve too sharply, but there was none of that, either."

"If the road was slick from snow or ice, it might not have left marks."

"Possibly. It depends on what time the snow started."

I thought back. "The snow was just starting when I left campus, which was at five. So the roads should have been clear for Kelly. Indigo said they spoke to her at two thirty that afternoon, and she was going to leave after her next appointment."

"I wonder who the meeting was with."

"I could check the Writing Lab portal."

"Good idea."

I got onto my laptop. "Nothing here—so it wasn't a student appointment. Unless somebody could delete an appointment to make it look as if it hadn't happened. Is that possible?"

"I don't know. It would require access to the system, which would mean one of you English adjuncts."

"Or Professor Waldron or Mr. Perkins." That was an unsettling thought. "No, wait. Kelly only put critique appointments in that database. Maybe it wasn't a student."

"Or if it was with a student, it wasn't for a tutoring session. Did Indigo know who the meeting was with?"

"They said they didn't. Do you think Kelly learned something important in that meeting?"

"No, I think the meeting was with the killer, and that's when he struck! What if he knocked her out or shot her full of tranquilizers?"

"Wouldn't the autopsy have shown signs of head injury?"

"There was probably trauma from the accident that could have masked an earlier blow. Remember the blood we saw?"

"I definitely remember that." The memory was more vivid than I would have preferred. "Wouldn't they know the difference between a newer injury and something a few hours old?"

"You may be right," Sid admitted. "*CSI* is always talking about antemortem, postmortem, and perimortem injuries. Before death, after death, and at the time of death."

"Okay, so he didn't hit her. And probably they'd have found a needle mark if she'd been drugged."

"Not if the killer injected her under a nail or on the scalp or someplace like that."

"Why would Kelly stay still for that?"

"Maybe there was an accomplice? One held her and one injected her?"

"Without making noise or leaving bruises? Let's make it simpler. Just one killer. What about coffee?"

"You want to take a coffee break now? This is just getting good."

I thumped him on the head, something it took practice to do without hurting myself. "What if the killer brought her drugged coffee, or some other drink? Though I don't know how somebody could drug her coffee without her noticing."

"It happens all the time," Sid said.

"True." Date rape drugs were alarmingly common on college campuses.

"The problem is, drugged coffee doesn't really go with the timeline. Unless we're picturing Kelly falling asleep at her desk, then waking up hours later just enough to stumble to her car, and then getting that far away before she crashed."

"You're right. That doesn't make sense."

"Unless… Okay, pretend I'm the killer. After Indigo leaves, I show up for our meeting."

"How could he be sure nobody would see him going into the Writing Lab?"

"I'm still at the speculating stage—we'll get to the arguing part later."

"Sorry. Carry on."

"So I go to the meeting carrying drugged coffee, which Kelly slurps right down because she's tired. Then I ramble on about something or another until she passes out."

"Okay."

"Then I lock the Lab door and lie low until it gets late enough that nobody is around."

"Not nearly as many people had keys then," I reminded him.

"Good point. So I'm not worried about anybody walking in on me. Maybe I even turn out the lights and sit in the dark. When I'm sure the coast is clear, I carry Kelly out to the car."

"How do you do that safely? If somebody had seen them, the whole plan would have been ruined."

"I'm not sure. Wait, what about one of those wheeled garbage cans?"

"Then there would have been garbage on her clothes—those things are never clean."

"Hey, I'm speculating here!"

"And I'm providing a reality check. Forget the garbage can and substitute one of those carts they use to transport heavy framed artwork and sculpture. The killer could have covered her with a tarp and nobody would know the difference."

"Oh, that's good."

"Except that now that I think of it, those carts have to be checked out. I saw a memo about it—apparently students were using them for races."

"Coccyx," Sid said.

We both drummed our fingers for a minute, then I came up with something. "What if the meeting didn't take place at FAD at all? Or if they met on campus and then went somewhere else? Maybe whoever she was meeting gave her a ride in his car, the way Lucas did with me the other night."

"Oh, that's better. So either he's already drugged her or he drugs her in the car."

"I think she must have been a little woozy when she left campus or she wouldn't have forgotten her phone."

"You forget your phone all the time."

"I do not. It's like once in a blue moon!"

He'd have rolled his eyes if he had any. "Anyway, no matter where he drugs her, he could just drive her around until she fell asleep. Then he could break her laptop, because he had to know there would be notes about the art theft on there."

"But now he's got two cars: hers and his. He can't leave hers on campus, but he needs his own to get home after he kills her."

"Okay, I'm not the best one to speculate about car issues. What do you do when you've got one car too many?"

I snorted. "I'm lucky if I've got one vehicle that's running."

"Focus."

"Sorry. What if they take Kelly's car instead?"

"Wouldn't she be driving?"

"'Hey, Kelly, you look beat. You want me to drive?'"

"That would work," Sid said.

"He drives around until she passes out, and then he heads for the spot he's already picked out. He destroys her laptop to get rid of any evidence that might be on it, gets out of the car, and pushes it over the edge."

"He must have been expecting her to die on impact or maybe to never wake up again."

"Kelly was stronger than he thought," I said, wishing I'd known her better.

"But he doesn't have a way to get home."

"Is there anyplace useful within walking distance?"

"Google Maps to the rescue!" Sid said and borrowed my laptop to access an aerial view of the area. "Hmm… There's not much around there."

"What's that?" I said, pointing to a blur that seemed to be the only structure nearby. It wasn't on the same road Kelly's car had been on, but only a thin strip of woods separated them.

He enlarged the picture, then went to Google Street View. "It looks like a log cabin."

"You think it might be a vacation place like this one?"

"I'll check the address." More typing. "Bingo! It's a rental and is currently available."

"Since I don't think anybody has been vacationing around here this winter, I bet it's vacant. What if the killer left his car there that morning?"

"How did he get to campus?"

"He could have called Uber or asked a friend to pick him up. 'Hey, Joe, my car is broken down on the road. Come get me, and I'll get my car towed or jumped or whatever later.'"

"So his car was there all day waiting, maybe under a tarp or something. After he deals with Kelly, he walks down the road a little way, ready to duck if he sees a car; goes into the woods to get to that cabin's driveway and his car; and drives home. Wait, wouldn't the driveway have been snowed in?"

"A lot of rental places have service contracts to keep the driveways plowed. Of course, he was taking a chance that the snow removal folks would find his car, but I bet he could have talked his way around that. The important part is that the spot where he went into the woods was far enough from the accident scene that the cops would have no reason to look there for traces of him passing, and of course, snow and wind would mean that all signs would be covered soon anyway."

"So he walks to his car and drives home. No muss, no fuss. Georgia, I think that's it. It's flawless!"

I enjoyed ten seconds of satisfaction before realizing the problem. "Sid, it's so flawless that I can't think of a single ossifying way to prove that that's what happened."

CHAPTER THIRTY-FOUR

That was the end of the speculation phase for the evening, though we kept on with the arguing for a while longer. We were convinced that our solution for how the murder was committed was the right one, but we couldn't come up with anything we could conceivably take to the police. Even if we went with our tried-and-true anonymous tip method, how would they be able to prove it?

Fingerprints in Kelly's car? The killer would surely have been wearing gloves—the only one in Falstone who didn't need to wear gloves every time he or she stepped outside was Sid, and he didn't have prints.

Traces of a car in the vacant cabin's driveway or of the killer in the woods leading to it? Sid was all for going out right then and there to look and only gave up when I went to online snow accumulation charts and reminded him of just how much snow had fallen since Kelly died.

If the killer had used Uber or a cab to get to campus that morning, the cops might be able to get a warrant to find out, but it wasn't something Sid and I could do. The only possible lead we had was that if an on-campus friend had given the killer a ride, and if I could figure out who that was, maybe I could get that person to confirm that somebody had been parked at that vacant cabin. That was predicated on that person being somebody I knew and who would talk to me, so the chances weren't good.

After a while, we gave up for the night and picked a movie to watch on TV, one which did not include murders.

It was aggravating to have gotten that far only to get stuck again, but as I told Sid, at least we'd made some progress. Probably. Surely we'd come up with something brilliant after a good night's sleep for me, and a good night's reading, web surfing, and YouTube video watching for Sid.

I was overly optimistic. The next morning, our minds were notably free of brilliance.

So we dove into weekend chores that had been put aside for detective work, going on the theory that our unconscious minds would be working as we washed, cleaned, graded, shoveled, shopped, and cooked.

Wrong again.

By Sunday night we were so desperate that we actually did get into the car to drive along the road Kelly's car had gone off, looking for traces that somebody had gone through the woods. We even went so far as to check out the driveway of the cabin but found it neatly plowed by some incredibly conscientious snow removal company. As a last ditch attempt, we turned up and down all kinds of roads, looking to see if there were some other place the killer could have hidden a car while leaving tire prints, a nice scraping of paint, or other useful physical evidence. That did nothing but waste gas.

Monday morning was almost a relief—I had definite things to do. There were papers to grade, classes to teach, and colleagues to be snubbed by. At least Caroline was speaking to me again, so we had a late lunch, gossiping about those who were snubbing me, and now snubbing her because she was with me. Sometimes I wonder if any of us really ever leave the behavior of junior high school behind.

Late in the afternoon, there was a knock at my office door and I looked up to see Indigo and Marissa. They weren't holding hands, but they were definitely standing closer than they had been before. I made a mental note to tell Sid. For somebody made completely of bone, he had a soft spot for young love.

"Hi, guys. Come on in."

They did so, closing the door behind them.

"I've got that class list you asked for," Marissa said, handing me an actual piece of paper.

"You could have e-mailed it."

"I only had your FAD e-mail address, and I wasn't sure how safe it is."

"Good point." Given the overabundance of suspects, our art thief could theoretically have access to my account.

"And I've got this," Indigo said, giving me another paper. "You remember how I put out feelers online for other people whose work had been stolen? Those are people who've been in contact."

"Great." Then I looked at the list. "Indigo, there must be over fifty names here."

"I know," they said apologetically. "They may not all be legit."

"Still, it's good to have," I said, trying to be sound more enthusiastic than I was. So many victims, so many suspects. This was starting to sound impossible.

"I put together a file of their stories so we can check them out, but that was too much to print. Do you have a secure e-mail address I can send to?"

"Sure." I gave them my home address. "Are all of these FAD students?"

"Only a couple, but I have friends at other schools, and they spread the word."

"Were these all stolen by our guy?"

"Who knows? There are a lot of these jackwagons out there. I didn't mention the name Scarlet Letter because I wasn't sure we should give out that much information."

"The earliest thefts Kelly found were by Scarlet Letter," Marissa said, "but that's not saying he didn't change his signature later. Even professional artists change signatures sometimes. This guy could have a dozen."

"You're probably right," I said. "How do you artists decide how to sign work anyway?"

Marissa shrugged. "It depends. Some people just go with a

name, but even then they spend some time deciding how to write it. Print, cursive, the kind of letters."

Indigo added, "It's like your brand or your logo, only more personal. I've had the same one for years."

"Me, too." Marissa looked embarrassed. "When I first started, I probably spent more time perfecting my signature than I did, you know, actually drawing anything."

"Yeah, we all do that," Indigo said. "Like jocks who practice their victory dances more than their touchdowns."

"And academics who spend more times on arcane titles than the actual paper they're writing. I guess nobody is immune. Anyway, thanks for all this. I'll see what I can find out."

The two of them looked at one another, and Marissa asked, "So what's next?"

"I'm not sure," I said.

"Don't you have something else you want us to do?"

"Not right now."

Indigo gave me a sharp look. "Are you trying to shut us out?"

"No and yes. No, I really don't have anything for you, but yes, I am trying to shut you out. Here's the thing, guys. When you volunteered to help Kelly, you were hunting for an art thief. But now I believe—we all believe—that we're looking for a murderer. And I've been having second thoughts about dragging you two into something that might be dangerous." The discussion about that had been one of the few useful conversations Sid and I had had the day before.

"I'm not afraid of this guy," Indigo said indignantly.

"Good for you. I am. I mean, I'm not giving up, but I am watching my back. This guy murdered Kelly even though as far as we know, Kelly didn't even know who he was. And that was just to keep him from getting caught as a thief. How far would he go to keep from getting arrested as a murderer?"

"I never thought of it that way," Indigo said and looked over at Marissa.

Marissa noticed, too. "Don't either of you get macho on me."

"I am in no way getting macho," I said. "But I am a professor, and protecting students is in my job description, more or less. Plus I've got a daughter not much younger than you guys, and if I found out one of her teachers was drawing her into danger, I would be more than a little upset." I could see that they both wanted to argue, but I didn't give them a chance. "Don't think I'm going at this alone. I've got someone who has my back."

"The person who hacked Bad Bobbie's computer?" Indigo asked.

I nodded. "Nobody here knows him, so he can do stuff none of us can do without becoming a target. And now that I think of it, there is something I want from you guys. More than one thing, in fact. First, keep your eyes open. If you hear anything else about art theft here at FAD, let me know right away. Indigo, if you could keep coming to the Writing Lab, that would be great because we'll have a non-suspicious way to stay in touch. Second, if anything happens to me, I'm counting on you guys to go to the cops. I'm going to e-mail all my files about this mess to you both, just in case. And third and most important: be careful. Don't talk about art theft anymore, don't put out any more feelers, and don't go off alone. The only people on campus that I'm a hundred percent sure are innocent are the three of us in this room, and Bad Bobbie." Though given Bad Bobbie's private project, maybe *innocent* wasn't the right word for her. But since I hadn't told Indigo and Marissa what Sid had found on her hard drive, I couldn't explain that to them.

I thanked them again and tried to look confident and eager to finish the investigation, but honestly, I was even more discouraged than ever. We already had just about every person on campus as a suspect, so I didn't see how knowing about more victims was going to narrow the field any further.

On the other hand, I knew Sid was as frustrated as I was and didn't have a job or a congenial lunch companion to distract him, and maybe he'd appreciate having something to dive into. So as soon as I got the files from Indigo, I forwarded them to him, along with an explanatory note. By the time I got home, Sid was hip-bone-deep in new data and only barely acknowledged my arrival. I warmed up leftover pizza, washed up afterward, did a load of laundry, called Madison to see how she was doing, watched some TV, and filed my nails, all to the sound of clattering at the keyboard. I stayed up later than usual, waiting to see what he'd find out, but was just about ready to call it a night when the racket stopped and he marched into the living room to slap a stack of paper onto the coffee table.

"No wonder our art thief is so hard to find," he announced. "He's been at this for years."

"Seriously?"

"At least five years, according to my calculations. Let me explain how I came to that conclusion."

"Or you could just skip to the end."

"Literature students could skip to the part where Romeo and Juliet die, too, but what fun would that be?"

"Many of my students would jump at that idea."

"We are made of sterner stuff," he said. "So as I was trying to say, I went through Indigo's list of art theft victims."

"They hadn't all been ripped off by our guy, had they?"

"No. Unfortunately, there are many sharks lurking in the Internet sea. Of the fifty-three names, I'm reasonably sure that eighteen of them hadn't been plagiarized at all. Either their ideas weren't all that original in the first place, or they were seeing copying when it was nothing more than a passing resemblance. Plus one guy copied a classmate's work and then claimed he'd been copied. Fortunately, others on social media have since called him out."

"Good." I paused. "Did you assist in that effort?"

He only grinned. "That leaves thirty-five who I think are actual victims. Of those, five had designs that were blatantly stolen by Scarlet Letter, four claimed ownership of Scarlet Letter designs that were very similar to theirs, and a couple who claim they had an idea that Scarlet Letter used."

"I've always heard that ideas are the easy part—it's the execution that's important."

"Agreed, and if the person being accused of stealing ideas was anybody else, I'd be more skeptical, but in this case, I'm inclined to assume the worst."

"Are all of these on City Riggers' site?"

"Not all. As far as I can tell, he started out selling his work on the kind of sites where designers upload their work and then people order custom-printed T-shirts."

"Like Green Globe, the site that banned Marissa?"

"Right. Those guys have hundreds, no, thousands of designs. I only looked through a handful, and that was enough to give me eye socket strain."

"Eye socket strain isn't a thing."

He ignored me. "So it's no wonder that people sneak in stolen designs without them noticing. Lately, though, there have been so many complaints that the sites are trying to address that. Unfortunately, sometimes they ban the actual artist instead of the thief."

"Like with Marissa."

"Exactly. Sometime in the past year, Scarlet Letter started selling designs to City Riggers, which I'm guessing earns him more money because it's a high-profile site. And as we've learned, they're known for not vetting the designs they sell or responding well to accusations of plagiarism."

"It's no wonder starving artists starve if companies steal from them! So how many more of Scarlet Letter's victims have you confirmed?"

"Eleven. Two of those eleven had pictures in Kelly's files, though she hadn't been in contact with them as far as I know."

"How many are FAD students?"

"None. They're not even all from art schools, though each of the schools involved has an art department: Suffolk University, New England College, Rochester. And FAD."

"They're all in New England."

"Right."

"Of course, if the art thief was stealing online, it wouldn't matter where they came from."

"Most of the artists claim to have been vigilant about posting anything online. But it only takes one slip in posting something or e-mailing it to somebody, who then posts it or e-mails it to somebody else. And so on. But I'm willing to believe that some of them really were that careful. And unlike Marissa, most of them never displayed their work at an art fair."

"Meaning that the thief had personal access to all of them."

"That many students, that many schools, over just a few years. Sid, you know what that means."

"I think I do."

"Our thief—and presumably the killer as well—is an adjunct."

Chapter Thirty-Five

That shouldn't have been a shock. After all, we'd already considered everybody at FAD to be a suspect, and a goodly percentage of FAD's faculty members were adjuncts. I still felt sick at the thought. Considering how my fellow English department adjuncts had been treating me, I shouldn't have felt any particular loyalty, but I knew how hard it was to try to make a living as an adjunct. Coccyx, even if the pay had been fabulous, the life itself was rough—working multiple jobs, having to rip up roots at short notice, getting so little respect from tenured colleagues.

That last thought triggered another.

"Sid, today I asked Indigo and Marissa how they chose their signatures. So why do you suppose the plagiarist picked Scarlet Letter?"

"From the Nathaniel Hawthorne novel, I assume," Sid said.

"You've read *The Scarlet Letter*, right?"

"I reside in a house with three English professors—of course I've read it. I didn't like it, which I know is blasphemy, but the man always comes off as a prig to me. Making that poor woman mark all her dresses with an A for adulteress. Or was it for adultery?"

"It was adulteress, but it could have been for either. A for apple, A for alligator…"

"A for alibi!" Sid joined in. "A for aardvark. A for academic."

"A for adjunct. Do you remember when I worked for Quintain University?"

"That was the one in New Hampshire, right? You hated that job."

"So much." I'd only stayed a semester, but that was more than enough. Adjuncts weren't taken as seriously as term or tenured professors at a lot of colleges, but Quintain took that divide to the extreme. "My ID badge there didn't say *Faculty*; it said *Adjunct Faculty*, so nobody would mistake me for a real professor."

"Seriously?"

"And the parking pass? It was the same color and design as a faculty pass, but they stamped a big A on it to make sure I didn't park in the faculty lot. I had to park in the student lots."

"That's insane, but while I'm happy to commiserate with you, I'm not sure why you're bringing this up."

"The *A* was in bright red ink."

"A scarlet letter."

I nodded. "So yeah, I think our Scarlet Letter is an adjunct."

"Of course, we've still got a lot of suspects, but it does limit the field some. There aren't as many adjuncts at FAD as there are students."

"Not by a long shot."

"So you think the thief worked at Quintain, too? Or do other schools do sacrum like that?"

"That's the only place I've seen it, but there's enough stigma at some schools that the allusion could have appealed to somebody even if they'd never been stamped with a literal scarlet letter."

"It's kind of a clue to how the person feels, too. I mean, Hester Prynne felt guilty about the adultery but also thought it was justified because she loved the guy and the resulting baby. So she's angry about the punishment. Also a little desperate. Right?"

"That's a fair interpretation," I said. "Write it up, with appropriate quotes from the book, and I'll give it a solid B."

"Please. It's totally A-level work! But anyway, maybe the thief feels a combination of guilty, justified, angry, and desperate."

"Then not just greed?"

"Anybody who was just greedy wouldn't be an adjunct."

"All too true," I admitted. Perhaps a little greed would have steered me in a more profitable direction. "Literary criticism aside, now what? I mean, you searched the offices of some of our adjunct suspects already."

Sid drummed his finger bones against his skull. "If you left me at FAD over a weekend, I might be able to get to—"

"You got to what, seven offices that one night? Multiply that by three for a weekend, which is being generous. Do you know how many adjunct faculty members we have? How many weekends would it take?"

He actually grabbed his laptop. "Okay, let me access the directory and add them up."

"Sid, no." When he started to object, I quickly added, "I swear I'm not trying to forbid you from doing anything. I'm just pointing out that it's not going to work. The semester would be over before you got to them all, and who knows if you would actually find proof in the thief's office. Someone who's been at this for five years is probably good at hiding his tracks. We need something to get the numbers down to something we can realistically handle."

More drumming of finger bones against skull. "Okay, how about this? We know Scarlet Letter stole at five different schools. What if I figure out which adjuncts taught at all of those schools?"

"How?"

"LinkedIn. People list all their employers there."

"Not everybody is on LinkedIn."

"Then online faculty lists—cached faculty lists for previous years. Social media, university papers and press releases, directories of professional organizations. The information is all out there, Georgia."

"I guess, but there are so many adjuncts at FAD, Sid. It's going to be incredibly tedious."

"I live for tedium! You turn in for the night and leave me to it."

I would have felt guilty about abandoning him, but he looked cheerful at the prospect. I think it wasn't just the fact that it was something to do—it was the fact that it was something nobody else could do. Nobody but Sid would be able to put in the hours a job like that would take. So I kissed the top of his skull and went to bed.

He was still at it the next morning, so I left him to go to work. When I returned after an uneventful day of teaching, critiquing, and looking at every adjunct I encountered with suspicious eyes, he was *still* at it. Only when I was washing up after dinner did he come into the kitchen.

"I'm done," he said in a flat, unemotional tone that was totally unlike him. His bones were disturbingly loose.

"Do you sound like that because you're tired?" He didn't get tired, or at least he'd never admitted to being tired before, but if anything would wear him out, it would be nearly twenty-four solid hours of research.

"No, I sound like this because I'm done. In every sense of the word. We have gone from too many suspects to none. Not a single, solitary adjunct taught at every school."

"You're kidding."

"I wish I were. Check out my spreadsheet." Sid loves spreadsheets almost as much as he loves dossiers. "Along the side are the adjuncts, other than yourself. Along the top are the schools from which we have confirmed art theft."

"Seems reasonable."

"I've got another spreadsheet with the schools where each adjunct has taught for the past seven years."

"Seven?"

"Just giving myself a margin for error. Then all I had to do was to check off the names. Easy, right?"

"I know a trick question when I hear it."

"Well, it would have been easy if anybody had taught at all five schools."

I ran down the list, more to humor him than anything else. "I see one person was at two of the schools."

"Several were at two. Some were at three, and two were even at four. But no one was at five. I didn't even get around to coordinating times to make sure they were at the right schools when the thefts took place. There was no need."

I looked down the list again as I tried to think of something comforting to say and got as far as the D's when I noticed something. "Hey, why isn't Owen Deen on here?"

"He's an English prof."

"So?"

"Scarlet Letter is an artist."

"Are you sure? Even I could take a design, scan it into a computer, and change the signature."

"Some of the changes were more drastic than that, and nobody had any art training in their background."

"Maybe they have natural ability that they've been hiding. Maybe they outsourced the dirty work. It won't hurt to look at their resumes, too, will it?"

"No, it won't! Give me a few more minutes!" He clattered off to his room and was gone for half an hour before he joined me in the living room. Now his joints were even looser than before.

"Nothing?"

He shook his skull so vigorously I was afraid it would roll right off his shoulders and handed me a new list. "Caroline and Renee were at two, and Owen and Dahna were at three."

"And I was only at one." He'd included me, and I had to respect his attention to detail. Except… "Wait, I've taught at Suffolk, too."

"That was distance learning, right? You taught your classes via computer."

"That doesn't mean I was never on campus. I haven't gone to Montserrat since you've been in town, but I do go every month to meet students whose issues I can't handle via e-mail and deal with paperwork and such. Some schools require even more frequent in-person visits."

"I didn't realize that!" Sid said. "Off to the Internet!"

I would have apologized for sending him back to the salt mines if I hadn't seen how tightly his bones snapped back together. He was delighted to have more work.

I admit that when I went to bed, I was worried about what I'd suggest if he didn't find somebody with connections on all five campuses, but as it turned out, the question was moot.

When my alarm went off the next morning, Sid was sitting at the foot of my bed.

"I've got it," he said and handed me a new and improved spreadsheet.

I rubbed sleep out of my eyes and took a look. He'd made it easy for me by circling one name in red.

"Dahna?" I asked.

"You were right about one of your colleagues having hitherto undiscovered abilities. It turns out Dahna Kaleka has a talent for art. Not to mention theft and murder."

.

Chapter Thirty-Six

"I know I told you to add the English adjuncts to the list, but I never would have suspected Dahna. Are you sure?"

"Are you impugning my research abilities?" He drew himself up stiffly.

"No, of course not. You rule the Internet, Sid, but this is hard to take."

"I understand. I even went back and double-checked a few of the adjuncts who'd been at four of the schools, just to be sure I hadn't missed anything, but Dahna is the only one. And yes, I made sure her work history matched the timeline. In all the thefts we know about, she was at the schools when art was stolen."

"Okay then. I'm convinced."

"I wasn't expecting you to take it so hard."

"I wasn't expecting the killer to be somebody I know as well as I do Dahna. I always liked her, until this whole tenure thing came up, and even then she hasn't been as nasty as Owen or Renee. The other killers we've found weren't so close to me."

He patted my hand sympathetically. "Look, there's still a chance we're wrong. I mean, this is purely circumstantial. We still need definitive proof."

"Any ideas for how we can get it?"

"I think I need another overnight at FAD."

"Tonight?"

"There's no reason to wait, is there? And I don't want you working at the same school as a murderer any longer than absolutely necessary."

I couldn't help trying to poke holes in Sid's theory as I showered, dressed, and ate breakfast. Had Dahna been able to hide artistic talent? Well, sure, anybody could have, and if she was Scarlet Letter, she would likely have taken pains to conceal it. Was she physically capable of lugging Kelly around? Certainly—she was a tall, strong woman. Would she have known a good place to push Kelly's car off the road? Of course. She'd been in Falstone more than long enough to figure something like that out. The only question that gave me real pause was the timing. What had compelled her to kill Kelly when it seemed that Kelly had had no idea she was the thief? To do so purely as a preventive measure seemed like a colder decision than I could picture Dahna making.

Sid seemed to have no such doubts, but then again, he'd never sat around and eaten Danish with her while talking about Shirley Jackson and complaining about students. The fact was, I'd liked Dahna a lot more than I'd liked Kelly, and that made me more than a little uncomfortable.

Our plan for the day was simple. I'd take Sid with me to class again—I'd used him for a writing prompt in a Tuesday-Thursday class, so now I could do the same in my Monday-Wednesday class. That would give me an excuse for bringing him back to campus and also for keeping him visible. The visibility made both of us happy. In my case, I needed a friendly face I was sure I could trust, and in his, he didn't want me to be without backup while a possible murderer was so close by.

We made it to my office without seeing Dahna, which was a relief, and Sid and I spent the morning behind a locked door playing online and grading papers, respectively. I really thought I might as well play games, too, for all I'd be able to get done, but apparently the years of practice paid off. When my alarm went off to let me know it was time to get to my classroom, I'd worked my way through a respectable number of papers.

Once Sid was posed comfortably in my desk chair, I wheeled him up to class. A skeleton on campus didn't get nearly the attention this time around—students get jaded very quickly. The first class went well, and since I still didn't want to risk running into Dahna, I skipped lunch and stayed in the classroom for the break before my next class. Giving the spiel with Sid the third time actually convinced me that FAD should add it to the curriculum permanently, if Professor Waldron didn't object. Of course, not all instructors had a skeleton handy, but they could substitute some other prop.

Once that class was over, I had office hours, and since I only have two chairs in my office, that meant disassembling Sid. By his request, I put his head on the bookshelf so he could keep watch while I met with students.

By the time that was over, I badly needed a bathroom break.

With Sid there to keep watch, I didn't bother to lock my door when I left. I really should have.

When I returned, Owen was sitting in my guest chair. Two cups of coffee and a plate of chocolate chip cookies were on the desk in front of him.

"Owen?" I said. "What can I do for you?"

"Can we talk?" he said, hanging his head. "I'd like to clear the air between us."

First Caroline, and now Owen. Of course, I liked Caroline and didn't much care for Owen anymore, but I decided I really should be gracious about it. "Sure," I said.

I sat down at my desk. Sid's skull was on the shelf where I'd left it, and I could tell that if he'd had a tongue, he'd have been blowing a raspberry at Owen's back.

As if he'd been practicing, Owen said, "I want to apologize. I've been borderline harassing you all semester, even though you've been very clear that you weren't interested. I just haven't been listening. If I'd realized you were seeing somebody else, I would have stopped."

"Owen, at the risk of repeating myself, let me remind you that my love life is none of your business."

"You're right, you're right." He took a deep breath. "I'm just disappointed and—But it's not about me. Other than me being the one apologizing, that is." He gave me the grin I used to find attractive. "The coffee and the cookies are a peace offering. I hope we can go back to being friends."

"Let's start with friendly colleagues," I said, but I did reach for the coffee cup. Before I could pick it up, I saw Sid's skull moving. He was shaking an emphatic *NO*. I took a cookie instead, and when Sid didn't react, bit into it.

Owen looked disappointed.

"This is good," I said. "Would you like one?"

"No, no. They're for you. The coffee, too. Black, just the way you like it."

Sid was shaking his skull again.

I touched the cup, then drew my hand back. "It's a little hot. Would you mind getting me some water from the bubbler to cool it down?"

"Sure, I'd be glad to," he said far too enthusiastically and rushed off.

"Don't drink that!" Sid whispered as soon as Owen was gone. "He was stirring it like crazy before you got here. Why would you stir black coffee?"

"I got the message, but I don't understand. Owen can't be Scarlet Letter. He was only at, what, three of the schools?"

"Maybe he's got a confederate. The thing is, he must be the killer or why would he be drugging you?"

"Maybe he had some other reason to kill Kelly. Maybe he tried to date her or—"

"Georgia! I don't care why he did it! We've got proof at last! Call campus security! Better yet, call the cops! They'll be able to test that coffee."

"Good idea." Then I had a flash of inspiration. "Or we could try to catch him in the act."

"What the patella are you talking about?"

"If he's the killer and we call the cops now, he'll know we're onto him and clam up. I mean, even if we get him for trying to drug me, we don't have any real evidence connecting him to the murder. Whereas if I play along, we might get him to say or do something that will really put him away."

When Owen came in a few minutes later, I was eating the last cookie and the coffee cup was empty. "It wasn't as hot as I thought," I said.

"No problem." He looked awfully happy for a man who'd been sent off on a meaningless errand, and looked even happier when I faked a yawn.

"Sorry. The day must be catching up with me."

"I know the feeling. I was up late grading papers myself." He regaled me with a couple of stories about his students' writing skills, and I followed with one of mine. Only I purposely got it tangled up as if I was having problems following my own train of thought. Owen couldn't stop smiling.

I was afraid he was going to sit there until I pretended to pass out, which I wasn't sure I could do convincingly, so I finally said, "Owen, I don't want to be rude, but suddenly I'm beat. I've got some work to do, but I think I'm going to lay my head down for a few minutes first."

"Good idea. Forty winks is just what you need."

"Thanks for the coffee and…" I faked a monster yawn. "And the cookies. Do you mind shutting the door behind you? I don't want anybody finding me asleep."

"You bet," he said, but I noticed he didn't push it far enough for the lock to engage.

As soon as I was sure he was gone, I closed the door more securely, then told Sid what we were going to do. At first he was unhappy, but the further I went with the plan, the more he liked it. It only took a few minutes to get everything set up. Then I put the door back the way Owen had left it and went to my desk to put my head down.

It seemed like I stayed that way for an hour, but Sid later assured me it was no more than fifteen minutes later when the door cracked up and Owen peered in. He stepped inside, this time locking the door behind him, and Sid saw he was carrying a tote bag. "Georgia?" Owen said.

It was all I could do to keep pretending to be asleep.

"Georgia!" he said a little louder.

I murmured something and shifted position.

"That's my girl."

It was harder to sit still for being patronized than it was for the worry he was going to hurt me. With Sid watching from above and the rest of his skeleton under the desk, ready to spring forth if needed, I knew that wasn't going to happen.

I felt Owen putting something on the desktop next to me, though I couldn't tell what it was. Then I heard him pouring something. "Should have bought something cheaper," he said regretfully, "but it'll be worth it." Finally, I heard him putting at least one item into my trash can.

He stepped away, and Sid told me later that he actually made a frame with his hands, the way movie directors supposedly do, to look over the scene he'd set. All I knew at the time is that he said, "Now is that any way for a tenured professor to act?" He chuckled to himself, then went back out the door.

I waited a few minutes before lifting my head. "What did he do?"

"He's not trying to kill you," Sid said indignantly. "He's trying to frame you!"

"For murder?" I looked at what Owen had left on my desk and realized what game he was actually playing. "That ossifying piece of sacrum!"

CHAPTER THIRTY-SEVEN

Twenty minutes later, there was a loud knocking at my door, but I pretended I hadn't heard it, even though I was no longer playing possum on my desk. Instead I had my laptop out and was working on a file. At least, I was pretending to work.

There was a second barrage of knocks, which I also ignored. A minute later, I heard a key being used.

I looked up to see Mr. Perkins staring at me, with Owen behind him with a look of glee that quickly turned to horror.

"Mr. Perkins?" I said, pulling my ear buds out. "Is something wrong?"

"You didn't answer the door," he said.

"Sorry, I didn't hear you," I said. "I like to listen to music when I work. What can I do for you?"

"Dr. Deen said there was a problem."

"What kind of problem?"

Mr. Perkins turned to Owen. "You told me there was something I needed to see. Would you care to explain further?"

"Um... I was afraid something was wrong. Georgia didn't answer my knock, either."

"Owen, you were just in here a few minutes ago," I said. "What did you think could have happened in that length of time?"

"I thought...I thought I smelled..." He swallowed visibly. "I must have been mistaken."

I continued to look as innocent as I could.

"Dr. Deen, if this is your idea of a joke," Mr. Perkins said,

"I find it in questionable taste at best. Dr. Thackery, is there anything wrong?"

"Not a thing," I said.

"Then please excuse my interruption."

"Of course."

He gave Owen a stern look and stomped off. Owen was about to leave, too, though it was more of a slink than a stomp, but I said, "Owen, would you stay a minute?"

"Um, sure. What's up?"

"This." I turned my laptop around so he could see the screen, then pressed the play button for the video I had queued up and ready. It showed exactly what Owen had done while he thought I was asleep. He'd put an empty beer can on my desk, and a half-filled one close to my hand. Then he'd put three more empties into my trash can. Sid, who'd been using my phone to take the video, had gotten a lovely close-up of Owen's smug expression as he made sure everything was just the way he wanted it.

The expression on the real Owen's face was far more satisfying to me. His eyes had gone big, and his skin was as pale as Sid's skull.

"Georgia, I didn't mean to—"

"I know what you meant to do, Owen. First you drugged my coffee. Which obviously I did not drink, though I did pour it into my water bottle so it can be tested for roofies or whatever you tried to dose me with. Then you came back and tried to make it look as if I'd been drinking on the job and had passed out at my desk. Finally, you dragged Mr. Perkins over as a witness. So you don't need to say anything about that. However, you are going to explain why you did it."

"You know why."

I leaned forward, ready to hear his confession. It wasn't what I was expecting.

He said, "I deserve tenure, Georgia, a lot more than you do. I don't have parents in the field who can get me plum positions."

"If my parents' connections could get me plum positions, don't you think I'd have one by now?"

He looked sullen. "I need this job."

"Enough to ruin my professional reputation by making me look like a drunk? You can't expect me to believe that's all you were trying to do."

For a second he looked as if he was going to hold it in, but I could see him reach the point where he wanted to talk more than he wanted to get away. I thought for sure that the real confession was coming. And again, it was, but not in the way I expected.

"Okay, fine," he snapped. "It's because you've been playing me."

"What?"

"All semester long you've been leading me on, and then I find out you're seeing some other guy."

"What are you talking about?"

"Don't play coy. I heard that other guy's voice at your house the night you said you were working. You've been making a fool out of me."

"You're jealous? Seriously, that's your reason? That's just pathetic, Owen. I thought you were—" I stopped just in time.

"Thought I was what?"

"I thought you were a worthwhile human being. Obviously I was wrong. I want you to stay the patella away from me."

"What are you going to do?"

"Nothing."

He started to relax. "You mean it? Georgia, I really appreciate this. I mean, actually—"

I looked behind him as Officer Buchanan stepped in.

"Is this the guy?" she said, jerking her thumb at Owen.

"That's him. He's all yours."

"You said you weren't going to do anything!" Owen said, looking indignant.

"I'm not doing anything," I said. "I called Officer Buchanan a few minutes ago, and she's taking over." I'd been nonplussed when she was the one to answer the phone when I called the police station, but if she really did think I had something to do with Kelly's murder, she'd compartmentalized that suspicion after I told her what was going on. To her I said, "Did you get the video I e-mailed?"

"Sure did. It made for some entertaining viewing. Have you got the physical evidence?"

"All ready for you." I handed her a shopping bag that held the coffee-filled water bottle and the beer cans Owen had planted on my desk.

"Dr. Deen, I would like you to accompany me to the station so we can have us a little conversation."

"But nothing happened!"

"Drugging another person without their knowledge or consent is against the law."

"It was just a prank."

"You call it a prank—I call it assault," Officer Buchanan said. "Are you coming quietly, or do you have a hankering for cuffs and a perp walk?"

"If you do a perp walk, can I film it?" I asked.

"I'll come quietly," Owen said. "It's just a misunderstanding, really."

Of course Mr. Perkins noticed Officer Buchanan escorting Owen out of the building, and even without the use of handcuffs, he knew something was wrong. He came rushing over for an explanation, which I was happy to provide.

"Then you think Dr. Deen is the art thief?" he asked.

I wished I could have said that he was beyond the shadow of a doubt, but even after all that, I didn't think he was.

"Are you sure, Georgia?" Sid asked for the umpteenth time when we were on our way back to the bungalow. He was huddling in his open suitcase on the floor of the passenger side of the front seat.

"Pretty sure. You heard him, Sid. He spilled his guts!"

"Nasty expression—makes me glad I don't have any."

"And yet you were gutsy enough to warn me."

"What are partners for?"

"Anyway, I don't think Owen was holding anything back. He

wasn't trying to conceal a theft or a murder—he was just trying to get rid of a competitor while getting back at me for not dating him. Or maybe he was getting back at me for not dating him while getting rid of a competitor."

"Now the only tenure he'll be getting is in jail!"

"That sounds like a tagline. Sid, have you been binge watching *Law & Order* again?"

"*Chung chung*," he admitted.

"At any rate, that puts Dahna back at the top of our suspect list. You should have gone ahead and gone sleuthing overnight. I'm fine."

"The patella you are! A friend—excuse me, a former friend—tried to drug you and frame you. You're shaky and upset and I am going to make sure you feel better. I can spend tomorrow night at FAD."

I really was shakier than I wanted to let on. Maybe I didn't much like Owen anymore, but I'd liked him enough at one time to date him, and having him turn on me the way he had left me wondering if he'd really changed or if I'd just been oblivious to what he was actually like.

Once we got back to the bungalow, Sid bustled me inside, pushed me down onto the couch with an afghan I didn't really need wrapped around me, and went to fix me one of my traditional comfort meals: a grilled cheese sandwich with cheddar cheese and a bowl of tomato soup. When I tried to boot up my laptop afterward to get a little work done, he grabbed it away and wouldn't tell me where he'd put it. Instead he put *Toy Story* into the DVD player, and when that was over, gave me hot chocolate and plopped the first Harry Potter book onto my lap and told me to read.

Sid did not end up spending the next night at FAD because my schedule was totally derailed. Before he could get me to bed, Officer Buchanan called to tell me that I needed to come to the station to give a statement. When I protested that I had a class to teach, she assured me that she'd already spoken to Professor Waldron, who'd called to find out what was going on with Owen.

So Waldron already knew not to expect me on campus and had said she'd make sure my class was covered.

Since that meant I was going to get to sleep late, Sid and I really indulged ourselves and watched another movie. Then we planned how I could work around the truth in my statement to the police.

It turned out not to be overly difficult. Once I switched from "Sid told me not to drink the coffee" to "I took a sip and it tasted funny" and from "Sid filmed Owen being nefarious" to "I propped my phone up to film Owen being nefarious," the rest was pretty much the truth. Officer Buchanan still seemed vaguely suspicious of me, but I was starting to think that that was her permanent state. She didn't mention Kelly at all, so I didn't either.

When I left the police station, I found a voicemail from Professor Waldron, requesting that I come meet with her as soon as possible. I should have realized she would want to talk with me—maybe I'd been even more shaken than Sid had thought.

I called her back, and she requested my presence on campus for an immediate conference. I wasn't thrilled by the idea, but I agreed, pausing only to text Sid where I was going. I'd hoped it would be a brief stop, but it ended up being a couple of hours before I got back home. Sid was waiting for me at the door, and I was pretty sure he'd been pacing.

"Coccyx, Georgia, where have you been?"

"I texted you that I had to go see Professor Waldron."

"I didn't expect you to be gone so long. You know I don't want you on campus alone with a murderer on the loose."

"You don't have to worry—I was nowhere near the English wing. Professor Waldron had me come straight to the administration building. I barely remembered where it was—I don't think I've stepped foot in it since my first day here."

"What happened?"

"Not only were Professor Waldron and the dean waiting for me, but they had the college lawyer, too."

"Whoa! What did they want?"

"The dean wanted to know what happened, Professor Waldron wanted to make sure that I was okay, and the lawyer wanted to make sure I'm not planning to sue FAD."

"Why would you sue FAD?"

"For money, presumably. Some people will sue at the drop of a hat. Anyway, I told them that I'm fine and that I don't hold FAD responsible."

"And it took that much time?"

"No, the part that took that much time was the lawyer trying to talk me into signing an agreement he just happened to have handy. It absolved FAD of any wrongdoing since the dawn of time, including—but not limited to—the death of the dinosaurs, the destruction of the Library of Alexandria, the sinking of the *Titanic*, and the canceling of the TV show *Firefly*."

"Seriously?"

"Not entirely," I admitted, "but it was definitely too vague for my taste, so I told them I saw no reason to sign. The dean tried to convince me delicately and the lawyer was less delicate, but I just wasn't interested. I mean, I'm not going to sue, but..."

"But what?"

"When I came to FAD, I had to sign a contract, and that same lawyer kept me sitting in his waiting room for an hour that day! Even though I had an appointment and showed up early. So no, I'm not signing his agreement. It's payback time."

"Good for you," he said approvingly. "Did you tell them you don't think Owen is the art thief?"

"Nope. It didn't come up."

"Good—we don't need any interference. But why didn't you mention it? I mean, you do have a tendency to tell people more than you need to."

"I do not! And especially not with a lawyer around. I think he'd have fainted if I'd brought up the concept of Owen having done anything else that might bring down legal ramifications upon FAD. I thought about talking to Professor Waldron about it afterward, but she stayed in the dean's office after I was dismissed, so I didn't get a chance."

"Okay. Then we're back on track for getting the dirt on Dr. Dahna, the real killer. Shall we lay a few plans?" He rubbed his hands together eagerly, if not quietly.

"Later. First, I want something to eat. And then I better get on the phone to Pennycross. You know how the academic grapevine works. If my parents haven't already heard about Owen, they will soon, and I want them to hear it from me first."

Eating went fairly quickly, but explaining what had happened to my parents; my sister, Deborah; and Madison took quite a while. Once that was done, Sid was ready and raring to plot. We spent the rest of the evening going over plans and contingency plans for how he'd get into Dahna's office.

CHAPTER THIRTY-EIGHT

Friday morning, I once again wheeled a Sid-filled suitcase into school. He had his phone in with him, with texting, e-mail, and camera apps to use in his evidence collecting mission. He also had a flashlight, a thumb drive, a pocket knife, a pad and pencil, and his lock pick set. He wasn't happy that all of it was tucked into my black satin evening bag for convenient carrying, but options at the bungalow were limited, and the bag was the right size and had a shoulder strap. I'd promised to get him something more appropriate the first chance I got.

Since I had no classes to teach and was still in avoid-Dahna mode, I didn't show up until right before my shift at the Writing Lab so as to keep opportunities for encounters at a minimum. I had a full slate of students, and if any of them had heard rumors about Wednesday's events, they were either too polite to bring it up or just not interested in the goings-on of instructors. So we stayed on topic the whole time.

But the minute my last appointment ended and the student walked out, Caroline popped in.

"Got you!" she said. "Don't you ever check your e-mail?"

"Sorry." I had seen her increasingly strident e-mails the night before, but after the cops, the administration, and my family, I just hadn't had it in me to go through the story again. "I just got the okay from the legal department to talk about it late yesterday." Actually, the agreement I had avoided signing had included a gag order, but obviously I didn't care about that.

"Then come join us for lunch."

"Who is *us*?"

"Me and Renee."

"Okay, sure." I could manage lunch as long as I didn't have to face Dahna. "Just let me drop off my stuff in my office."

Caroline walked with me, apparently unwilling to risk my getting away without sharing the dirt, and was so intent on that she didn't even comment on why I was wheeling around a suitcase.

Caroline said Renee had already gone to The Artist's Palette to make sure we got a good table, and when we arrived, we spotted her waving from a corner booth. Evidently her curiosity about my misadventure had pushed aside her competitive, tenure-focused instincts. She'd already gotten food from the serving line, and Caroline insisted on treating me to the club sandwich and salad I picked out.

"Sure you want coffee?" Renee said with a grin. "It could be drugged."

"Renee," Caroline said in an appalled tone.

I sighed but said, "It's okay. I know you guys want to hear about what happened. I would, too, in your place."

"Eat first," Caroline said, and I decided it would be impolite to disobey. Besides, I was hungry.

As soon as I'd finished, I repeated the story once again, though with more profanity than I'd used with the police or college administration. "Is that what you guys had heard?"

"Pretty much," Caroline said. "Except for the part about Owen pouring booze over you while you were pretending to be passed out."

"I heard it wasn't booze," Renee said with a wrinkled nose.

It took a minute for that to sink it. "Oh, yuck. There's no way I'd have been able to stay in character if he'd done either of those."

"I bet he would have if he'd thought of it," Caroline said. "What a slimeball! Did you know he's been suspended until the formal outcome of the investigation? Without pay!"

"Professor Waldron said something about that yesterday. What are they going to do about his classes?"

Caroline looked a bit embarrassed, but Renee was matter-of-fact when she said, "Dahna, Caroline, and I are each taking over one, and somebody at Montserrat is going to handle his online classes."

"We'd have checked with you first," Caroline said, "but we thought it might be a little awkward for you to be teaching one of Owen's classes, under the circumstances."

"Maybe more than a little." If Owen's students had any fondness for him, they might not be entirely happy with me.

"Besides, we can use the brownie points," Renee went on. "You're already way ahead on that score, what with catching a scumbucket in action."

"I didn't think of it that way. I'd really rather get the job on my own merits."

"Don't listen to Renee," Caroline said. "If you get tenure, it'll be because you're an extremely qualified candidate, not just because you caught an art thief."

"Actually, I'm not so sure I did catch an art thief. Owen hasn't admitted to any of that, has he?"

"Not that I know of—I just assumed."

"And I've never seen any signs of him having more money than he should."

"He sure doesn't spend it on his clothes," Caroline quipped. "Did he dress like a bad Western hero when you dated him, Georgia?"

"Oh, it's totally him," Renee said. "They found a student's sketchbook in his office—had her name in it and everything. He was probably scoping it out for more designs to steal."

"Color me relieved. I'd hate to think we had more than one scumbucket on campus," Caroline said.

The conversation drifted into other directions after that: Renee's wedding plans and the perennial favorite of complaining and/or bragging about students. I think I managed to keep up my end, but my heart wasn't in it. I was too busy trying to decide if I'd caught an art thief—and murderer—almost by accident.

Chapter Thirty-Nine

Sid had no such doubts. I'd gone back to my office after lunch and found him at my desk reading, and I explained what Renee had told me.

"But Sid, if that sketchbook is the one Marissa left with Kelly, then doesn't it mean that Owen took it after killing her? And drugging her, drugging me... You think it was a coincidence?"

"One," he said, raising one finger bone. Being Sid, he literally popped it off and held it up. "If that's Marissa's sketchbook, then the real killer could easily have planted it in Owen's office." He put the finger bone on the desk and pulled off a second. "Two, drugging people is hardly an original method." He put the second finger down. "Three, we know Owen never worked at three of the schools where Scarlet Letter stole designs." Third finger on the desk. "Four, the real killer must have been at all five. And by 'real killer,' I mean Dahna because she's the only adjunct that fits the bill." Another finger down. "And five, I have a hunch and my hunches are never wrong." He picked up the handful of fingers, tossed it into the air, and let them re-form to give himself a high five.

"Are you really that sure?"

"Maybe not a hundred percent, but enough so that I'm not giving in yet. And this could all work in our favor. If everybody assumes Owen is the thief, then Dahna is going to let her guard down because she'll think she's safe. It's the perfect night to search her office."

"Or maybe she'll decide that she's dodged a bullet by having Owen handy to blame, and she'll give up theft and murder."

"Then she'll have to get rid of the evidence soon, so it's the perfect night to search her office."

"I'm guessing that you still want to search her office tonight?"

"You can bet your tailbone I do!"

No students showed up for office hours, which was fine with me. I kept going over the evidence in my head, looking for where we could have gone wrong. Since there were all kinds of places we could have gone wrong, that kept me busy most of the afternoon. It didn't help when Marissa texted to say that she'd gotten her sketchbook back—hers was definitely the one found in Owen's office. I was glad that she'd recovered it, of course, but it was plain from her texts that she, too, thought Owen was the thief. That only gave me fresh ammunition for dithering.

I ended up staying considerably later than I usually did, and even with my office door closed, I could tell the English wing was emptying out for the weekend.

"Georgia, why aren't you going home?" Sid finally asked.

"Hmm… Oh, it is late, isn't it?"

"Wow, so convincing. Go home."

"You know, I was thinking that I could just stay with you for the search."

"No! If Dahna catches you, it could be dangerous, and if security catches you, you could be arrested and will almost certainly lose your shot at tenure. If Dahna catches me, I'll collapse and nobody would believe her. If security catches me, I'll collapse and nobody will believe them. Go home."

"But I could stay here in the office while you search."

"Or you could go home so nobody spots your car in the parking lot and wonders why you're still here."

"But—"

"No buts. And in my case, that's literal." He tapped the back of his flesh-free pelvis. "Georgia, the problem is that you're doubting yourself."

"Always."

"Then you have got to learn to trust your gut."

"My gut is tied up in knots."

"Well, trust my gut, and mine says it's Dahna."

"Sid, you don't—"

"I don't what?" he said ominously.

I swallowed my intended comment about his lack of a gut. "You don't understand how nervous I am about leaving you here alone."

"I'll be perfectly safe. I'll wait here until I'm sure nobody is around, and I'll text you as soon as I find out anything. Go home."

"I'm going." Admittedly, I didn't go swiftly, but I did pack up and leave only after confirming our plans one more time. Well, maybe one and a half because I think I repeated some parts.

But eventually I was wearing my coat and winterizing accessories, had left Sid in my office, and was halfway to the exit when I heard somebody call my name. I turned around to see Dahna coming toward me.

Given the acid rush of fear that shot through me, apparently my gut agreed with Sid after all. The only reason I resisted the impulse to scream and flee was because I didn't want her to chase me, and I was pretty sure she was smart enough to interpret "scream and flee" as a sign that I'd figured out she was the killer.

"Hi, Dahna," I said, trying to sound normal. "What's up?"

"I was just finishing up at the Writing Lab and realized we'd never discussed staffing it from now on. With Owen... gone, it will be more difficult."

"Oh, I never even thought about that."

"I am not surprised. It must have been a frightening experience. You are very clever to have thwarted him."

"I was mostly lucky," I said. "And you're right, we need to work out staffing the Writing Lab, but can it wait until next week? I'm on my way out, and we should bring the rest of the department in on the discussion."

"Of course. I just thought that you should have the first choice of the extra hours since we other adjuncts are taking over Owen's classes."

"I heard, and it was the right decision, but we should all have a shot at the extra Lab hours."

"You are very gracious. Perhaps Professor Waldron will want to call another meeting on Monday."

"That's a great idea—why don't you suggest it to her? Just let me know about the timing, and I'll see you then." I had to turn my back on her to walk toward the door, and it wasn't easy, especially not when I could see her reflection in the glass door in front of me. It looked as if she watched me the whole time, but at least she stayed put instead of pursuing me with an ax. I didn't really relax until I got outside, and even then I looked behind me to ensure that she hadn't followed.

It was already full dark, and the sky was clear the way it only is when the weather is extra frigid. I walked quickly both from excitement and because I wanted out of the cold. I should have been more careful, Sid pointed out later, but in my defense, I was sure that Dahna couldn't be anywhere near me. So I wasn't paying particular attention when I turned the corner to go to my minivan.

Just for a second I sensed that somebody was behind me. Then I saw stars brighter than those above, and an instant later, felt the pain from the blow to my head before sinking into the snow.

CHAPTER FORTY

I woke up cold. Not just the-covers-slipped-off-during-the-night or the-heat-is-set-too-low chilly, but draining, painful cold. I was shivering so hard it took a while for me to realize that I wasn't in my bed at the bungalow. I didn't know where I was. It was so dark I wasn't even sure my eyes were open at first. I was lying on my side on something hard, and my head hurt so much it took me a while to notice that my hands and feet were bound.

At least my hands were tied in front of me so I could feel around enough to be fairly sure that I'd been left on rough concrete, and it was inside...somewhere. Unfortunately, it was somewhere without heat.

I know what it can mean when a woman wakes up in a place she doesn't remember going. So as best I could, I checked to make sure all my clothes were intact. When I'd verified that I was still wearing jeans, long underwear, flannel shirt, sweatshirt, and all the usual undergarments, I breathed a bit more easily. I just wished I had my coat, hat, and gloves, too. A pillow and blanket would have been welcome, too.

With that off my mind, I tried to untie my feet, which would probably have been possible if my hands hadn't been nearly numb from the cold. Chewing on the rope binding my hands didn't do a thing, either. I abandoned the effort and twisted around in hopes of seeing something.

Though the room was inky dark, I spotted a tiny line of light along the floor a few feet away. I hoped that meant it was a door, and I started scooting my way in that direction. I'd hoped to lever myself upright somehow once I got there, but my ankles were tied too tightly for that to happen. The best I could do was to get up on my knees, which got me high enough to reach the knob, but of course it only moved a fraction of an inch. There was a rattling, and I decided it was chained shut from the outside.

I lay back down and put my face right up to the crack in the door. "Hello! Is anybody out there?" There was no response. "HELLO! I'm stuck in here." Nothing. I continued to yell until my throat started to hurt, but nobody came. Then I rolled over onto my back and used my feet to pound against the door. Still nothing.

The walls on either side of the door felt like ridged, bare metal, frigid enough that it almost hurt to touch. Hadn't I seen university storage buildings with corrugated walls? Did that mean I was still on campus? I switched to kicking the wall for a while, which made a cacophony of sounds, but nobody came and it made my head ache more.

I hated to leave my one area of light, but I was going to have to find another way to get somebody's attention. The kicking had warmed me up some, but not enough, and I was far from certain that I could make it through a whole night of below-freezing temperatures. Plus there was the off chance that I'd find something useful that I might use to cut myself free. So I started wriggling like an inchworm well past its prime and aimed for what I thought was the center of the room. At some point, I ran into a pile of something in bags. From the smell, I was guessing it was something landscape-related—grass seed maybe or fertilizer—but whatever it was, it wasn't going to help me.

I managed to crawl on top of the sacks, thinking that they'd be a little warmer than the concrete, and I was still trying to convince myself that it was working when I heard a noise at the door. It opened, and I had just a second of seeing distant streetlights when somebody shone a flashlight in my face.

"Look who's awake," a familiar voice said.

"Renee?" I said. "How did you find me?"

"Easily. This is where I left you. Though obviously I should have hit you harder."

Coccyx! I wasn't being rescued after all. "HELP! HELP! HELP!"

"Oh, shut up! The campus is closed down for the night, so there's nobody to hear you anyway."

"Why are you doing this?" I asked, still trying to see past the light in my eyes.

"I'll pass on the explanatory monologue if you don't mind. And don't try anything stupid. I've got a gun."

Renee? How had Sid and I gone so far wrong? She'd only taught at two of the schools involved. "You're Scarlet Letter?"

She moved enough that I could see the pistol in her hand and aimed the flashlight at my hands and feet. "At least the knots held."

"She's awake," another voice said, and Dahna stepped inside. "You said you knocked her out."

"Next time, you do the dirty work," Renee snapped.

"You're the one with experience with violence," Dahna shot back.

"Whereas an art thief is such a law-abiding citizen?"

"Better to be a plagiarist than a murderer."

"At least I had the balls to do what I had to. I didn't drag innocent people into my mess."

"What innocent people? Certainly not you."

"I'm talking about Jeremy. You know damned well he had no idea what you were up to."

"Is that what he told you? And you believed him?"

"My fiancé doesn't lie to me!"

I had a vague idea that as long as they were fighting with one another, I would be better off staying quiet. Plus I was confused enough that I had nothing to say anyway. If I was interpreting their sniping correctly, Dahna really was the art thief, but Renee had killed Kelly. And Jeremy was involved, too, somehow. Or maybe whoever had hit me had scrambled my brains.

Dahna and Renee glared at one another, but Dahna was the

one to relent, possibly because of Renee's weapon. She said, "It is of no possible difference now. What are we to do with Georgia?"

"I think the answer is simple. If she lives, all three of us go to prison."

"People do not get sent to prison for plagiarism. I had nothing to do with Kelly's murder, and I suspect Jeremy did not either."

"And I had nothing to do with your art theft, but at this point, we're all accessories to everything. If not in the eyes of the law, then in the court of public opinion. Are you ready to lose your job? To abandon your life's work?"

"No, but…"

"I'm not, either, and I'm not throwing away Jeremy's chance at tenure. Why do you think I took care of Kelly in the first place?"

"I will never understand why you had to do that. She would never have caught me or Jeremy."

"Georgia almost did—Kelly would have sooner or later."

"I do not think that's true. Kelly had no idea, and Georgia wouldn't have even gotten involved if Kelly hadn't died."

"How was I supposed to know Georgia was terminally nosy?" Renee gave me a look. "Emphasis on terminal."

"This is not a joke!"

"No, but the way you're acting is. Stop playing Hamlet. You knew exactly how this was going to end as soon as I told you Georgia didn't believe Owen was the art thief. Once she's gone, we can move on with our lives. Jeremy gets tenure, and if we're lucky, you or I do, too. I get married and take care of my dogs, and you can keep stealing art. Just keep Jeremy out of it from now on out. All we have to do is get rid of Dr. Nosy here."

"Georgia has a daughter. The girl will be an orphan."

"That's not my problem. The kid will be grown in a couple of years, anyway. Until then, her grandparents can keep her. She'll be fine."

Dahna hesitated. I held my breath, hoping that she was going to balk, reject Renee's plan, and save me. But what she said was, "How shall we do it?"

That was my cue to start yelling again, though I didn't expect it to do much good. It didn't. They had me gagged with Dahna's scarf in seconds, and continued their discussion as if I hadn't screamed.

Renee said, "I'd really like it to be an accident, but that's not going to fly again. The cops are going to be suspicious enough after how that idiot Owen muffed it. If he hadn't let Georgia see him drugging her coffee, she'd be out of our hair already. Nobody would have believed anything she said if they thought she was a lush."

That explained how Owen had come up with his plot. Now that I considered it, it had been uncharacteristically devious for him.

"How did you convince him to help us?" Dahna wanted to know.

"He doesn't know anything about us. He just wanted to get back at Georgia. All I had to do was act sympathetic and listen to him whine about how she'd done him wrong. Then I made up a story about how a guy I knew had gotten his revenge on a colleague, and pointed out that the plan would work perfectly in his case, too. He did the rest." She went on. "Anyway, I was thinking about faking a robbery. That bungalow she's staying in is plenty isolated. We'll take her laptop—which we should do anyway, just in case she's got anything incriminating on it—and anything else she might have that's worth stealing. Tie her up, kill her, and get out of there. With luck, she won't be found for days. Or maybe we could set a fire."

"What about her car? We should not leave it here."

"We'll use it to take her to the bungalow. I'll follow in my car—I'm parked right next to her."

They went on to discuss myriad details like keeping gloves on; disposing of the property they were going to steal; and whether they should shoot, bludgeon, or stab me. I could see why Renee had been so successful in killing Kelly. She wasn't the type to leave anything to chance.

The mention of my van reminded me that Sid was still in my office, waiting for his chance to search Dahna's office. Or maybe he was already searching it. I didn't know how long I'd been unconscious.

I tuned back in when Renee said, "You untie her. And Georgia, don't try anything stupid. I've still got a gun."

By that point, I couldn't have done much if I'd wanted to. My ankles had been bound so tightly for so long that they were nearly without sensation, and my legs weren't much better. Renee had used some sort of nylon cord to tie me up, and she had to loan Dahna an uncomfortably large knife to cut me loose. Unfortunately, she left my hands bound.

"I will help you get up," Dahna said.

I shook my head.

"Do not be stubborn, Georgia."

I wasn't being stubborn—between stiffness and returning circulation, my legs weren't up to the job, which she realized as soon as she tried to get me upright.

"Her legs must be asleep," she said.

"Then you're going to have to carry her," Renee said.

Dahna made a face. "Where is her coat?"

"Back there with her purse and other stuff," Renee said, gesturing with her gun.

For some reason, that made me angrier than their calm discussion about how to kill me. I understood why Renee had taken my satchel. Like most women, I carried a wide assortment of useful objects, and of course, my phone was in there. But once she'd searched my pockets, there was no reason to take my coat. That was tantamount to torture, and finding out that it had been in the building with me the whole time only made it worse. Had I been able to move properly, that gun might not have stopped me from going after her.

Dahna handed my satchel to Renee, then put my coat around my shoulders and buttoned it so it would stay on before helping me stand up. By that time I was able to stumble forward with her support. Renee waved us ahead, and followed, no doubt with the gun aimed right at my unprotected back. On the good side, Dahna was so focused on helping me walk that she didn't notice that the scarf they'd used to gag me had slipped down and a discreet tug pulled it the rest of the way off. I wasn't going to start calling for help yet, but I would be ready if I got the chance.

They'd stashed me in some sort of storage building in an isolated corner of the FAD campus, far away from any dorms where students might be looking out the windows, and apparently security didn't bother with it, either. Maybe it was the time of night. I still hadn't seen a clock, but it felt like midnight. Or maybe it was too raw out for the guards to care—it was snowing again and the wind was blowing it right into my mostly unbuttoned coat. Our progress was slow, which was fine with me, but Renee was getting impatient and there was a limit to how much I was willing to risk being shot.

We turned a corner toward where I'd parked that morning. My minivan and Renee's car were the only vehicles in the lot. At least, I'm pretty sure it was my minivan—I couldn't speak for the lump next to mine.

"What has happened?" Dahna said.

"Why are you stopping?" Renee came up beside us, and then she, too, stared.

The cars were covered in snow. No, not just covered. Buried, from tire to hood level, with more snow blown against the windows. There was just barely enough of the roofs showing to tell which car was which.

"What did you do?" Renee demanded, shoving me.

I almost answered before remembering I was supposed to be gagged, so I just grunted my ignorance.

"I don't understand," Dahna said. "There was some snow this afternoon but not enough to do this. Even a snowplow wouldn't—"

"Shut up! I don't know what's going on, but we've got to get out of here. Where's your car?"

"On the other side of the English wing."

"Come on!" Renee shoved both of us this time, and once we were moving, cursed freely at our slowness. This time I was actively stalling. I could only think of one way my van could have been buried. Or rather, only one person who would have buried it.

Renee kept pushing and prodding as we went, but as we turned the corner, we saw another snowy mound in the middle of that parking lot. "Oh no!" Dahna moaned. "My car as well."

"We've got to dig one of these cars out!" Renee said. "Have you got a shovel in your trunk?"

Dahna shook her head, and Renee cursed Jeremy, who apparently had broken hers and not replaced it. "I bet Georgia has one." She started pulling us back to the other lot.

Then we heard something. At first I thought it was a car, and I was about to try to break free and yell for help at last, but it was the wrong kind of engine. A few seconds later, it came into view. It was a snowblower, the kind that attaches to a lawn tractor.

I later read that eight miles an hour is considered speedy for a snowblower, and I doubted this one was going that fast, but it seemed to zoom toward us, headlights illuminating the snow it was throwing like icy diamonds. Dahna and Renee just stared at it at first, then tried to run away, still dragging me along.

Dahna tripped and fell, and I went down on top of her, digging my knees into her back as hard as I could to pin her to the ground. Renee turned to grab me, but I screamed out, "HELP! SHE'S GOT A GUN!"

I thought Renee was going to shoot me, and she did, too, but the tractor was overtaking us too quickly and she took off running.

The tractor slowed as it reached me, but I yelled, "I'm good! Get her!" It sped up again, and the chase was on.

Renee was making a mad dash to escape, but the footing was treacherous, and more than once she went down only to pop back up again. In the meantime, the tractor was slowly gaining on her, and finally she turned and aimed her gun at the driver.

The tractor braked, and the driver stepped off and went toward her.

"Stay right there! Stop!" she yelled.

The driver ignored her.

There were gunshots, spaced too closely together for me to count, but she soon ran out of ammunition. The driver stopped just a few feet from where Renee was still pulling the trigger, slowly pulled down his hood, peeled off a ski mask, and let it fall to the ground.

Even from a distance, I could tell Renee had drawn in breath as if to scream, but instead she slid to the ground in a dead faint.

The driver turned, and of course it was Sid, but the expression on his skull was like nothing I'd ever seen before. I almost recoiled myself, but the fury was gone in a second, and it was Sid's smiling face again. He grabbed the gun and my satchel from Renee, and trotted toward us.

"Are you okay?" he asked.

"I'm fine."

"Who is that?" Dahna said and twisted under me. I pushed harder to keep her face to the snowy ground.

"Are you all right?" I asked Sid.

"I think she nicked a rib, but chicks dig guys with scars. Let's get you untied."

"Renee's got a knife you can use."

"She's lucky I don't use it on her," he said, with just a shadow of his previous intensity. He started back in her direction, but the sound of sirens sliced through the night. Somebody must have heard the gunshots.

"Go!" I said, and Sid dropped my bag and Renee's gun and ran for it.

It was a few minutes before the police reached us, and I wasn't overly surprised to see Officer Buchanan leading the pack. They got me off of Dahna, who was still cowering on the ground, cut me free, and cuffed her. After that I lost track of exactly what was happening in the incredible confusion as the combination of relief, adrenaline crash, cold, and bone-tiredness caught up with me. I started to wobble, and two police officers had to stop me from keeling over.

"I better get Dr. Thackery inside," Officer Buchanan said. "And somebody can take Doctors Turner and Kaleka to the station."

Renee was stonily maintaining her right to silence, but Dahna resisted the officer taking her away long enough to say, "Georgia, you must tell them. I am not a killer. It was Renee who killed Kelly. You must tell them."

I just glared at her. "Would you have cried at my funeral the way you did at Kelly's?"

She just stared at me.

"Get that ossifying piece of sacrum out of my sight," I said and turned my back on her.

CHAPTER FORTY-ONE

Officer Buchanan insisted I get into the ambulance that had shown up to go get checked out at the hospital, and since my head was pounding, I didn't argue with her. The EMTs were all business, and so were the people at the emergency room, but I could tell that there was a lot of gossip about the case going on behind the curtains surrounding my bed. A doctor quickly determined that while I had a mild concussion, no stitches would be required for the big goose egg on my head. My wrists and ankles were rubbed raw and I had a wide variety of bruises, but there was no sign of frostbite or any other permanent damage from being in an unheated building for so long. The combination of pain meds and finally feeling warm again, thanks to a heated blanket, put me to sleep almost before the doctor finished her diagnosis. I woke briefly as I was being moved from the ER to a regular room, and at various points when nurses came in during the night, but by the time I woke up all the way, it was daylight.

Mr. Perkins was sitting in a chair next to my bed, reading.

"Good morning, Dr. Thackery," he said cheerfully.

"Good morning," I responded automatically.

"I hope you don't mind my being here, but Professor Waldron had a commitment she had to keep and tasked me with making sure that you were recovering from your ordeal."

"That's very kind of you."

"Not at all. Is there anything you need?"

"Is my phone handy?"

"Of course." He handed me my satchel and added, "I believe it is in here. I heard several alert buzzes from it earlier."

I'd received a slew of messages from Sid from before he rescued me. He'd started texting about an hour after I was attacked to see if I'd made it home okay, and had kept doing so with increasing urgency. The last text said that he was coming to look for me. He hadn't texted again since. I told myself it only meant that he'd left his phone somewhere or he'd run the battery down, and there was nothing to worry about. Unfortunately, I didn't entirely convince myself.

"Is there anything else?"

"I do need to go to the restroom, but..."

"For that, I shall summon a nurse." He stepped out, and though I expected to have to wait for attention, a nurse arrived promptly to help me get up and go to the bathroom. I was stiff and a little sore, but otherwise fine, and the nurse promised to rustle up something for me to eat, which sounded better than any medicine at that point.

Mr. Perkins returned once I was back in bed and decently covered, and wonder of wonders, he had a cup of coffee for me. "Black, if I remember correctly."

"Mr. Perkins, you are the best department secretary at FAD." I took a sip and added, "In fact, you're the best department secretary of any college in the United States."

He allowed himself a smile of satisfaction.

"I understand you're waiting for breakfast," he said, "but if you're up to it, I would appreciate an explanation of last night's events. Professor Waldron is most anxious to hear."

"I wouldn't mind hearing more of that story myself," said Officer Buchanan, who'd opened my door without knocking or making any noise whatsoever. Now that she knew I hadn't killed Kelly, I shouldn't have been bothered by that, but I still found the woman uncanny.

To give myself a chance to weigh whether or not I should hold anything back other than the obvious Sid-related bits, I took a big sip of coffee, but by the time I swallowed, I'd decided to be frank and open. Mostly.

I started with learning about Kelly's investigation, which I attributed to finding the pictures in the file combined with conversations with Indigo and Marissa. Officer Buchanan wanted to know why I hadn't come to her.

"One, I had no proof and didn't know who the art thief was. Two, I didn't want to hurt FAD's reputation until I was sure somebody on campus was involved. And three, I had the distinct impression that you suspected me of killing Kelly and would have considered anything I said to be dubious."

She chuckled. "Well, I did believe some of your answers about the night you found Ms. Griffith's body were less than forthcoming, but people lie to the police all the time for all kinds of reasons, most of which aren't criminal. Just in case, I checked you out with my colleagues in Pennycross, and they said your family is pretty respectable and they'd be mighty surprised if you were doing anything like killing anybody. In fact, a Sergeant Raymond said you had a habit of stumbling onto crimes, which you then solved. I thought if I made you nervous enough, you might do the same here."

"Excuse me? You sent me after a killer?" I was going to give my sister an earful about her boyfriend Louis Raymond telling tales on me, too.

"It seems to me that you made your own decisions and went into it with your eyes open."

"Well, maybe. But if you were so sure that Kelly was murdered, why didn't you investigate yourself?"

"I had my reasons."

"No, no, you do not get to be enigmatic and mysterious anymore."

She chuckled again, but it was more rueful this time. "Fair enough. The fact is, I felt like there was something about that accident that didn't ring true, but I couldn't put my finger on what it was, and my chief didn't buy it. I even told him about Kelly's investigation, but he just didn't see how stolen pictures could lead to murder."

"Wait, you knew about the art theft?"

"Not the details, but that she was investigating. You remember Kelly and I lived in the same apartment complex? When she got started with this mess, she came to me for advice, but I had to tell her that even if stealing designs was against the law, it wasn't really a police matter the way stealing an actual painting would be. Once she found evidence of the plagiarism, the victim could take it to court and sue for infringement, but unless somebody stole a physical object, there wasn't much I could do."

"And you didn't think that had anything to do with her death?"

"Of course I did. Which is what I told my chief, but there wasn't the first shred of evidence that Kelly's death was anything but an accident. I wasn't lying when I said I was waiting for the blood test results. Which have returned, by the way. Nothing showed in the standard tox screen, but after that character Deen tried to drug you with GHB, I had them test for that and a few other nasties, and sure enough, Kelly had been drugged. Now, you go on and tell me how you figured out who it was."

My breakfast arrived, so the rest of my story was punctuated with bites of cheese omelet, fresh fruit, and toast. I was glad of it, because as I got closer to the end, it got harder to avoid mentioning my sleuthing partner, and I needed the extra time to think.

I started by explaining why I started looking at my fellow adjuncts. "The name 'Scarlet Letter' was the clue. FAD treats us adjuncts pretty well—"

Mr. Perkins cleared his throat.

"In fact," I said, "they treat us better than any place I've ever worked. If they'd give us enough hours to qualify for benefits, it would be just about perfect." He could clear his throat about that all he wanted. "It's different at a lot of other schools. I've been at some where the tenured professors barely acknowledged our existence, and—" I stopped. "Sorry, it's a sore spot, and not really relevant right now. The point is, I remembered a school where my parking pass was marked with a big red A."

"A scarlet letter," Officer Buchanan said.

"Or A for adjunct." I explained Sid's spreadsheet magic as if it'd been my own doing. "It turned out that the only adjunct who'd been at all five schools was Dahna. So she had to be the thief."

"But not the killer?" Officer Buchanan said.

"That's right, though I didn't know that then. I'd been assuming they were one and the same, but the pieces didn't fit together quite the way I'd expected. As far as I can tell from things Renee and Dahna said last night, Dahna got the idea to steal T-shirt designs when she was dating Jeremy and went to him to get help with graphics. When they broke up, they stayed partners in the plagiarism business, even after he and Renee got engaged."

Officer Buchanan said, "Dr. Turner is pretty insistent that her fiancé never knew that the design ideas Dahna brought to him were stolen."

"I think she's fooling herself. Maybe Jeremy didn't know at first, but the later Scarlet Letter designs were so close to the originals that it's hard for me to believe that he never saw them, no matter what he told Renee. At any rate, Renee heard the gossip about Kelly investigating art theft, and realized that Jeremy could lose his job. When it was just an adjunct job, she was willing to accept that he and Dahna were hiding their tracks. But then tenure for Jeremy came into the equation, and an opportunity like that was too valuable to risk. So Kelly had to go."

"She says her fiancé didn't know about that, either."

"That I'm willing to believe. From the way we—" I faked a cough and took a swallow of orange juice. "From the way I worked out the murder, Renee could have handled it all by herself." I explained how Sid and I thought it had been done.

"So you had the method and the motive, and thought you had the killer. Why didn't you call me then?"

"Because there was still no proof. Then the stuff with Owen happened, and I wasn't so sure anymore. It took a while for me to convince myself that Owen wasn't the thief and unfortunately, I let that slip in front of Renee. So she decided she had to take care of me, too, and convinced Dahna to help her. I don't know if Dahna realized that Renee intended to kill Kelly, but I'm sure she figured it out afterward." Which explained her unexpected tears at the memorial service—it had been guilt, not sorrow. "And of course, she was perfectly willing to kill me."

"But somebody rescued you last night. Any idea of who that could have been?"

"He was on a school snowblower, wasn't he? I thought he was part of the maintenance staff."

"No, the maintenance people have all been accounted for, and the shed where the snowblower was stored had been broken into."

"Then maybe a student pulling some sort of prank. The cars in the parking lot were all buried in snow, you know."

"We saw that, and we thought of a student, but nobody's come forward. And you didn't get a good look at the guy?"

"No, I never saw his face. What did Renee say?"

"She said it was somebody wearing a ski mask, with a skull mask under that."

"It must have been a good one to make her faint like that," I said with a hint of malice. I'd really enjoyed seeing Renee pass out. "All I know is that the guy took off right about the time we heard the sirens—I never even got a chance to thank him."

"And I'm guessing that even if you did know which student it was, you wouldn't want to get him into trouble anyway, under the circumstances."

"Well, he had just saved my life."

Officer Buchanan and Mr. Perkins both wanted me to elaborate on a few things, which I was willing to do. I thought I was doing a good job hiding the fact that I had a partner until the very end.

"That seems to cover everything," Officer Buchanan said as she put her pad away. "There's just one little detail. I know doggoned well that somebody has been at that bungalow with you. I've seen movement in there during the day and way more tracks in the snow than one person would leave."

"Then you're the one who's been spying on me! We—" I faked another cough that fooled nobody. "I was scared to death when I saw your footprints. Isn't that trespassing?"

"As it happens, the folks who own the place asked me to keep an eye on the place over the winter, so that's what I've been doing."

"That was before I moved in."

"That's true, but the Benstommes never got around to calling and asking me *not* to keep an eye out."

Coccyx, she was tricky.

"So I'm asking again," she said, "and I realize it's not really any of my business, but I would like to know. Who's been out there with you?"

I was trying to choose between lying—knowing that I'd probably be found out—and refusing to answer—knowing that she wouldn't rest until she got an answer. Help came from an entirely unexpected quarter.

"It was me," Mr. Perkins said.

We turned to him in surprise and confusion—Officer Buchanan was surprised and I was sure as sacrum confused.

"I appreciate Dr. Thackery's—Georgia's discretion," he went on, "but there's no reason to be reticent about our relationship under these circumstances."

"Your relationship?" Officer Buchanan said.

He reached over and put his hand on top of mine. "Yes, our relationship."

I nodded but couldn't think of a single word to say.

"Then you've been together…"

"Since February," Mr. Perkins said. "Valentine's Day, in fact." He actually squeezed my hand.

"He brought me chocolates and roses," I said, thinking I should offer details of my own to add verisimilitude. I thought his first name was Justin, but if I was wrong… "He's very romantic."

Officer Buchanan didn't look completely convinced, but after a moment she shrugged and said, "Okay, then. That clears up a lot. I just wish you two had told me sooner."

"We've kept it quiet because we were concerned people would be worried about favoritism, given my role in the department and the fact that a tenured position is open."

"And people around FAD gossip so," I said. "We wanted to keep it private."

"Okay, no law against that," she said with an air of finality. "I'll let you know if I have any more questions."

"We'll be happy to help in any way we can," Mr. Perkins said.

The two of us continued to beam like lovebirds until she was well out of eyesight, then Mr. Perkins swiftly pulled his hand away.

"That should keep her off your back," he said smugly.

"I don't know what to say."

"No need to say anything. We all have our secrets. You have kept mine, and if you have one you wish kept, I am more than happy to assist."

"But what—?"

He lowered his voice to a husky whisper I never would have suspected him to be capable of and half-sang, *"Don't you want to play a glitter game?"* Then he cocked his head to one side, looked at me from under his surprisingly lush eyelashes, and puckered his lips.

I flashed back to the pictures Sid had shown me from the fan site for Pteriwinkle Gleam. Mr. Perkins wasn't just mimicking the pose—it was his pose! Sid and I had been amused by the idea of Mr. Perkins being such a big fan of the glam group but had never realized that he was the lead singer himself.

"How did you know I'd found out?" I asked, not letting on that I was just now catching up.

"I could hardly be the best department secretary of any college in the United States if I didn't have decent security on my computer. I wasn't sure who'd been into my system, but given the fact that you were in the midst of an investigation, you seemed the most likely suspect. Since your project had been sanctioned by

Professor Waldron herself, I could hardly complain, but I confess I was anxious for several days afterward, awaiting the inevitable snickers as the news spread via the faculty grapevine. Not that I'm ashamed of my former identity, but I would not wish my fame—if I might call it that—to detract from the gravitas of the department. But the snickers never came."

"I didn't tell anyone. And won't."

"Your discretion is sincerely appreciated."

"There is one thing."

"Oh?"

"I downloaded your albums from iTunes, and it seems to me that while 'Glitter Games' is great, I actually think 'Man-child Mania' is even better."

He actually smiled.

Chapter Forty-Two

Once a doctor came by and said it was okay for me to leave, Mr. Perkins helped me navigate the paperwork for being released from the hospital and drove me home. My minivan was already there, which he'd arranged somehow, and I think he'd have spent the rest of the weekend with me if I hadn't insisted I would be fine. I finally had to tell him that I was going to invite my mysterious companion over once he was gone to get him to leave. Even then, he checked the refrigerator and pantry first to make sure I had plenty to eat. Maybe he really was the best departmental secretary in the country.

As soon as the door was shut behind Mr. Perkins, I called out, "Sid? Are you here?" I'd texted him several times since Officer Buchanan's visit, but there'd been no response.

There was no response to my calling out, either. I knew he wouldn't have stayed quiet if he'd heard me and I know his hearing is excellent even without ears, but I still went running through the house, looking under every bed and inside every closet, hoping to find him. I was peering into the washing machine when I heard a light tap at the door.

I didn't even stop to look through the peephole, just threw open the door.

He was still in the clothes from the night before and was covered in snow, but I didn't let that stop me from dragging him inside and hugging him as tightly as I could.

"Georgia, stop! You're getting yourself wet!"

"I don't care."

"You're going to catch cold."

"I don't care."

"You're going to break my ribs!"

That I cared about, so I let him go and helped him out of his ensemble, which I now realized was a complete mishmash of garments: a Deadpool hoodie, a pair of tie-dyed pajama pants, a Pikachu Laplander hat, and pink rain boots decorated with ducks.

"Where did you get this stuff?"

"I raided the lost-and-found box in Mr. Perkins's office," he said as he pulled off the hoodie, which was tight even on someone with his BMI. "And is that really your first question?"

"Sorry. I'm not thinking straight. I have much better questions." I pulled him over to the couch. "How did you know I was in trouble?"

"I tried to text you after you'd left, just to let you know I was okay and to tell you I really like that Squirrel Girl graphic novel. When you didn't text me back, I tried again, but you still didn't reply. I knew something had to be wrong.

"How did you find me?"

"It's a long story, and it would have been a lot shorter if we had one of those phone locator apps."

"We'll download one later."

"Good. Anyway, by that time the building was empty, so I got to a window and saw the minivan was still in the parking lot. I figured that maybe that meant you were, too. I searched everywhere in the English wing before deciding you must be outside or in another building and went to get something to wear in case somebody saw me."

"You're a genius, even if your mittens don't match."

He grinned. "I knew Kelly's killer—Wait, was it Dahna?"

"Nope. Renee."

"So much for my hunch."

"They were working together, so you were half right."

"Huh. Another team supreme."

"More like a match made in hell. I'll explain later. You go on."

"Since I knew the killer—who I now know was Renee—had used Kelly's own car to stage an accident, I was afraid she'd do the same with yours. I was thinking about slashing the tires and was looking in the tool shed for something to use when I found the snowblower. It was all gassed up, so it was easy to make sure your minivan couldn't leave. I didn't know who those other cars belonged to, but they were the only ones left in the lot, so I buried them, too. I was riding around looking for you when I saw the path in the snow, and you know the rest."

"Not quite. How did you get home and why didn't you text me that you were okay?"

"The answer to the first part is that I walked. My sense of direction sucks, so I had to follow the roads to get here, and of course I had to hide a lot. Still, I beat you home so you shouldn't be all superior. I've been hiding out back, waiting for you to show up. And I didn't text you for the same reason I didn't break into the bungalow. I left my stuff in your office at FAD. I was kind of distracted."

"I don't blame you. And one last question. Did you know that you are the best friend anybody ever had?"

"They must have hit your head harder than I thought. I nearly got you killed!"

"Coccyx, Sid. You saved me!"

"You wouldn't have been in danger if—"

I put my hand over his moving jaw. "You saved me, Sid. This investigation was as much me as you, and if I can't order you around, then you can't keep taking the blame for my decisions. Partners, right?"

He mumbled something, so I removed my hand.

"Partners," he said. "Fist bump?"

"Fist bump!" That was followed by another hug, and then my explanation of what had happened to me and what I'd found out along the way. I tried to fuzz over the worried-about-freezing-to-death and barely-able-to-walk parts, but Sid wasn't fooled. I was pretty sure that if either Renee or Dahna ever made it out of jail, they'd be getting a pretty horrific visit from Sid. Personally, I never wanted to see that terrifying expression on his face again.

"Dahna and Renee should be going away," I concluded, "but it looks as if Jeremy is mostly in the clear, which hardly seems fair. Okay, he'll lose his job at FAD and probably won't ever get another teaching job, and he might be sued for plagiarism, but he's still an artist. He can keep painting. The notoriety might even help him sell paintings."

"I'm not so sure about that," Sid said. "When I spent that first night on campus, I flipped through some of Jeremy's sketchbooks. You know how Indigo dates every sketch? Jeremy does that, too."

"So?"

"So even with my untrained eye sockets, I could tell his most recent sketches weren't any good. Jeremy must have thought so, too, because he'd drawn X's over them. He'd done the same thing to nearly every sketch for the past six months."

"Ouch."

"This is my guess. He was happy to take the money from modifying T-shirt designs, especially when he got engaged to Renee, who wanted a big wedding. But he was humiliated, too, because they were other people's ideas, and even worse, they weren't what he considered real art. It all combined to give him a massive case of artist's block. Which I hope is permanent."

"I almost feel sorry for him. Except for the part about him stealing Indigo's artwork, making Marissa nearly starve, and possibly being an accessory to killing Kelly."

"Not to mention nearly killing you."

"Yeah, let's not mention that. Especially not to my family."

"You know they're going to find out."

I sighed. "You're right. Let me get the phone—I may as well get it over with." By the time I was done with that, e-mails had started coming in from Caroline and Lucas, and I had to respond promptly to stop her from coming over with a pizza and beer and him from bringing lasagna, wine, and tiramisu. I appreciated them thinking of me, but by that point, all I wanted was some soup, an old movie, and an early trip to bed, secure in the knowledge that Sid was watching over me.

The next morning, I got a call from Mr. Perkins to arrange another meeting with Professor Waldron and the dean, this time at the bungalow. Though the lawyer wasn't mentioned specifically, I wasn't at all surprised when he showed up, staggering under the weight of an enormous fruit basket.

In a bizarre rerun, the dean wanted to know what happened, Professor Waldron wanted to make sure that I was okay, and the lawyer wanted to make sure I still wasn't planning to sue FAD. And again I explained and reassured, though I wouldn't sign the lawyer's newly expanded agreement any more than I would the last one. This time, however, Professor Waldron chased the lawyer off by asking if he and the dean would wait in the car while she took care of another matter.

Apparently they'd been warned, but I was confused when she sat back down on the couch.

"Doctor Thackery," she began, "I realize that this may not be the best time to tell you, but the decision about tenure has been made. Even before last night's events, the choice was down to you and Dr. Craig."

Obviously Renee and Dahna were off the list now, I thought, and nodded.

She took a deep breath. "I'm afraid that I've decided that Dr. Craig is the better candidate."

I had only the briefest flash of disappointment, followed by an almost shocking rush of relief. "Caroline is a great choice," I said sincerely. "Her work with graphic novels fits perfectly with FAD's sequential arts curriculum."

"That's true, but in all honesty, that wasn't the primary reason for my decision."

I hated to ask the next question, but I needed to know the answer. "Was it my reputation? For becoming involved in crimes and so forth?"

"No, not at all. I quite admire your adventurous spirit." She gave a brief smile. "Not to mention your unwillingness to be bullied by our college lawyer."

"Can I ask what the reason was?"

"It seems to me, Dr. Thackery—May I call you Georgia?"

"By all means," I said, though I didn't think I'd be asking if I could call her Martha anytime soon.

"Your understanding of literature is both broad and deep, and you are an excellent instructor, Georgia. In fact, in discussions with Mr. Perkins, he pointed out that you are much like a younger version of me. But while I'm in the waning years of my career and content with my position at FAD, the best of your academic achievements are yet to come. You should certainly not settle for a position in a small art school."

"That may be the nicest rejection I've ever received."

"Consider it not so much a rejection as a challenge. I expect great things from you, Georgia. Do not disappoint me." Then she swept out my door.

A moment later, Sid came in.

"Did you hear?"

He nodded.

"So no tenure for me."

"I'm sorry, Georgia."

"I'm not."

"You're not?"

"I'm really not. I mean, I do want tenure some day, but not at FAD. It's a great art school, and if my specialty were sequential art like Caroline's, I'd be as happy as a clam there. But if I were stuck in Falstone long-term, I'd end up just as bitter as Kelly was. Not to mention the weather! I'll finish up the semester and maybe stay through the summer session—I'm not going to leave them with only two English instructors—but I'm going to start looking for someplace else for the fall. Are you disappointed? I know you like being able to go out in the snow."

"Meh. It's been fun, but after that walk home, I've decided that the outdoors is overrated. And shoveling is getting boring."

"Using the snowblower, too?"

"No, that'll never get old. But when the time comes, I'll be ready to move on. Wherever you want to go."

"Wherever *we* want to go. I meant it when I said we're partners, Sid."

"What if you and some guy get together? You and Mr. Perkins made a darling couple."

"No, thanks."

"What about Lucas?" he said delicately. "You like him and he did find me worth painting, which is a point in his favor."

"Closer, and he is pretty cute, but I don't think so. You know that when I told him about our investigation, he wasn't interested in helping."

"Really?"

"Not at all. How would somebody like that fit into my life?" Despite what my sister said on the phone the day before, I did not go out looking for murders, but when chance brought one my way, I wasn't going to ignore it. "Besides, he flunked my litmus test."

"Which is?"

"Okay, this is going to sound silly."

"Not to me. I have no romantic experience of my own to judge you against."

"What about that online flirting you haven't told me about?"

"I'm still not telling you about it."

"Fair enough. So whenever I date a guy and think maybe he could be 'the one,' I try to picture him doing nothing with us."

"Doing nothing?"

"Hanging out at the house, doing laundry, reading, watching TV, grocery shopping. I mean, that's real life—not the dates and nice dinners and all that. I just can't see Lucas sitting around with us."

"You don't think he'd like Madison?"

"Of course he'd like Madison—everybody likes Madison. I mean I can't imagine telling him about you."

"Me?" His jaw fell open.

"Of course you. How could I make a commitment that doesn't include you?"

"Georgia, you can't reject a relationship because of me."

"Yes, I can." I held up one fist. "Team supreme!"

"Team supreme," he said in choked voice as he returned the bump.

"Sid, you can't cry."

"I'm not crying. I'm just... Hey, let's crank up the Pteriwinkle Gleam and celebrate!"

Maybe Sid can't cry, but he sure can dance.

ACKNOWLEDGMENTS

My daughter Maggie, for explaining the workings of art school.

My daughter Valerie, for helping to make sure my younger characters don't sound like they're my age.

My ever-patient husband, Steve, for acting as alpha reader.

My BFFs Charlaine Harris and Dana Cameron, for beta reading under ludicrous time constraints.

Sara Weiss and Art Taylor, for making sure I didn't mess up every detail about the adjunct lifestyle. (Any mistakes I did make are mine alone.)

Robin Burcell, for doing the same when it comes to police procedure. (Again, the mistakes are all mine.)

The Facebook hive mind, for answering the most random questions with accuracy and speed.

LEIGH PERRY takes the adage "Write what you know" to its illogical extreme. Having been born with a skeleton, and with most of her bones still intact, she was inspired to create Sid and write the Family Skeleton Mysteries. *The Skeleton Paints a Picture* is the fourth in the series. As Toni L.P. Kelner, she's published eleven novels and a number of short stories and has coedited seven anthologies with *New York Times* bestselling author Charlaine Harris. She's won an Agatha Award and an RT Booklovers Career Achievement Award and has been nominated for the Anthony, the Macavity, and the Derringer awards. Leigh lives north of Boston with her husband, two daughters, a guinea pig, and an ever-increasing number of books. You can visit her online at **LeighPerryAuthor.com**.

CPSIA information can be obtained
at www.ICGtesting.com
Printed in the USA
BVOW09s0812220917
495262BV00002B/2/P